THE BOY

CHALK PATH BOOKS

Published by Chalk Path Books
www.chalkpathbooks.com

First published 2011
Revised and extended edition published 2013

ISBN: 978-0-9574711-1-5

10 9 8 7 6 5 4 3 2 1

Interior art copyright © 2013 Christopher Cavill
www.cloudpine451.blogspot.com

All stories copyright © 2001–2013 Peter Kendell

THE BOY

and other stories

Peter Kendell

Illustrated by
Christopher Cavill

chalk path books

Contents

Acknowledgements

I WROTE THE STORIES WHICH COMPRISE *THE BOY* OVER A TWELVE-YEAR period, mostly when I was supposed to be doing something else. I expect that full-time professional writers often find themselves doing something else when they are supposed to be writing. Or, in other words, You Can't Win.

The first edition of this collection of stories was published on Amazon Kindle as an experiment. I felt that there was little to lose, and perhaps something to gain, by putting my efforts in front of a potential worldwide readership, however modest the book's sales might turn out to be. Unfortunately, that original publication fell short of what it might have been, even though I had done my best to remove the worst of its glitches and typos.

It was this: the cover, which I made myself, was *awful*. *Terrible*. I know what good artwork and layout look like and the original eBook of *The Boy* had neither of these things. This present edition is a different matter altogether and I should like to thank everyone at Chalk Path Books for their help and expertise in producing it.

Especially, I must extend my grateful thanks to Chris Cavill for his beautiful artwork. Every time he's sent me an illustration I've been struck anew by the way he has seen something in a story that I hadn't noticed was there and realised it brilliantly in pen, crayon and paint. He has transformed a mere assemblage of words into a distinctive work of art.

Peter Kendell, Summer 2013

For Christine

THE VALE SCHOOL

THE BOY

The Boy

'HAVE YOU EVER SEEN A GHOST?' GEOFFREY THURSLOW ASKED ME one rainy Saturday afternoon in late October, as we sat on opposite sides of the staff-room fire enjoying a brief respite from boys and ink and noise and O-levels.

'No, I can't say I have.' I put down my notebook and looked up at him, sitting back in his leaky leather armchair, pipe in hand. He was wearing an ancient brown tweed jacket and cavalry twill trousers and was looking even more the middle-aged bachelor schoolmaster than usual.

Geoffrey pushed his glasses back onto the bridge of his nose.

'I suppose most people would say the same. And yet, if you were to ask them if they believed in ghosts, you'd probably get a different answer.'

'People take many things on trust. Or because they're attractive or comforting to them. I mean, if you say that you believe in ghosts, that's another way of saying that you believe in an afterlife, which is something many of us would like to believe in, even if there's no solid evidence for it.'

'Yes, Jack, you're right. And so very sensible and rational too. I wonder if you'd admit to the existence of ghosts if the shade of Jacob Marley came clanking through that door right now?'

We both glanced at the staff-room door.

'It's much more likely that Jenkins minor will come clanking through that door with a summons from the Head.'

'Or carrying a message from Matron about missing socks. But; did you ever think about writing ghost stories, rather than those penny-bloods you turn out?'

'No, not really. There are quite enough explainable mysteries in the world already for me to have fun with, without my needing to invoke the Beyond or the Powers Of The Occult. And besides, how could anyone possibly write a ghost story that was better or more frightening than, say, *The Mezzotint*? Or anything else by M.R. James for that matter? I certainly couldn't.'

'Very true, very true.' Geoffrey was not the kind of person to wink. Wry remarks like that were the closest he got to it.

'I suppose that one of the things about ghosts – if you admit their existence at all, that is – is that they act as a form of *momento mori*; a reminder that you are going to die. All the ghosts I ever read about or heard of were of people who died with some aspect of their life not finished or settled.'

'Like Jacob Marley in *A Christmas Carol*, you mean.'

'Well, yes. He died having accumulated a huge pile of money that was no good to him and which he could have used to help the poor starving people around him. He then had to suffer the torment of not being able to succour them after his death.'

'He couldn't take it with him.'

'Quite. Except for several fathoms of iron chain.'

'Anyway, they died and there was something wrong with their lives and they couldn't be allowed to go on to the proper afterlife until that wrong was put right. But they had to die first.'

'That is the usual pattern, yes.' I reached for my notebook again.

Geoffrey fell silent. He eased himself out of the armchair which had somehow become his unofficial property and shambled over to the window, through which could be heard the sounds of healthy young middle-class English manhood playing rugby football. His stooped figure was silhouetted against the grimy panes of the window as he gazed over towards Rugger Bigside where the first fifteen were engaged in a school match against nearby Wayland College.

'Forbury is doing well. He'll be playing for the Varsity in a couple of years' time.'

A cheer echoed across the playing fields. They'd be throwing buns in Hall later. Thank heavens I wasn't on tea duty that week.

Geoffrey sighed and meandered his way back to his chair. He sank into it, bent forward to look at the fire and sighed again, then straightened up suddenly as if he had come to a decision. He looked directly towards me.

'Jack, I'm going to tell you about something that happened to me a while ago – last year, actually. It's not raw material for one of your blasted books either, although it was one of them that started the whole thing off.

'It was a Saturday afternoon rather like today, windy and rainy and altogether pretty beastly. I'd gone into Town, even though the first fifteen were playing at home, to get a few bits and pieces. Matron had said that the laundry had rejected three of my shirts as being too far gone for them to wash without them falling apart so I popped into Marks and bought some more.

'It was quite foul when I came out so I made a dive for the teashop opposite…'

'The Kozey Kettle?'

'That's the one. The place was packed – it was half-past three and the weather being so bad had brought lots of people in off the streets, I suppose. Anyway, I couldn't get a table to myself, so I had to sit at one which was already occupied. I didn't take in the other person except to notice that she was a middle-aged woman with a few shopping bags piled around her and that she had her nose buried in a book.

'I ordered tea and a rock cake and arranged my own things between my chair and the wall. I couldn't see much as my glasses had misted up so I took them off and wiped them. Then for the first time I took a proper look at the person I was sharing the table with.'

'Or whose privacy you had invaded.'

'If you want to put it that way, yes. The first thing I saw was the book she was reading. I'd expected it to be one of those popular romances – *Bills and Spoon*, or whatever it is. But actually, it was one of yours.'

'Oh yes? Which one?' Professional interest, you know.

'Let's think. Does *Blood Bath in Battersea* ring a bell?'

'No! You know damn well it doesn't!' It's only jealousy on Geoffrey's part. I keep telling him there's much more money in school textbooks than crime novels.

'I know. It was one of those country house murder stories. *Death and Tennis* – that's it.'

'I got a Silver Dagger for that!'

'So you've often told me. Anyway, I was looking at the book's cover when I became aware that the reader herself was looking back at me. A pair of shrewd eyes were regarding me in an amused manner over the top of the book.

'"You can borrow it after me, if you like," she said.

'"No, no, that's quite all right," I replied, embarrassed. "It's just that I know the author. He's a colleague of mine."

'"Is he, now? Tell me, is he a very wicked cruel man, this Fabian Greene, to think up all these nasty ways of killing people?" she said.'

'I hope you said "yes",' I interjected.

'No I didn't. And it's a funny thing, because I really can't remember what I said. Or what she said after that. All I can remember of our first meeting is that we chatted and that somehow everything she said seemed witty, or funny, or true or all of those things, and that she made me feel as if I was witty and funny also. Which you've got to admit is unusual for me.'

I should perhaps say at this point that Geoffrey was perhaps the most bachelor-like bachelor I had ever met. His life seemed to have consisted of babyhood, school, then university and then straight back to school again, as a schoolmaster. I often wondered if he had ever experienced what you might call real life – life outside the cloisters of school and university, I mean – at all.

'When I looked at my watch it was half-past five and I had ten minutes to get to Hall in time for tea duty. I made a hasty, clumsy, farewell to my companion and dashed out of the teashop door, only just remembering my shopping. I haven't run so fast since I was an undergraduate.

'I was in such a blind hurry I very nearly bowled over a boy who was standing just outside the door. He wasn't one of ours – a good thing too, else he'd have been in trouble for staying out after five o'clock. I apologised to him and suggested that standing in doorways wasn't the most sensible thing to do. He stared back at me vacantly. I decided he must have been slightly concussed by my having crashed into him, so I gave him a shilling and ran on up the hill to School.

'I can't say I gave the matter of the boy, or my teatime friend, much thought over the week that followed. I had quite enough to do with trying to get Holloway major to draw a proper distinction between Plutarch and Pluto. Have you got him this year?'

'Yes, I have.'

'Hmmm. Well, anyway, it was a busy week and there was no School Match that Saturday so, without knowing quite how I got there, I found myself standing outside the Kozey Kettle again. And there she was, sitting in the window, reading a book. No, not one of yours this time, something with women's names in the title. I tapped on the window and she saw me and beckoned me in.

'I made some fatuous joke about trashy romances not being quite her style. She became quite cross with me and told me very firmly that her book was most certainly not a trashy romance of the *Wills and June* variety but a subtle satire of the kind that was probably well beyond my ability to appreciate. I was suitably contrite and bought her a slice of carrot-cake in recompense.

'Again, we seemed to be able to talk extraordinarily easily. We volleyed *bons mots* and epigrams between ourselves like – like two table-tennis players who are each trying to make sure the other doesn't miss the ball. Yes, that's it.

'I wasn't on duty that week, so we were able to go on talking until the staff very pointedly started stacking the chairs and tables around us. We agreed to meet the following week at the same time and place.

'As I strolled up the hill towards School in the semi-darkness, I slowly became aware that I could hear the footsteps of someone following me. I had heard about muggers, of course, but I decided I would rather turn and confront the criminal, if such it was, than suffer the doubt of not knowing who was behind me. The streetlights were coming on, so I stopped under one and turned round.

'There in front of me, strangely lit by the orange light above us, was the boy. The same boy that I had bumped into outside the teashop the week before. I thought he must be after another tip, so I said "Sorry. I only give shillings to war veterans," meaning to make a joke of it. But he just stared up at me with the same vacant expression that had been on his face the week before. I remember that his nose was running and I wanted to tell him to blow it.

'"Are you all right?" I asked him. He continued staring at me. It was beginning to disturb me, that stare. There seemed to be nothing behind it. Nothing behind his eyes, I mean. I made one more try.

'"Do you live nearby?"

'He made a kind of inarticulate sound in the back of his throat. "Ah-ah," or something like that. Then he suddenly turned and ran off.

'"Oh well, that's that," I thought, and carried on back to School.

'I can't tell you with what eager anticipation I looked forward to the next Saturday. Even the unsettling encounter with the mysterious boy didn't bother me as much as it might have done if I had not been so looking forward to my next meeting with Marjorie, for that was the lady's name. There was something, though, that had me slightly unsettled. Something about the boy's face. Not its blank idiocy, although that was disturbing enough, but the fact that, somewhere in the back of my mind, I thought I'd seen it before.'

'We see lots of boys.'

'Yes, of course, but even the stupidest one has managed to pass his Common Entrance or else he's exceptionally good at sport, like young Forbury out there. No, I wondered if there hadn't been a boy who was disabled or mentally handicapped, or whatever we call it now, in the village when I was growing up, and this boy was reminding me of him.

'The week passed slowly enough, but the next Saturday I presented myself at the Kozey Kettle at half-past two. To my annoyance, the boy was standing outside the clothes shop next door, leaning against the doorway and playing with one of those blasted yo-yo things. He looked up at me with a slack-jawed grin and made that "ah-ah" sound in his throat again. I gave him a sharp look in return and entered the teashop.

'Marjorie was there, waiting for me. "It's a lovely day," she said. "Why don't we go for a spin?" She had a blue car parked outside in the High Street. A Ford Anglia, I think it was, with a radiator grille like a great big grin. I hopped into the passenger seat and we drove slowly up the Vale, enjoying the brilliant autumn sunshine and the colours of the trees. And chatting. I learned that her full name was Marjorie Wallis; that she was a widow, that her husband had been a solicitor and had died two years previously, leaving her well provided for.

'I told her about myself, as her little car weaved its way through the villages of the Vale. It was a novelty for me to meet a woman who was prepared to listen to me talking for longer than five minutes without finding some reason to escape my company. I supposed that she was a captive audience, so to speak, and anyway she had her driving to keep her occupied.

'We stopped outside one of those combined Post Offices *cum* General Stores *cum* tearooms that you find in small country towns. I rushed round to the driver's door, opened it and handed her out of the car; which courtesy she received very graciously indeed. But there was a shock waiting for me. Inside the tearoom, loitering by the counter, was… the boy.'

'The same boy?' I said.

'Yes, the very same boy. Staring at me with the same idiot grin, his head tilted oddly to one side, making the same obscene noises in his throat. "Ah-ah, pa-da, ga-ga." I felt disgusted, and ashamed.'

'You mean you felt ashamed of your disgust.'

'Yes, I do. But I was unnerved too. How on earth could the wretched child have reached the Post Office before us? How could he have known where we were going? I hadn't known myself.

'"Geoffrey, are you feeling unwell?" Marjorie asked. I made up some excuse about feeling a little carsick, which wasn't very tactful of me. Actually, she was a very good, steady, safe driver.

'We found a table, and when I looked up again at the counter the boy had gone. I pulled myself together and decide to forget about the intruder and concentrate on enjoying myself. Marjorie was the same marvellous company as ever, and after a while I pushed him to the back of my mind. We drove back as it was growing dark and she dropped me outside the Lodge, arranging to meet in the lobby of the Regal cinema the following Saturday.

'Only one thing spoiled the following week, apart from 5B's total lack of interest in Ovid, that is. It was late Wednesday evening: I was getting ready for bed, when I heard an odd scratching sound coming from outside. I supposed it was cats.

'I flung up the window to take a look. Outside, leaning against the Lodge gates, was that hideous boy, looking up at my window and making those awful ugly sounds – "Pa-da, ah-ah, ga-ga, da-da, ah-ah." He was sucking his thumb and I saw to my horror that he had taken his member out of his trousers and was fiddling with it.

'"Clear off!" I shouted. "Clear off now, you horrible creature, or I'll call the police!"

'He took his thumb out of his mouth, gave me a mocking wave, and sauntered off into the darkness. Yet again, I was struck by the conviction that I had seen him somewhere before. I didn't sleep at all well that night, and I expect the Fourth Remove caught the sharp edge of my tongue the next day.

'I'm not going to tell you about every single time I encountered the boy. Marjorie and I saw *A Hard Day's Night* at the Regal the next Saturday. It was the most infernally noisy film I've ever seen, but Marjorie said that we should try to keep up with what the young people were interested in. I couldn't understand what it was all about, myself – there were no tunes to speak of and you couldn't make out a word of what they were saying. We had a bit of a disagreement over it.

'All the same, our relationship flourished. Did anyone here notice, by the way?' Geoffrey asked me.

'You can't keep secrets in a boarding school. There may have been one or two remarks made.'

'By Harries?'

'Yes. And Twemlow, too. I soon shut them up.' I poked the fire and added some coal from the blackened old scuttle. The sounds of cheering and the referee's whistle coming in from outside reminded us that the rugby match was nearing its end.

'Well, I don't care. And it's all over now.'

'How did it finish? I mean, if you don't mind telling me.' The shouting and cheering were reaching a deafening pitch outside the staff-room window. It appeared that School had won, and that Forbury was being given his Colours.

'No, not any more, although I was rather cut up about it at the time.

'As I said, Marjorie and I continued to get on terrifically well and it was becoming clear to me that, if things carried on the way they were, marriage could well be on the cards. Yes, me, Geoffrey Thurslow, a married man! Imagine! We spent many afternoons in the front room of her house, a nice bungalow on the Wantage road, reading to each other, talking, even watching her television set. She was a football fan, did I say?

'I'll never forget our first kiss; in the back row of the Regal, while we were pretending to watch *The Dam Busters*. I felt like an adolescent all over again...'

Geoffrey fell silent for a minute of two. The fire settled in the grate with a soft rustle.

'But still there was the boy; ever-present, always appearing at the worst times, blighting my happiness. Sometimes he had a crutch; occasionally he was in a wheelchair, usually he was on his own two feet. And always with that terrible empty expression and horrible sub-human cry – "pa-da, ga-ga, ah-ma, ah-ah, da-da."

'Then Marjorie had to go away for a week or two. To see a sick aunt, she said, although I think that what she really wanted to do was to give herself an opportunity to think things over. I thought that when she returned I might, if I could gather up my courage, propose to her. I helped her to pack her things and waved her off, the red tail lights of her little Ford Anglia disappearing into the night.

'I had, of course, wondered about the apparent connection between her and the boy. Her marriage had been childless, I knew, and she had no relatives living nearby. Besides, the boy seemed to be able to appear in one place or another without actually needing to *travel* between them. But, all the same, it was true that I had never seen him before I met Marjorie. It could have been coincidence, of course, but it was all so uncanny – his suddenly turning up just like that and the nagging familiarity of his face.

'Marjorie had been gone a few days, and I was sitting in my study one afternoon doing some marking when I heard a familiar noise outside. I went to the door of the Lodge, both knowing and dreading what I would find. Sure enough, there he was; chewing on a stalk of grass and scratching his head.

'"This has got to stop," I said to myself. I told the boy to come inside and led him to my study and sat him down. I took out some lemonade and a packet of ginger nuts from the cupboard and gave them to him. He ate and drank like an animal, scattering crumbs and sloshing lemonade on the carpet.

'"Who are you?" I asked him. "What's your name, where do you live?" And still he said nothing, nothing coherent at any rate. Just that hateful "ah-ah, pa-pa, ga-ga, da-da," over and over again.

'This went on for several minutes. I was at my wits' end – I couldn't see how I was going to communicate with this boy and get to the bottom of the mystery.

'"Look here," I said. "This can't go on. Why are you here? Please, please, tell me. *What do you want from me*?" And I held my hands out to him in a gesture of supplication.

'The boy looked up at me from where he was sitting with his plate of biscuits and glass of lemonade on the floor beside him and gave me a broad smile – oh, the most beautiful winning smile you ever saw. He leapt up from the chair and flung himself at me, throwing his arms around me and hugging me as hard as he could, and saying the same word over and over again. I folded him in my arms and kissed him on the forehead.

'We held each other tightly for what seemed an age and then he got up and walked – unsteadily, for he had a withered leg now – out of the room. I sat and thought for an hour or two about what he had said to me, and then I wrote a letter. It was the hardest letter I have ever written in my life.

'Jack – we were saying that a ghost is the shade of someone who has died, but whose life was somehow incomplete, unfinished.'

'Yes.'

'First the life, then the death, then the haunting.'

'Well, yes.'

'But what if the life were a terrible, a most abominable life, but the person who lived it were not yet born?'

'That would be different. It's hard to see how you could be haunted by the ghost of someone who had never actually been alive.'

'Quite so. And yet… In that letter I told Marjorie that it would be absolutely impossible for us to meet in the future. I wrote it brutally; I wanted her to hate me for it. I told her I had only been after her husband's money, that I found her physically repugnant and that now that I had unexpectedly come into some money of my own I didn't need to see her any more. It worked, too; I believe she moved away in the spring and I never saw her or the boy again.'

'But why? You and she were getting on so very well, you said.'

'Yes, we were. We had sometimes joked about what our children might be like; for she wasn't so old that she couldn't have had children. But as I sat in my study that long afternoon, something that had been only a suspicion in the back of my mind up to that point froze into a cold certainty. I *knew* what our child would be like. I had *seen* him, outside the Kozey Kettle and the Masters' Lodge, the Regal cinema and Marjorie's house. I knew his face. It resembled my own face, when I was a boy.

'I suppose I'd had an inkling of it already, in the distorted sounds he was making – "ah-ah, ga-ga, pa-pa, da-da." Our son would be crippled, handicapped, disabled. He would be the most terrible burden, mocked and derided, pointed at in the street. I couldn't face that. I'm a coward, I know, and who is to say that such a life as he would have had would not have been a worthwhile one?'

'But what was it that he said, in your study, that finally convinced you?'

'*Daddy*. He called me *Daddy*. Over and over again, with more love in his voice than you can possibly comprehend. I can't forget it. I can't forgive myself. I could have been that boy's father, but I turned him away. I denied him his life.'

Geoffrey stared into the fire. Outside, the match was over and the boys were rushing in out of the cold and wet. Soon it would be time for tea.

First Term Only

W HAT'S IT ABOUT THIS TIME, THIS NEW BOOK OF YOURS? THE usual murder and mayhem?'

'Pretty much, yes. It's another police procedural, actually.'

'What; the prickly Inspector Gorse and his faithful sidekick Mull? Solving yet another donnish malefaction in Cambridge?'

'That's it. The readers like reading them; I like writing them. My publisher absolutely loves selling them!'

'Quite so, Jack. It keeps you off the streets, at least.'

My friend Geoffrey Thurslow and I were sitting on the bench under the big oak tree outside the Old Buildings, enjoying our pipes and a companionable afternoon talk. It was an especially fine summer's day and wonderfully peaceful, as all the boys had been packed onto buses first thing after Chapel to go and play soldiers up and down the Vale. Waving rifles (unloaded) at each other, building camp fires, that sort of thing. Some boys love the CCF – the Combined Cadet Force – some loathe it. Field Day really brings it out in them. I said as much to Geoffrey.

'Yes, I've noticed that. What about that boy you were so worried about – young Twiss?'

'Oh, he'll be fine.'

'That's a relief. We talked about him more than once last year, if I recall. I suppose that some of them just take longer to settle in than others. As a housemaster, you'd see more of that than me, of course.'

Yes, indeed. As a housemaster, my duties include the pastoral care of the boys. School House – my own responsibility – has fifty of them, ranging from hulking great young men of eighteen years to little boys, some scarcely weaned, of just thirteen.

It's always a difficult time, introducing the new boys to School life at the start of the autumn term. They turn up at the gates two hours before the older pupils; anxious boys and even more anxious parents. Some hide their anxiety better than others, naturally. If the father is an Old Boy this can help, although some fathers so put the wind up their sons with their own reminiscences of school that the poor little chaps are half expecting to be caned for some minor offence before they even cross the threshold. I find it helps to choose the kindest and most sensible of my prefects to keep an eye on the new boys. A housemaster may well have eyes in the back of his head – he wouldn't last five minutes if he didn't – but boys pick things up that adults miss, like the onset of bullying, for example.

This term started off much like any other. Once I had got rid of the stiff-upper-lipped fathers and their tearful or frightfully-brave wives I took the new boys into my study and offered them tea and cakes. My wife Muriel was there, too. Her presence helps reassure the more worried kind of boy.

I cast my eyes over the ten of them. They were a fairly typical bunch. Boys of thirteen vary widely in their maturity, both physical and mental. Wheeler, for example, five foot eight inches tall and bulky with it, came with a tremendous sports report from his prep school and would be playing in the under-fourteens very soon, I could see. He would settle in very easily. Parsons, lanky, bespectacled and abstracted, had won a scholarship and would doubtless be going up to Oxford in five years' time. Hodgson, short, round and cheerful, would be the class clown. And so on. But Twiss…

'Didn't he have a teddy bear with him when he came?'

'Yes. It's unusual, but well within the rules.'

I should explain: When a boy gains entrance to The Vale School, his parents are sent a long list of the clothes and various essentials he is expected to bring with him on his first day. Shirts, shoes, collars, studs, trousers, coats, socks, suits and sports kit. And other things, like pens, pencils, geometry kit, prayer-book, Bible, trunk and tuck-box. Most parents – the better-off ones, anyway – simply go to one of the big department stores and make a bulk order of everything. The less well-off make do with what they can get at Marks and Spencer, and the house matrons – the more understanding ones, that is – very sensibly overlook any minor exceptions to the rules.

At the very end of the list is this item:

One Teddy Bear (First Term Only)

Some of our new boys are very young for their age.

Twiss, I could see, was going to be a problem. Uniquely in my experience he had not only brought a teddy bear with him, he was *carrying* it, holding it by one paw. In front of all the other boys, too. I could imagine the things that would be said and done to him in the dormitory that night, and the way that spiteful rumours – for thirteen-year-old boys can be incredibly spiteful – would spread around the school. I resolved to have a special word with Hume, my new Head of House, about him. The prefects could at least try to do something to help him through what promised to be a difficult few weeks.

I gave the new boys the usual pep talk: 'I'm Mr Jackson, and I'm the housemaster of School House; everyone calls me "Jack", but not to my face. Play fair by me and I'll play fair by you. My study door is always open; come to me, or Mrs Jackson, at any time if you have a problem or just need to talk about something that's troubling you.' As I say, the usual stuff. Then I handed them over to Muriel, and she took over all the unpacking and organising.

I briefed Hume and the other prefects over a glass of sherry that evening. They promised to do their best, but I wondered if that was going to be enough. And, as the first weeks of that autumn term passed, I could see that it was not going to be enough. My colleagues would have a quiet word with me in the staff-room; Twiss was not doing very well. Muriel would mention that his clothes and other things kept going missing. Whenever I saw him, he seemed to be on the verge of bursting into tears. We had persuaded him to leave his teddy bear – whose name was Mr Gruff, by the way – in the dormitory; although I half expected that he too would mysteriously disappear, the way Twiss's collars, socks and sports kit did. But no. The bear, it appeared, was considered sacrosanct. Sometimes I entirely fail to understand boys, even though I was one myself, once upon a time.

One afternoon, two or three weeks into that autumn term, I was passing the first year dormitory when I heard voices. Now, there's a strict rule that no boys are allowed in the dormitories, without special permission that is, between nine o'clock in the morning and nine in the evening, for all kinds of very sensible reasons. So I was just about to storm in and deal with the offenders when I stopped. I recognised one of the voices. It was Twiss's. I resolved to deal kindly with him as he had probably been ragged by his fellows and had gone up to the dorm, despite the prohibition, for some respite.

Then I realised that something was a bit strange. One of the voices, as I said, belonged to Twiss, but I didn't recognise the other. I was half-relieved that he had found a friend at last and half-annoyed that they had both broken a clear school rule. The peculiar thing was that I didn't know the second voice. It didn't sound like a boy's voice at all – not a first-year's at any rate. I listened for a moment.

'It's Stapledon, now.' That was Twiss.

'What's he done?' That was the other voice, deep and hoarse.

'He took all my books and threw them round the Arts Quad. I lost my History essay and got given a detention.'

'Do you want me to do something about it?'

'I wish you would.'

That was enough. I flung open the dormitory door. There was Twiss – small and weedy, frightened as a rabbit caught in the headlights of a car on a country road – sitting on his bed, but where was the other boy? I looked around; the dormitory was empty. I was not going to look under the beds, naturally. I had my housemasterly dignity to maintain and sometimes it's better not to let on about everything you suspect.

I sent the boy downstairs with no more than a reminder that rules were rules and were to be obeyed and then I looked around the dormitory again. Nobody else was there, I'm sure. Just ten iron-framed beds, five chests of drawers, a hanging cupboard. And Mr Gruff, of course, in his usual place on the pillow of Twiss's bed.

It was a day or two later that I heard about what had happened to Stapledon, a rough but basically good-hearted chap in Rogers's house. It seemed that he had been heard screaming in the night – a nightmare they supposed. But when the lights were turned on they revealed a trembling Stapledon shivering by the dormitory window. Down his left side were three long scratches. Whatever had made them had torn right through his pyjamas.

'Sounds like a case for your Miss Dorpleston,' Geoffrey said to me the following day. I had a look in Stapledon's dormitory and found a nail sticking out of one of the cupboards – a nasty thing. The school carpenter fixed the cupboard, Sister patched up Stapledon and that was that.

But after that, more odd and unsettling things happened. Hume told me that he'd had a word with Hamley about teasing Twiss. Hamley was a fifth-former who was blessed with an infinite supply of sarcastic wit. Despite Hume's warning he hadn't stopped tormenting the boy and shortly afterwards had been found with deep cuts and abrasions, caused by a rake we supposed, in the gardener's shed where he had gone for an illicit cigarette.

Then there was Mr Trevor, the third-form Classics master. I had never liked the man, and I couldn't understand why he had chosen teaching as a profession. He clearly hated children, particularly adolescent boys. I wondered if he had had a terrible time at school and had taken up teaching so he could wreak his revenge on the boys – or substitutes for them – who had tortured him in his own schooldays.

I was not surprised to hear that he had several times reduced poor Twiss to tears in his Latin classes. No doubt the boy had forgotten everything he had ever known about fourth declension nouns under Trevor's remorseless stare.

And there seemed to be a kind of inevitability about it when I heard that Mr Trevor had lost control of his car while driving down the hill into Marlborough and had been taken into hospital with serious injuries.

The atmosphere in the school was starting to become strained. After what happened to Williams, who had been heard shouting at Twiss to "Come on, damn you," during a cross-country run and shortly afterwards had been very badly scratched about the face – on barbed wire, we presumed, as the local farmers had been wiring their hedges to keep out the dogs – and Lessiter's horrible accident in the kitchens after he told Twiss to "eat up or he'd never grow into a man," I decided that I had to take action.

I called Twiss into my study one evening during Prep, and asked him to bring Mr Gruff with him.

'Now look here, Twiss,' I said. 'I know it's not been easy for you these past few weeks. Lots of boys have a difficult first term, but everybody finds their niche in the end. This school is big enough for everybody.'

'Yes, sir,' he replied, staring at the carpet.

'This teddy bear of yours, Mr Gruff. Have you known each other long?'

'All our lives, sir.'

'You stick by each other, don't you? You're best friends.'

'Yes, sir.'

'You'd do anything for each other, wouldn't you?'

'Yes, sir.'

'And yet it's possible to go too far, you know. It's completely the right thing to stand by your friends, but not if people get hurt. I'm sure you take my meaning.'

'Yes, sir.'

'Good. Then there's someone I'd like you both to talk to, if you wouldn't mind. You and Mr Gruff.'

'Sir?'

'I'm going to leave you three together now for half an hour or so. Just come and find me when you're ready.'

'As it turned out,' I said to Geoffrey, 'I could see that neither Hume nor I would be able to solve young Twiss's problem for him.'

'Who did you get to talk to him, then? A psychiatrist? Like your psychological detective, what's-his-name?'

'Sigmund Spofford, you mean?'

'Yes, the chap in *Dagger of the Mind*.'

'No – this was someone much more appropriate. I had Twiss and Mr Gruff talk to Lionel.'

'Lionel? Lionel who?'

'Lionel Bear. I've kept him in my study all these years. He was given to me when I was a baby and we've gone everywhere together ever since.'

'Let me get this straight. You left Twiss and Mr Gruff alone in your study to talk to your forty-five-year-old teddy bear?'

'Yes. I don't know what Lionel said to them, but he can be pretty stern at times. Much fiercer than me, Muriel always says.'

'And that's all you did?'

'That's all I had to do. And it worked; you've seen the results for yourself. No more nasty accidents around the school. A much better atmosphere altogether. Young Twiss is out there now, somewhere in the Vale, terrorising the locals with a Lee-Enfield rifle and having a whale of a time with his friends. Admit it; you never liked Trevor either.'

'Well, I'll be…' Geoffrey knocked the dottle out of his pipe onto the side of the bench. The summer sun, shining through the leaves of the oak tree, dappled the ground around our feet. It really was a most beautiful afternoon.

The Secret

'ANOTHER ONE?'

Geoffrey Thurslow nodded. 'Thank you, Jack.' I picked up our glasses and carried them over to the bar. 'Two pints when you're ready, Fred.'

'Right you are, sir.' The landlord took the glasses and refilled them. The Badger's Rest is my local, partly because it's near to the cottage and partly because Fred knows how to look after his beer, which is supplied by Fullers' Brewery of Chiswick. We're a fair distance from the metropolis, I know, but London Pride travels pretty well so long as it is given a few days to settle.

When I got back to our table one of Fred's boys had cleared the plates away and Geoffrey was sitting back comfortably, puffing away at his pipe. That's the other reason I patronise the Badger's Rest – there are no silly rules about not smoking in the bar. What's the point of a public house, I say, if you can't smoke and drink in it?

Geoffrey took his glass. 'Cheers!'

'Cheers!' I rummaged in my jacket pocket for my pipe, refilled it and lit it with a taper from the fire, and we sat companionably for a while. People came and went, families looked in, saw the haze of blue-grey smoke that hung around our heads, tut-tutted and went into the garishly decorated family room next door, where their children could eat hamburgers and chips and play on the games machines. Fred's a canny businessman and he does his best to keep all his customers happy, not just old fogies like Geoffrey and me.

We hadn't seen each other for a few weeks and so we were catching up on each other's news; though, to be frank, neither of us had actually done a very great deal since we had last met. It's enough at our age just to be able to meet up in the pub from time to time and talk about the old days. It must have been the mention of somebody we'd known at The Vale that jogged my old friend's memory.

'I've got something for you.' Geoffrey reached into his top pocket. 'I just remembered. Something for the *Valetudinarian.*' He passed a letter over to me. It carried a Berkshire postmark.

'Hatch, match or dispatch?'

'A death I'm afraid, Jack. It's one of yours. Chap called Sellars.'

Oh, how I hate that kind of letter. As editor of the magazine of The Vale School Old Boys' Association – the *Valetudinarian* – I have to expect that I will receive such a letter from time to time. There are always ten or so obituaries to insert in every yearly edition. It's worse, though, when the death has occurred among one of my boys – one of the four hundred or more who lived in School House during the thirty-five years that I was House Master. I suppose I should be grateful that I was there in peacetime and never had to stand up in Chapel every Sunday and read out the names of those Old Boys who had died in one war or another and whose names would one day be added to the Roll of Honour on the school's War Memorial.

I started to read the letter. It was from the deceased's son, who had himself left The Vale School only five years previously to read Social Engineering at some red-brick university or other. Social Engineering? What sort of subject was that? Nothing that would improve the state of the country, I was sure. Whatever the evanescent nature of the course the young man had taken, the contents of the letter were clear and coherent enough. At least some of the things he had been taught at The Vale School had stuck and he could still organise his thoughts well enough to write a decent letter. The facts were plain enough – his father John Sellars, sometime Head of School House, had been killed in a motor accident near Swallowfield in Berkshire on the fifteenth of September. That was just over two weeks ago, then.

Sellars... Of course I remembered him, even though he had left school thirty years ago. He had been Head of my house and a School Prefect, after all. He must have been only in his late forties or early fifties when he died – unfairly young, especially so when I considered that I was still in pretty good condition myself, despite having celebrated my eighty-third birthday this year.

Geoffrey leaned across the table. He must have seen the mist in my eyes, for he said quietly, 'I know, Jack. It's a brute, isn't it?'

'It's always bad when they die before their time. Always bad...' I took a pull at my pint.

'His son was at The Vale too, wasn't he? Duncan, was it?'

'Yes that's right, in the 1980s. He was in Griffiths' House, not mine. I wonder why he wrote to you?' I had a shrewd idea why he hadn't written to me.

'He didn't write to me. He wrote to the Head. I had told him that I was coming down to Dorset to see you, so he passed the letter on to me.' Oh yes. I should have locked more carefully at the envelope.

'The family'll be well provided for, I suppose.'

'Yes, I'm sure they will be.' Every now and then Old Boys send me news of their progress – from first jobs to partnerships, from footloose travellers to men of property, from wild youths to pillars of the establishment. They tend to lead lives of solid achievement, our Old Boys. I suppose those who are less successful tend not to write to me. No doubt there are many stories of failed promise and unfulfilled lives that I don't get to hear. Just the same, I print the stories in the magazine and I expect they encourage people to excel in their own ways. I tucked the letter absent-mindedly into my coat pocket. I was feeling uneasy. There was something... something at the back of my mind, waiting to come into focus. Something about John Sellars.

'Come on Geoffrey. Let's head on back.' We finished our beer, picked up our coats and to a cheery 'Thank you, gentlemen!' from behind the bar made our way through the blustery autumn wind the short distance down the lane back to the cottage, making a stop or two along the way as old men do when they have had three pints to drink and the weather is on the chilly side. When we got home, it was to find that my wife had lit the fire in the sitting-room and settled herself in the corner with a book. Two mugs of tea were waiting for us by the hearth. Muriel knows Geoffrey and me very well indeed.

People sometimes ask me why I moved away from the Vale of White Horse when I finally retired from teaching. 'After all,' they say, 'you must have liked it there. How long were you at The Vale?'

'Nearly fifty years,' I reply.

'How could you bear to leave?'

And I explain that, although being a senior master at a Public School is a good life, it's not the only life. Not for me, anyway. Some masters enjoy playing games, some go on expeditions, some compile crosswords, some collect antiquities. I write mystery novels under the name of Fabian Greene and I don't mind admitting that I'm pretty good at it. I must have had over fifty of them published by now and I've enjoyed my fair share of success – radio plays, TV adaptations, a couple of films, that sort of thing.

It was the royalties from my detective stories that bought the cottage, not my school pension. It's the repeat fees from the television shows that have allowed Muriel and I to enjoy a very comfortable retirement, taking holidays whenever we feel like it and still having enough money left over to help our children when they need it. Not for us the life of a Mr Chips, dosing quietly away in genteel poverty just outside the walls of the school. That's Geoffrey's preserve. He never married, although there had been talk once, many years ago, that he might. Only he and I knew the truth about that, and we never talked about it, not even on the occasions, three or four times a year, when he drove his old Rover the hundred miles or so down from Oxfordshire and came to stay with us for a few days.

So we moved away, to Dorset and the coast where Muriel could mix with people who had absolutely nothing to do with education (to her great relief). I could enjoy the sun and the wind and the rain, and look at the sea whenever I wanted, and do a little writing, and keep in touch with the old world – kept at an appropriate distance – via the expensive new computer that was installed in the study which I had had built on to the side of the cottage.

The computer... Sellars... Now it came into focus at last.

'Geoffrey. Would you come into my study for a moment?'

'I've just got comfortable.'

'No, come on.'

Geoffrey grumbled, but he stood up and followed me into the study. 'You haven't brought me out here just to show me your nasty new toy again, have you?'

'Sit down, old chap.' I pointed to a wickerwork chair in the corner of the room, next to the display case where I keep my literary trophies. Geoffrey sat there and scowled at me while I turned on – or "booted up", as my IT instructor likes to phrase it – the machine. After a minute or two of mysterious buzzes, clicks and whirs the logon screen appeared and I entered my name and password. This process mystifies Muriel, which annoys me. She's an intelligent woman and could easily learn to use the computer just as well as – or better than – I do. I clicked on the Mail icon and my email magically manifested itself, all the messages I had received neatly arranged in reverse order of delivery with the newest one at the top of the list.

Now then... about a week ago, wasn't it? I scrolled down the messages... and there it was. I clicked on it and it opened in a new window. (I know the jargon, you see.)

'Look at this.'

Geoffrey peered over my shoulder. 'I can't see a thing. Can't make it out. You read it.'

The room was cosy and warm, but I felt a chill as I read the message out aloud:

Dear Mr Jackson,

Please excuse my not writing to you properly. I got your email address from the School magazine. I'm afraid that I have some bad news to pass on to you. My father, who was in your House from 1966 until 1971, died last week in a car crash. I expect you'll want to put something about him in your magazine, I'll send you something in the post.

Yours sincerely,

George Campbell

'Campbell...' Geoffrey mused. 'We had lots of Campbells. I suppose you remember this one? If he was in your house, I mean.'

Yes, I most certainly did. My mind may have been a little befuddled earlier by the effects of three pints of best bitter and a generous helping of Fred's chicken and leek pie but it had recovered its clarity now. I swivelled the computer chair around and faced Geoffrey.

'We kept it quiet at the time.'

'Sorry? What do you mean, you kept it quiet? What did you keep quiet?'

'You'll see. It's an odd story and so far as I know only Sellars, Campbell and myself knew about it. We didn't want any kind of scandal and it was possible in those days to have people promise to keep things under their hats and actually stick to their promises. They wouldn't go running off to the papers just because someone waved a cheque-book at them.'

'Many did, though, even then. What about the Profumo affair?'

'Yes, I know, but not the kind of people who were at The Vale. It wasn't the form. People had more decency and a proper respect for authority.'

'More reticence, anyway.'

'Just as you like, Geoffrey. But listen...'

There were never two boys so different as Sellars and Campbell. Sellars weighed over twelve stone when he first came to The Vale as a thirteen-year-old and none of it was fat. He was extraordinarily strong, and to go with his strength he had an excellent eye for a ball and a passion for games of all sorts. While no genius, he had no problems with keeping up in class so long as he applied himself. Geoffrey remembered him as being somewhat dense, but as my friend's chief subject and dearest love was Latin this was perhaps not to be wondered at. Very few boys managed to live up to Geoffrey's standards of scholarship and anyway Sellars' true home was on the football field or in the fives or squash courts. He was tough and aggressive and the kind of boy who could take a loose assortment of players and mould them into a team. It was no surprise to anybody when he became School Captain of Football when he was in the Fifth Form and still only sixteen.

Campbell was another case altogether. He was tall and lanky and gawky and thin and walked with an odd drooping posture. He always looked as if he was as if he was about to fall asleep and that often led the boys and the staff to assume that there was something wrong with him – before they got to know him, that is. In fact, he had won the top scholarship of his year and, when he applied himself or his interest was aroused, was capable of the most extraordinary work. Once, I remember Hedges the Lower School maths master coming to me in a state of great excitement – 'Jackson! Look! It's your young Campbell! Look at this!' He showed me an exercise book full of abstruse symbols that meant nothing to me whatsoever.

'Very good, Hedges. What is it?'

'What is it? What is it?' Hedges chirped at me. 'Fermat's Last Theorem. He's proved it! Nobody's been able to do that, ever. Not for hundreds of years! Look!'

I looked. I had no idea what Fermat's Last Theorem was, nor whether Campbell had proved it, nor whether this was a good or a bad thing to have done.

'Very good, Hedges. Very good.' (Actually, I still don't know whether Campbell had proved it or not. I saw a television programme about it a year or two ago which said that an English chap who was working in America had done it, so I suppose that either Campbell hadn't really proved it after all, or he hadn't been able to prove that he'd proved it.)

Chalk and cheese, apples and oranges. Two very different boys. We prided ourselves at The Vale School that we could bring out the best in every boy, and as a rule we did pretty well. I think that the school was big enough to contain both boys and, had things been arranged differently, they would not have clashed so disastrously. But they were not.

For a start, both boys were placed in my House. We allocate new boys to Houses on a sensible basis, taking into account parents' preferences (if the father is an Old Boy he may well want his son to enter the same House as he once lived in), the existence of siblings (a boy may – or may not – want to occupy the same House as his elder brother) and whether boys who were at the same Prep School want to stay together. After that, boys with no predetermined preferences are spread around the Houses in such a way that the good sportsmen and the good scholars are evenly distributed. It was no surprise and only fair that, having been given a superb footballer one year, I should get no more outstanding players for a while, but be handed an academic type the following autumn.

That was the root of the problem. Sellars was a year senior to Campbell. Why was this a problem? There were two reasons. First, the brighter new boys moved immediately into the Fourth Form, while their less academically distinguished comrades spent a year in the Third. This meant that Campbell and Sellars took many of their lessons together, despite their year's difference in age and seniority. I've no doubt that Campbell's effortless academic superiority and patronising air towards those who were less gifted than him grated on the older boy.

The second reason lay in the way that sporting contests between the Houses were organised. As you might expect, we had things like inter-House cricket matches, squash tournaments, swimming competitions, track days; all that and more. The boys who were good at games got into their House teams and enjoyed themselves. The ones who did especially well were awarded their House Colours and strode around the school grounds wearing them and feeling that they were mighty fine fellows. But it was felt – and rightly so – that there should also be an opportunity for those boys who were never chosen for their House sides to make a contribution and so the House Standards competitions were introduced.

They worked like this: each term had its own corresponding sport – gymnastics in Winter, athletics in Lent and swimming in Summer. For each sport a set of attainments were put in place – a first-year might be expected to climb a twenty-foot rope in five seconds, or run a hundred yards in eighteen seconds or dive for a brick at the bottom of the deep end of the swimming pool. They were set so as to be challenging, but nevertheless achievable by the average boy if he was prepared to make a decent effort. Every time a boy achieved a Standard, a point was awarded to his House. The points were totted up at the end of the competition and the House with the most points won. Of course, there were some boys in each House who got all their Standards with no trouble at all, and others who struggled to gain more than one or two. It was generally felt that, so long as a boy did the best he could, and showed a respectable amount of House spirit he would have shown himself to be a good sort. The prefects chivvied those boys who had not gained all their Standards down to the gym, the track, or the pool and encouraged them to win more points for their House.

It was a good basis for a competition, I think. No boy could earn any more points for his House than any of his fellows, however good he was, and the results reflected more the ability of a House's prefects to motivate and organise their charges than the brilliance of any particular individual.

'I kept well clear of all that nonsense,' Geoffrey said.

'It wasn't nonsense.'

Geoffrey shook his head. 'All right, Jack. But it brought out the worst in some of the boys, even if it brought out the best in the others. Take your man Sellars, for example.'

So Geoffrey had noticed, then. It was inevitable that when he entered his final year at The Vale, Sellars should not only become a House Prefect, but also Head of School House, if for no other reason than the need to do something about the lamentable state of our trophy cupboard. If anybody could lift our sporting results, it would be him. It worked, too. We won the House Rugby hands down, and came second in the Gymnastics Standards, despite Sellars being no gymnast himself.

He was tireless; sweeping School House every afternoon for all the boys who still had Standards to earn and urging them on as they suffered on the various instruments of torture with which the gym was equipped. I would go down there regularly and give him my support, and I couldn't help but notice that his keenness and encouragement sometimes tended to turn into bullying and intimidation. I had had a quiet word with him once or twice to go easy on some of the less able boys. Of course I never saw Campbell in the gym, or on the rugger pitches either, and I don't recall that he ever earned School House more than a desultory point or two in all the years he was with us. This did not at all endear him to Sellars.

The other housemasters would come up to me in the Staff Room. 'No chance for us this year, eh Jack?' I'd smile and say that it was School House's turn at last for a little sporting success.

Christmas came and went, with its School Play and Carol Concert. Then it was Lent Term, with chilly winds and snow on the ground. The Athletics Standards competition started after half-term and ran for four weeks. The initial six-week series of my Miss Dorpleston mysteries was being performed on the wireless, I recall. It was the first time any of my detective stories had been adapted into dramatic form and I was eager to hear what the BBC Repertory Company had done with them. It was ten past three in the afternoon and I had just settled down to listen to their production of *The Lady's not for Spurning*, when there was a heavy knock on my study door.

Blast, I thought and, 'Come in,' I said.

It was Sellars in his sports kit, red-faced and furious. He glared at me as if I was a particularly obnoxious fourth-former.

Geoffrey interrupted; 'They *are* obnoxious.'

'So they are, Geoffrey. But let's get back to the story.'

With a sigh, I turned the wireless down. 'Do take a seat, Sellars,' I said.

The boy remained standing. Although the room was warm I could have sworn that I could see steam rising from him. 'Sir,' he said. 'I want your permission to beat Campbell.'

This must seem like an extraordinary request these days, when corporal punishment is forbidden in schools, but it was not so very uncommon then.

'Why?'

'He's the most dreadful slacker, sir.'

'That is unfortunate Sellars, but not sufficient cause to punish him.'

'He has told me a direct lie.'

Ah. That was more serious. Campbell's total lack of interest in sport was down to the way he was made and there was nothing much we could do about it. Lying to a prefect was another thing altogether. At The Vale we preferred to teach our pupils to tell the truth, rather than how to lie effectively, as seems to be the case so often nowadays.

'Very well, Sellars. I shall need some time to consider this. Would you and Campbell please come and see me tonight at nine? I shall listen to what both of you have to say then.' Sellars left the room, still fuming, and I turned the wireless back up. I saw no reason why a squabble between two boys should interrupt my listening.

'Was it any good?'

'The programme? I thought it was execrable. Totally lifeless. They made Miss D. sound like a ninety-year-old moron.'

'Oh dear,' said Geoffrey, sounding rather less upset than I would have liked.

They had had a row, of course. Sellars had gone barging about the House in his usual way, flushing reluctant sportsmen out of their comfortable studies and into the changing rooms, to put on running shoes and shorts and go down to the chilly athletics track and have another try at the 220 yards, or whatever Standard it was that they hadn't earned yet. He had found Campbell in his room, reading a book with his feet up on his desk and listening to choral music on the wireless. He had told him to get off his anatomy and get into his kit and to show some doubly-qualified House Spirit for a change. Campbell had ignored him; except for turning his wireless up a notch. Sellars had lost his temper at this point and, although he didn't actually strike Campbell he pretty much forced him to his feet and out into the changing rooms. He probably threatened him with a week of polishing the prefects' shoes or some other form of punishment. Sellars claimed that Campbell had told him that he would see him by the high jump – which was the one Standard that he thought the six-footer might be able to achieve – in ten minutes. He never turned up and Sellars found out later that he had gone to the Music Department instead and played Scarlatti sonatas all afternoon, still wearing his plimsolls.

'He told me he was going to the field and he didn't. He never meant to. He was lying to me, sir!'

I considered. The accusation was serious, and it seemed to be well-founded. Campbell was a sixth-former, and consequently high standards of probity and integrity were expected from him. On the other hand, there was Sellars' bullying manner to consider. Campbell could claim that his promise to go to the high jump was forced from him under duress.

'What do you say, Campbell?'

'I say he should jolly mind his own business. If he spent less time running around the place shouting at people about his stupid Standards he might have a better chance of passing a few A-levels next term!' Campbell, like so many academically clever boys, had absolutely no tact. A-levels were as much of a *bête noire* to Sellars as sports were to Campbell. If only they hadn't been exactly one year apart!

'How do you mean?'

'You see Geoffrey; if they had been in the same year then Campbell would almost certainly have been a prefect too, and Sellars would not have been able to demand that he go to the sports field and threaten to punish him if he didn't. If Campbell had been two years younger than Sellars, he wouldn't have dared to disobey him. Or if they had been in different Houses or Sellars had been younger than Campbell, then again the problem wouldn't have arisen. But from Campbell's point of view he was Sellars' equal and he saw no need to show him any deference or respect at all. There was a lot of that sort of thing about in the late 1960s.'

'All that awful music, you mean.'

'Yes, and the Paris Riots of 1968. It was all very unsettling. In the following year, the prefects tore up the punishment system altogether.'

'Good Heavens!'

'It meant a lot more work for me.'

Sellars had been an idiot, coming to me. It meant that I was involved, for Sellars' authority derived from me, and if I didn't back him up then his credibility – and mine too – would be in danger. Somehow, I needed to find a way out of this *impasse*.

'Why can't you two come to some agreement? Settle it now? Admit you've both got a bit steamed up?'

'I will, sir.' That was Campbell.

'No! He has told a deliberate lie to a School Prefect! Either I must beat him or you must, sir.'

I was coming to that conclusion myself. It would have been a very bad idea to let Sellars, who had a powerful squash player's right arm, cane Campbell, especially as he had such an obvious grudge against him.

'Very well. If you cannot agree to shake hands and admit that you have both made a mistake, then I shall have to punish Campbell. But I must tell you, Sellars, that you have fallen a great deal in my estimation over this. A very great deal.' That was my way of punishing Sellars.

'We're going to win the Athletics Standards, sir. That's what matters. I'm going to make sure of it.' Sellars' determined expression made this seem very likely. And if I were being honest, I should have to own up to the fact that I was enjoying School House's new run of successes, and I knew that it was mostly down to Sellars' efforts.

'So you're going to get Mr Jackson to do your dirty work for you, are you?' Campbell sneered. The hostility between the two boys was at its most palpable. Neither could or ever would see the other's point of view.

'That's enough, Campbell!' I said. The boy was going too far.

'Sir, before you cane me for this, I think there's something you ought to know.'

'What's that?'

I leaned across to Geoffrey.

'Campbell told me something about Sellars that I will never tell you or any other living soul. Not even now, even though both he and Campbell are dead. It was astonishing and very, very horrible. They both had sons, and it would be the most appalling thing if they were to learn from anybody other than their own fathers what I learned from Campbell that evening. I hope their fathers never told them.'

'Was it...?'

'No. Please don't ask. All I'll say is that Sellars looked very sick indeed, and I had to send a boy over to fetch Muriel to take him down to the San.'

When Sellars had gone I turned to Campbell. I had absolutely no idea of how to deal with him. 'I should bloody well thrash you for what you've just done. I hope you're proud of yourself.'

'He made me say it, sir. I didn't want to.'

You didn't have to say it, I thought, but kept my thoughts to myself.

'How did you find out, anyway?'

'Our sisters... they go to the same school. Girls talk, you know, sir.'

'Why would your sister tell you a thing like that?'

'She wouldn't have, I'm sure. Only, one day in the hols I was telling her what a beast Sellars is and what he was doing to me, and she told me what I told you, and she made me swear never to tell a living soul. You won't tell on me will you, sir?'

'I will not. But in your turn you must promise that you will never repeat to anybody what you have told me this evening.'

'Yes, sir. Sorry sir.'

I looked at the boy, still standing by the bookcase. He looked as pale and ill as Sellars had, and even though I despised him for what he had done, I felt pity for him too. What a heavy burden that knowledge must have been!

Both boys stayed on at The Vale, although I suggested to each of them individually that it would be the right thing for them to leave. I would have preferred it if we could have expelled them; but on what grounds? It was totally inconceivable that I should tell anyone what I had learned, so we would have had to send them down for trumped-up reasons. Sellars never spoke to Campbell again. He left at the end of the year with a modest set of A-level results and spent three years at a provincial university, gaining a third class honours degree and going straight into his father's business, where he prospered. Campbell was not made a prefect – he was temperamentally unsuited, I told his parents – and he moved on to a life of academic research, and modest fortune, as so many very clever but socially maladroit boys do. That might have been all there was to tell, except that when the Internet took off in the mid-1990s it turned out that he had registered some patents which were a key part of the system, and he became very rich, moving to the Thames Valley and living and working quite near to his old adversary who was by this time a well-established businessman.

The second letter arrived a day or so later. I showed it to Geoffrey.

'Good heavens! What an extraordinary thing!'

'Yes. Most extraordinary. So extraordinary and unlikely that I think we should go to Berkshire and take a closer look. What do you think?'

Geoffrey, Muriel and I piled into the Saab and I drove us up to Oakingham, which is the town where Sellars and Campbell had both lived. We didn't like it much. There was nowhere decent to have lunch, even though the town was full of pubs and restaurants. In fact, I've never seen anywhere so thoroughly spoiled as that town. It must have been a pleasant enough place fifty years ago, before the corporations and the money and the housing estates arrived, but now it was drab and dreary, traffic-choked and cramped. In the end we gave up on it, and drove out to the west. Swallowfield, where the accident had occurred, was three or four miles away, to the south of Reading.

When we reached Swallowfield we found that there was still a bunch of wilted flowers lying by the side of the road, where it made a turn to the east. It had been a few weeks since the crash, so the grass had started to grow back over the tyre marks on the verge, but the scrapes on the wall and the newly-replaced section of wooden fence behind it told a story which I could read easily enough. Standing on the verge we could see that the entrance of the drive which belonged to the house which stood on the inside of the apex of the bend was a dangerous place to turn out from – so dangerous that the owner had fixed a two-sided mirror to a post on the far side of the road so he could see cars coming from both directions.

It had made the front page of the *Oakingham Times*. Two middle-aged businessmen, both driving powerful German sports cars of the same make and colour, had collided on the bend. Each had been going at an estimated sixty miles per hour. Both cars were in excellent mechanical order, and easily capable of rounding the bend in the dry conditions which pertained at the time of the accident. One had been driven by Sellars, one by Campbell.

'What do you make of it?' asked Geoffrey, when we regained the warmth and safety of the Saab. I didn't answer immediately, but started the car and drove down the road a little way, reversed in a side-entrance and came back slowly.

'Look straight ahead,' I said, and 'Oh, yes!' Muriel said immediately afterwards. Geoffrey, who was sitting in the back seat, didn't see what we saw from the front, so I carried on past the bend and stopped in a lay-by. My two passengers changed places and I turned the car round again.

'Keep your eyes on the road ahead,' I told him. Geoffrey stared forwards. We passed the corner for the third time.

'Ah... I see,' he said. 'It's like something out of one of your books, isn't it?'

'So each driver saw what he thought was the reflection of his own car in the mirror that was fixed by the side of the road. He didn't realise that it was actually the other driver's car that he was seeing. What time did the accident happen?'

'Seven-fifteen in the evening. It was just getting dark. Twilight is always the most dangerous time to be out on the roads. Both drivers must have known that road very well – the paper said it's a popular route if you want to get from Oakingham to Basingstoke and avoid the traffic on the A33. Campbell was ploughing along, saw Sellars' car, thought it was the reflection of his own car in the mirror and not another car coming in the opposite direction, and took the bend a bit wide.'

'While Sellars, who was on the outside of the bend, made the same mistake and, as he was going pretty quickly too, he decided to cut the corner a little.'

'And the result was that they met on the crown of the road at a combined speed of one hundred and twenty miles per hour.' Muriel shuddered. 'No wonder they were both killed instantly.'

We were drinking coffee in the sitting-room of the cottage. It was dark outside and Muriel had drawn the curtains and turned up the radiators.

'I read somewhere,' I said, 'that's there's no such thing as a coincidence. So many things happen in the world every day, every second, that even the most extraordinary improbabilities are really very commonplace indeed. Suppose that there was a million to one chance that you would, oh I don't know, meet a man from Mars on any particular day. Now there are over fifty-five million people in this country alone, so several of them could be shaking hands with Tars Tarkas, Jeddak of Thark, right now.'

'You mean, Flying Saucers Really Have Landed.'

'Don't be silly. You know what I mean. It wasn't so very unlikely that Campbell and Sellars would end up in the same prosperous part of the country, nor that they, having made their piles, would buy similar Porsche sports cars.'

'Yes – but why should they meet on that particular day on that particular bend in the road?'

'It was a day like any other. Any day would have done.'

'It's still too much. Too... bizarre, too wrong.'

'I agree.'

'Could Campbell have been blackmailing Sellars, with the knowledge he had? You still won't tell me what it was?'

'If I told you, you'd only wish I hadn't. Believe me Geoffrey, you're better off not knowing.'

'If it was as terrible a secret as you say, are you sure that Campbell wasn't using it against Sellars?'

'Why should he? He had plenty of money. And why then, and not before when he wasn't so well off?'

'They were both the same in so many ways – dogmatic, never paying much attention to other people's opinions or feelings.'

'Could we have helped them, while they were at The Vale?'

'They would never have seen eye to eye. Their happening to clash the way they did was just another coincidence – in other words, not a coincidence at all. The same goes for the accident, don't you think?'

'If only we could be sure...'

'If you two don't cheer up soon,' said Muriel, 'I'll send you both off to the pub!'

How many people are there left who know Sellars' secret? I wondered, as I lay awake in bed that night. It had been many years since I had let that fearful knowledge disturb my sleep, but it came back to me with full force now. It was the stuff of nightmares, and I was rather afraid that I would be suffering upset nights for some weeks to come. Thoughts kept turning over in my mind – about the secret, of course, but about other things too. There were ramifications and consequences to consider.

For example, were Campbell's and Sellars' sisters still alive? They both knew the secret and I prayed that they had not let it get any further than it had already. But if they too had died like their brothers in an unlikely accident that only left me and maybe their sons. And, if I were the only one left alive who knew the secret, I could be sure that the knowledge of it would die with me, for I will never tell it to anybody. There is another possibility, however, and it worries me. Suppose there is somebody who, without knowing the secret themselves, knows that I know it and needs to be sure that its last owner can never pass it on? What about Sellars' son? Was he told about it? Or that I was privy to it? Surely not. But can I be sure? Could it be that I too will suffer an untoward end some day? And perhaps Muriel as well? It would be too dangerous to make enquiries, however discreet, so I shall never know.

There is just one other thing that bothers me. As I said, I've been a successful writer of mystery stories for forty years or more, and published more than fifty books. Could it be that somewhere in one of my tales I have let slip, unconsciously of course, some little detail that an alert reader could use to discover what Sellars' secret was? No author knows more than half of what goes into his stories and any writer who claims that he understands himself and his writings completely is either deluding himself or a liar. The secret has been lurking in the back of my mind for over thirty years. Who knows what effect it might have had on the workings of my imagination or the way in which I may have chosen to tell a story? I simply cannot tell whether I may have inadvertently revealed the truth about Sellars, and I know no safe way of finding out.

There is, however, one thing of which I am certain. I do not think that I shall ever again drive in the twilight.

A MATTER
OF
DISCIPLINE

A Matter of Discipline

WHAT ON EARTH IS GOING ON IN SCHOOL HOUSE?'
'Going on? What do you mean, "going on"?'
'You know what I mean.'
'I'm not sure that I do.'

'I'm sure that you do. The whole bloody place is going to the demnition bow-wows.'

'Very funny. Come on. We're late for Physics. Don't want old Haystacks getting in a sweat about it.'

'Dead right. He's sweaty enough already.'

It hurt me of course, and if I had been more alert I'd have coughed loudly or dropped a book to let those two boys know I was nearby. As it was I had eavesdropped on them quite by accident. I had been sitting at my desk in the Sixth Form Arts School, idly working up a new sub-plot for one of my novels, when they passed by the open window, chatting as boys do. One of them was Watson from Roberts' House and the other was one of my own School House boys, George Whybrow.

The mid-morning break was coming to an end. I would have to put my notes aside in a moment or two and get ready to resume revising the social history of the Industrial Revolution with one of my Middle Sixth classes. They would be taking their A-level examinations in only another few weeks, so the die was cast for most of them – they would pass or fail on the basis of their inborn talent combined with their application to their work. Or otherwise, naturally. All the same, a good course of revision can turn a fail into a pass, or lift a grade C result to a B or even an A. It can make the difference between entering Oxford or Cambridge and having to settle for a lesser university. It's no exaggeration to say that whole careers have been made or thrown away in the A-level examination room.

I looked again at my notepad. My jottings were making little sense, and I found myself wondering why I had ever tried to create this set of stories featuring the adventures of an alchemical detective in sixteenth century London. It had sounded such a good idea. Kit Huntingdon, natural philosopher and occasional alchemist, solving crimes in the intrigue-ridden courts of Henry Tudor and his daughters Mary and Elizabeth and his son Edward. There was so much story potential there – Kit would be walking a tightrope, in perpetual danger of being denounced as a witch and trying to avoid being sucked into the fierce religious disputes of the time, while putting his quasi-heretical skills to good use in the untangling of the devious political schemes and stratagems for which the Tudor courts were renowned. The story I was working up – *The King of Spain's Weird* – concerned the Spanish Armada, the Inquisition and a false soothsayer. It was full of interesting ideas and it should have practically written itself, but it wouldn't. The plot wouldn't gel, the characters refused to act in a consistent way and – worst of all – I kept getting my historical facts wrong. Which for someone who calls himself a historian is a very serious matter indeed.

Nicholas Nickleby was an A-level English set book that year. That explained the silly Dickens quote which that wretched Watson had misused. I should have laughed at the boy's foolishness and left it at that. But I couldn't; and I'm sorry to say that I was not a great deal of help to my History class that morning.

For there was definitely something wrong with School House. My House. I had been in charge of the everyday pastoral care of the sixty boys who lived in the oldest and most traditional of the Houses of The Vale School for six years now. Generally speaking, they had been good years and I could look back on my time there as having been a success. It wasn't all down to me; my wife Muriel had taken on the job of House Matron and I had been fortunate in my prefects and Head Boys. Some years were better than others, of course, and it was certainly true that one boy could exert a disproportionately bad influence on his fellows and drag the whole tenor of the place down. That was why we had a punishment system.

If, as a potential parent perhaps, you read the Prospectus of The Vale School you will see that there is a clear statement that we have a policy of no compulsory fagging. The great Public Schools still keep it, I know. In the halls and corridors of Eton or Harrow, Winchester, Rugby or Marlborough a prefect's cry of 'fag!' will summon a stream of small boys eager to pass the Senior Study door ahead of the rest and escape having to perform some menial task for their superiors; such as making toast or cleaning shoes or washing sports kit. It is said to encourage the development of appropriate hierarchies and to ensure that even boys from the wealthiest homes have at least some experience, just once in their lives, of the simpler housekeeping jobs. It also causes much innocent amusement among our transatlantic cousins when they hear a distinguished member of the House of Lords declare that 'Lord So-and-so was my fag at Fettes.' It confirms their belief that the British Public School system is a hotbed of all kinds of deviant behaviour.

That is as may be. And while it is true that there is no *compulsory* fagging at The Vale; nevertheless there are ways and means around this. In School House for example, a minor infraction of the rules is punished by the awarding of one or more so-called Obligations, which are recorded on a chart which is affixed to the Senior Study door. Any boy who has undischarged Obligations can be made to do such lowly tasks for the prefects as making toast or cleaning shoes or washing sports kit – in other words fagging is used as a means of maintaining discipline, rather than as a reminder that there are dirty jobs to do in this world, and that people have to do them. I am not sure that this is a good thing; this making a penance out of necessary labour and offenders out of those who do it, but it is the way things are done here. The system is run by the prefects and I make sure that they do not abuse it.

There are further sanctions available to deal with more serious offences, but I will come on to them presently.

The trouble came down to this: Discipline had almost completely collapsed in School House. Only last week someone had torn down the Obligation chart from the Senior Study door. Boys ran around the place just as they pleased, shouting and swearing at the top of their voices. School House boys were late for their lessons, were missing their books when they did get to them and usually hadn't done their homework. I was taking considerable flak in the Staff Room – so much so that I'm sorry to say that I was beginning to avoid going there at break times, preferring to return to my study in School House. Not that that was very much better. The sound of highly-amplified popular music echoed up and down the stairs and out of the windows, disturbing my studies. 'What is that noise?' I asked Morrison, my Head of House, one day.

'The Grateful Dead, sir. They're a new group from America.'

'The Grateful Dead? Why are they grateful? Who is dead? What does it mean? I hope it's nothing to do with drugs.'

'It's only a name, sir. It doesn't mean anything.'

'Neither does that awful racket they're making. Get it turned down. It's deafening!'

'I'll see what I can do, sir.'

The prefects – and they weren't a bad lot, just out of their depth – seemed unable to control the juniors. I later found out that they were tending to avoid School House themselves, just as I avoided the Staff Room, going back with their friends from the other Houses and eating muffins and drinking instant coffee in their studies instead.

It all seemed to come down to one group of Fifth Formers, led by an objectionable lout by the name of Simon Parrott. It would sound like one of the stories I used to read in the *Gem* or the *Magnet* when I was a boy if I were to say that he was spoiled and rich, but in fact he was neither of these things. His father was a department store manager in Derby, I believe. He was very intelligent, I am sure, but he had no idea of how to apply his intelligence and so he easily became bored. With boredom came what Edgar Allen Poe called the Imp of the Perverse. He always had an objection, which he would express as if it were a perfectly valid reason, to doing as he was told. You could argue with him for ever, and get nowhere. Or you could simply tell him and, if you were a master or a prefect he would do it, with a sullen or cocky air. This was bad enough when he was a new boy, or in the Fourth Form, but by the time he had been at The Vale for two years and entered the Fifth, he thought he had no need to obey anybody. To add to the problem, the malaise was beginning to spread. It only took one abstracted or tired prefect to overlook one of his transgressions, and that would be taken as justification for him to do it again, and for his friends – for he had friends, surprisingly – to do it as well. 'You didn't punish Parrott for running on the Chapel Flags,' some oik in the Fourth would say, 'so why are you picking on me?'

It came to a head at the start of the Lent Term. The boy had been beaten before, but only by the prefects. They are carefully supervised when they administer corporal punishment, so they are more likely to wield the cane too gently than with an excess of force. These punishments had had as little effect on the reprobate as you might have expected, culminating in an unfortunate episode which had left

Clayton, who was a soft-hearted chap, much more upset than the offender he was supposed to have disciplined. I called Parrott into my study.

It must have been clear to him the moment that he entered the room that he was in serious trouble. I had turned the picture of the Queen which hangs over the fireplace around, so that it faced the wall. It emphasises the grave nature of what is about to happen that the Queen of England's image should not be exposed to the sight of a boy's beating. It also gives the boy advance notice, so that he can prepare himself mentally for the ordeal to come.

Actually, the Queen's picture – the Annigoni portrait – was the only part of the room which was as it had been the previous year. Muriel, who spent a good deal of her time trying to make me a little less schoolmasterly, had had my study redecorated and rearranged the previous summer. I had to say that she had made some remarkable improvements. My desk was now much better lit by the leaded windows which looked over the tennis lawns beyond, my bookcases were neatly organised and completely re-indexed and my two Parker-Knoll armchairs had been reupholstered and moved from their original positions by the door to new locations on either side of the bay window in the opposite wall. She had, with that infallible woman's touch of hers, transformed a stuffy room full of stuffy thoughts into a light and airy place.

Parrott slouched though the door, slamming it shut behind him, and stood in the middle of the floor with his hands in his pockets and his head tilted to one side. His mouth was moving – he was chewing gum or something like that. I decided to waste no time with him.

'Parrott, we both know why you are here today. Would you kindly spit out whatever you are eating into the waste-paper basket.' The youth spat.

'Now remove your jacket. You may hang it on the back of the door.' Moving with an insolent slowness, Parrott took off his coat and hung it up.

'Thank you. Now bend over the right arm of that chair and wait.' I pointed to the left-hand armchair. I myself am right-handed.

Again with that infuriating lassitude, Parrott did as he was told. I got up from behind the desk and went to the cupboard where I keep the instruments of correction. I unlocked it, and took out a medium-weight kooboo with a straight handle. As you might expect I use a number of different canes, some suitable for the delicate boy, others of a substantial nature, more appropriate for the older offender. This was the stick which I usually employed with boys from the Fifth Form. I removed my own jacket and my schoolmaster's gown, hanging them on the back of the door, and took my usual place to the front of the armchair where Parrott was kneeling.

I looked carefully at him. He might have entertained the idea that he could use that oldest of schoolboy devices, the exercise book slipped into the seat of the trousers, but if so he had thought better of it. One of his friends had probably warned him that I was not so stupid as not to know about such tricks, and that the beating which I would administer following its discovery would be far worse than it would have been otherwise.

I was not disposed to be gentle with Master Parrott, so it was indeed fortunate for him that he had not tried to mitigate the effects of the punishment which I was about to give him. Or so I thought.

I gave the boy six strokes, fully swung. In other words, I pulled the cane all the way behind my shoulder before sweeping it down and striking him with it. It is the length of the swing which mainly determines the force of the blow. Ask any golfer. The results, however, were not quite what I had expected.

Usually after such a beating the boy is a little short of breath and gets up from the kneeling position with a certain amount of care. Then he and I shake hands, and he thanks me before taking his jacket and walking – slowly, as a rule – from my study and closing the door silently behind him. This time it was different. Parrott practically jumped to his feet.

'Is that it? Thanks sir.' He sauntered over to the door, across the room, grabbing his jacket and slinging it casually over his shoulder. He yanked on the doorknob, strode out into the passageway beyond and pulled the door shut behind him with a loud bang. I believe he was whistling as he returned to his study.

Whistling! I was staggered. I had just given Parrott six of the very best and he had leapt up and strolled out as if we had just been taking afternoon tea and having a fireside chat. I looked at the cane where it lay on the desk. I picked it up and flexed it. There was nothing wrong with it that I could see. I gave it a trial swing through the air. It made the customary sound. Was there something wrong with my arm? No – apparently not. There was no pain or discomfort there. I had not strained it recently. I locked the kooboo back in its cupboard and shook my head. I was absolutely sure that Parrott had not put anything down his trousers. As I said, I am not a fool and I had been a housemaster for over six years.

By the end of the day the whole of School House knew that old Jacko had lost his form and that a caning from him was nothing to fear any more. By the end of the following week it felt as if I had caned half the House, with the same dismal results as with Parrott. By the end of the first Half of that Lent Term I was beginning to feel a little desperate. Things were, I was sure, beginning to be said in the Staff Room, the Bursar's Office and the Headmaster's Study.

I saw the school doctor; an old quack to be sure, but he gave me a clean bill of health. I spent some time in the gym during the evenings when it was quiet, doing a little weight-lifting. I ordered a complete new set of canes from the Midland Educational Company, but they were no better or more effective than the ones I had already. In the end, I did what I should have done to begin with. I talked to Geoffrey Thurslow about it.

'What do Rogers and Jenkins say?' asked Geoffrey.

'I… I don't want to talk to the other housemasters just yet. They might see it as a sign of weakness, you know.'

'Quite so, quite so. And you say the beatings have had no effect at all?'

'Apart from making me look like an idiot, no.'

'Well, hmmm. Can't say I'm in favour of this corporal punishment anyway. Boys don't learn though their bottoms, do they?' He chortled at his own joke.

'Or any other way, so I hear.' I was feeling testy.

'Now, now. All right, here's an idea. Why not test it on me?'

'What?'

'Try it out on me. Where do you put the horrible miscreants when you're going to give them a whacking?'

'Over the arm of the chair you're sitting on.'

'All right.' Geoffrey stood up. 'So they take their jackets off?'

'Yes.'

'And they kneel down so?' He crouched down by the side of the chair.

'Pretty much. Forward a bit. Yes, that's it.'

'All right, Jack. Take a swish or two.'

63

'What?'

'Give me a couple. Swish me.'

I studied Geoffrey's skinny buttocks, outlined in beige cavalry twill. He turned his head to the left and grinned at me. 'Go on. I won't tell anyone.'

'Do you really mean this?'

'Of course.'

'You've been caned before?'

'Of course. I went to school, didn't I?'

'Very well.' I fetched a 36-inch dragon cane from the cupboard. 'I warn you Geoffrey, this is meant to hurt.'

'Stop messing about and get on with it!'

I took careful aim and placed a couple of blows on Geoffrey's rear. 'Go on! Give me a few more.' I obliged him, *con brio*.

Geoffrey stood up with no obvious signs of discomfort. 'Well! Either my backside is a lot tougher than it used to be, or you housemasters have forgotten how to use the cane!'

This was getting ridiculous. 'All right, Geoffrey! If you're so tough, try it out on me.' I kneeled down over the arm of the chair, gripping the opposite arm with my hands as I had seen the boys do. Geoffrey lifted my jacket up over my back, exposing the seat of my trousers. 'Aren't you supposed to take this off?'

'Yes I am. I'd have given one of my boys an extra two for forgetting it.'

'Then so will I.'

As I had supposed to be the case with Geoffrey, I hadn't been caned since my schooldays. Unlike Geoffrey I was – or so I had thought – a skilled practitioner of the supple art. I hoped that my friend would remember that when it comes to administering a caning consistency is all; consistency of force and consistency of positioning. I had no wish to be struck on the back or on the legs. I need not have worried.

The dragon cane swooshed through the air and landed fair and square on me. I was expecting to suffer a red-hot burning sensation from the cut, but apart from a mild impact I felt very little. Nor did the next blow have any more effect. Geoffrey may not have been experienced in the use of the cane, but he was no beginner either, the cuts being spread evenly across my anatomy. After the sixth, seventh and eighth he stopped. I stood up.

'Where did you learn to use a cane like that?'

Geoffrey's face was flushed – from exertion, perhaps. 'Oh, nowhere. It's a knack, you know.'

'It's not much of a knack, then. I hardly felt a thing.' I took the instrument from Geoffrey. 'There's nothing wrong with this.' Indeed there was not. It had cost me thirty-one shillings and sixpence.

'No – it's a very good one.' How did Geoffrey know that? Subject masters like him did not use the cane at The Vale. Such matters were always referred to housemasters such as myself. I decided that I would rather not find out where Geoffrey got his knowledge from and let the matter drop.

It was nearly the end of the Lent Term. It had been the worst time of my life, and that includes my first term at Ercall College when I was bullied incessantly and remorselessly. My own morale and that of the boys in my charge had fallen to an all-time low. It seemed as if Parrott and his cronies thought that they were running the House, not me, and could do as they pleased. Why not expel them, you say? It was coming to that; but how could I admit my failure to the Headmaster or to my fellow housemasters? Had I been younger and less experienced I would not have minded calling for help. As it was I kept up a stony front which repelled all thoughts of assistance. I was seriously considering resignation. I could see no way out of the situation.

In the end it was Geoffrey who saved the day. He knocked on my study door one Saturday afternoon and bounded in cheerfully. I was sitting behind my desk, morosely leafing through *Crime and Punishment*.

'Jack, I've got it!'

'Well don't give it to me.'

'Ha-ha. No, listen. I know why the cane isn't working. It's the chi!'

'The what?'

'The chi! C-H-I. Chi! It's energy!'

'What are you talking about? I've plenty of energy.'

'It doesn't look like it. Anyway, listen. I told Brian…'

'Brian who?'

'Brian Thurslow. My brother.'

'You've got a brother?'

'Yes. His name's Brian.'

'You never told me.'

'You never asked.'

'And you told him?'

'Yes.'

'Why. What business was it of his?'

'He's filth!'

This was past bearing. I stood up. 'Geoffrey, have you been drinking? What do you mean, he's filth? Do you hate him? Why did you write to him about me, then?'

'Sit down, Jack. He's filth. F-I-L-T-H. Failed In London, Try Hongkong. He set up in stockbroking in the Square Mile, but it didn't work out. The family sent him out to the Far East for a second chance.'

'So you have a wastrel brother in China. How does that help me?'

'There are more things in heaven and earth, you know. Listen and learn, Jack. You've been having problems with discipline since the start of the school year, haven't you?'

'You know that.'

'What happened, in here, in the last summer holidays?'

'I read *War and Peace* for the tenth time. Is that relevant?'

'Not so far as I know. What else happened? Look around you!'

I looked around me. 'Muriel had the place done up. I like it.'

'Yes! The room was rearranged!'

'So what?' I was getting annoyed.

'So everything! You've been losing chi! Wasting energy!'

'What the hell are you on about?'

'I wrote to Brian, as I say. I told him, in passing, of what was happening here. He sent an airmail back, asking me how the room was laid out. I sent him a plan.

'Then he went to this business acquaintance of his, who helped him arrange the furniture in his office. Brian's been doing ever so well, you know, since he met this chap. Making money hand over fist – says he's going to retire soon. It seems that the way you set out the tables and chairs and windows in a room has a critical effect on your fortunes. Brian's was all wrong before this chap helped him because the chi – the energy – was leaking out through the window. As soon as he moved his desk to the right place all the energy and all the money landed on the top of it, instead of in the street outside, and stayed there.

'It's the same with you. All the discipline, all the order, in this room is being dissipated because the armchairs are standing by the window. Move one of them over here by the door and use that one for your canings, and everything'll be fine. Look!' Geoffrey showed me a piece of rice-paper, with a plan of my study carefully drawn on it in black ink. 'Come on! I'll help you move your things.'

Geoffrey and I heaved and pushed the heavy old armchair back into its old place by the door. 'Are you sure about this?' I asked him. 'By the window was much better. I could see what I was doing with the cane, and get a good swing.'

'Believe me. Now then!' The chair was by the door, looking rather out of place and in the way. 'We'll move the other stuff later. Let's try it out!'

'On you?'

'No fear! Isn't there an offender somewhere who's due a jolly good whacking?'

I was about to answer when there came a loud crash from outside the door, followed by a stream of imprecations which I will not repeat here. Geoffrey shot out, returning a few moments later holding Parrott by the left ear. 'Here's your man. He's just smashed the Quiet Room table.'

'All right. Get over that chair, Parrott. Mr Thurslow will stay and observe.' I went to the cupboard and fetched the dragon cane, although I had little hope that it would do any good. When I returned, Parrott was in position over the chair arm. I could see him smirking and pulling faces. He was sure he was in no danger. Geoffrey was standing on the other side of the chair. I took up my usual stance, pulled back the cane to its fullest extent and swung it as hard as I could at his posterior.

'Yarooh! Christ! Hell!' Parrott yelled and stood up. He rubbed his backside with one hand.

'Get back down, Parrott. Mr Thurslow, if you please.' Geoffrey took hold of the boy's hands and forced him back over the arm of the chair.

'Thank you.' I swung the cane again.

I gave Parrott thirteen strokes in total – a full baker's dozen – that afternoon, and sent him directly to his dormitory. The boy's shrieks and howls of pain had echoed up and down the stairwells and passageways of School House, bringing an eerie silence which persisted long after he climbed slowly up to his bed, to clutch at himself and drench the pillow with his tears. Muriel saw to him later, and the bruises had pretty much subsided by the time he went home a week later at the end of term.

Geoffrey and I finished moving the study furniture in accordance with the plan his brother had sent him. 'It's called Feng Shui,' Geoffrey said.

'It's an ancient Chinese art, making sure that your living and working spaces are harmoniously disposed.' I looked at the room. 'Ancient Chinese fiddlesticks,' I said. 'All we've done is put everything back exactly the way it was before Muriel redecorated it!'

'So we have. Tell me something, Jack. When you moved in here, after old Crockers left, did you change anything?'

'No. It seemed… right as it was.'

'And do you think *he* changed anything when he moved in here, fifty years ago?'

'I can't say.'

'I bet he didn't. Those old scholars knew things we don't know any more, whether they were Chinese, Celtic, Anglo-Saxon or whatever. Call it Feng Shui, call it instinct, call it what you like, you'd be a fool not to pay attention to what they said and did.'

And that is more or less the end of the story. Muriel never believed my explanation of why I had undone all her good work in my study, but as the atmosphere of the House that Summer Term was the best I had ever known it – especially as Parrott did not return after the Easter holidays – she forgave Geoffrey and me. I wanted to write to Brian to thank him personally, but Geoffrey dissuaded me. It appeared that he was a very private person who, like Mister Badger in *The Wind in the Willows*, hated Society. I have my own theory about which you are free to speculate, but which I would rather keep to myself.

THE GIFTS
OF THE LADY

The Gifts of the Lady

BLOODY HELL! OUR GEOFF'S IN LOVE! HE'S ONLY GONE AND GOT himself a girlfriend! That's what it is! Ha, ha, ha!'

'Shut up, Harries. Don't be so bloody vulgar.'

'Shut up yourself, Jacko. Anyway, it's true. Geoff's got a tart! He's a lovestruck loon; that's what he is!'

Harries was an obnoxious twerp, but I thought it very likely that, in this case at least, he was right. My friend Geoffrey had been behaving a little… oddly recently. Not that I was going to admit it to Harries. What a silly little man he was! All puffed up with pride just because he'd won his sergeant's stripes in the war, and been in the invasion force on D-Day. Didn't he realise that that was eight years ago now? The war was over. There was peace – a dangerous phony sort of peace, with America and the Soviet Union glaring at each other across the Atlantic Ocean, armed with horribly deadly weapons, and us, Little England, stuck in the middle and feeling as if we were everyone's target. All the same, it was peace of a kind.

I knew – because he had once told me in an indiscreet and not altogether sober moment – that Geoffrey Thurslow's contribution to winning the war had been infinitely greater than Sergeant Harries could ever guess; but I would never tell anyone else and neither would Geoffrey. Not all civilians were shirkers, as anyone who gave it a moment's thought would realise, and not all fighters necessarily wore blue or khaki.

Harries banged his way out of the Staff Room, leaving me its only occupant. I had a free period coming up, and should be getting on with marking 5B's essays on "What were the chief reasons for the execution of Charles I?" especially as I wanted some free time this evening to visit the Regal cinema. They were showing *Genevieve* that week. I reached for the pile of grey-green exercise books with a sigh. At the top of the heap was Clerestory Minor's opus. I groaned in anticipation, picked up the grubby book and searched its thumb-marked pages for the essay in question. It began:

> *Charles 1 was too busy having fun to rule the country properly. He wanted Ship Money. My father says he had a mistress who sold oranges, her name was Nelly Gwynne and he was very fond of her and didn't let her starve but Cromwell and the Roundheads...*

I put it down with another, deeper, sigh. Where could I possibly begin; apart from drawing attention to the fact that the idiot boy had got his Tudor and Stuart kings mixed up, that he had obviously paid no attention to what I was trying to teach him and that he had better try again? I would have to have a quiet word with his housemaster.

I could not possibly face the task of reading another such effort if it were to be along the same lines as Clerestory Minor's. It would only drive home to me the fact that I was not doing as well as I might when it came to dinning the facts of English History into the heads of a class of fifteen year-olds who had not the slightest interest in the subject. It could be wretched work. My only consolation was that I was not the only schoolmaster at The Vale who was encountering difficulties at the moment. We teachers love to complain about our lot – spending our lives trying to convey precious knowledge to a crowd of adolescent philistines who are much more interested in girls, rugger or cricket than the mysteries of the structure of the carbon molecule, or the poems of Ovid, or the foundation of the East India Company. It is the same for the other professions too, no doubt. But there was something... something in the air that was distracting the pupils and us and making it harder than usual to concentrate on our studies.

I stood up and crossed over to the window. It was propped open, serving the dual purpose of letting the fuggy, tobacco-laden air of the Staff Room out and the heady scents of the school gardens in. It was, and had been for the past three weeks, the most beautiful English summer imaginable. Soon, indeed, it would be Midsummer's Day and a perfect June would reach its glorious zenith. But there was more than simply the perfume of summer in the air, although that was fine enough – the flowers in the carefully-tended beds outside the window, the fragrance of new-cut grass drifting over from Cricket Bigside where Haynes was preparing the square for the First Eleven's match against our rivals from Marlborough. Leaning out, I breathed deeply and felt the essence of summertime flowing into my lungs, infusing my blood with a tingling urge to go, to be, to do. Even more than that, there was something else, which I can only describe as a heightening of physical and spiritual desire. I wanted to love. I wanted... I desired to become close to somebody; to lie next to her in a soft bed, or on a high eyrie perched at the top of the world, and to share my longings with her. I had not experienced such yearnings since I had been half my present age; just a boy. These feelings were coming close to overwhelming me, that summer. I often found that I was murmuring AE Housman's words of sweet nostalgia to myself:

When I was one-and-twenty
I heard a wise man say,
'Give crowns and pounds and guineas
But not your heart away;
Give pearls away and rubies
But keep your fancy free.'
But I was one-and-twenty
No use to talk to me.

If I, "Jack" Jackson, a celibate thirty-two-year-old history master at a minor Public School in the South of England, felt this sensuous urge so strongly, what must it have it been doing to the boys in my charge whose blood was seething and bubbling in their veins, hot from the springs of youth? How could they bear to be confined so – in dormitories and classrooms, laboratories, studies and cloisters? How could they give their full attention to the desiccated tasks and arid disciplines of the school syllabus, when all their instincts must have been pleading with them; begging that they be allowed to rush out into the verdant air, and run, and swim, and swoop, and fly and search, search, search for somebody to adore? No wonder they were unsettled. I certainly was.

And so might Geoffrey be; even he. For all his tweedy devotion to the study of his beloved Latin and Greek, for all his impassioned desire to keep those beautiful old languages alive in his heart and in his pupils' hearts, there had to be a part of Geoffrey, I knew, which lived in other spheres than those occupied by the stolid prose of Julius Caesar, and which wished for more earthly joys than the contemplation of a perfect iambic pentameter could afford him.

For Harries, coarse and objectionable though he might be, was no fool, and he was shrewd enough to notice that Geoffrey's manner was more distracted than usual, and in a different way. There were none of us who hadn't at some time or another been cannoned into in one of the corridors or quadrangles by Geoffrey, walking fast with his head down, lips moving as he recited some piece of Latin verse to himself; or tried to carry a yard-high pile of books from the Master's Lodge to his classroom. But at least when this happened Geoffrey, covered with confusion and embarrassment would stammer his apologies and, more likely than not I, or whoever it was, would go down on our knees and help him to pick up his things. That was the old Geoffrey. The new Geoffrey wandered about in a random fashion, often with his hands clasped behind his back and a curiously absent expression on his face. His eyes, I remember, often seemed to be out of focus; as if he were seeing the world at a greater or lesser distance than the rest of us. Harries had seen this before in other men – so had I, for all that – and he recognised the symptoms. So did I; or so I thought I did.

Was Geoffrey affected by the same sensations that we all felt? That the world was out there, waiting expectantly for us, breathlessly hoping that we would run to it and embrace it? Did he too hear the call of woods and hills, streams and valleys, entreating him to leave his house of brick and stone and make his bowered home in their nestling folds? Or was it, as Harries said with a knowing leer, just a woman?

It was quite impossible for me to ask my old friend directly, of course. I would have to use my eyes and ears instead. You may say it was none of my business, but a boarding school is a funny place and things work differently here. It's a closed world, an environment where the pace of life is usually slow and steady but where emotions, denied an external release, often flare up very rapidly, only to die down again just as quickly. In such a confined place it's not possible to keep a secret for long.

'Hang it!' I said (*Hang Whitewash! Hang Spring Cleaning!* said the voice of the Mole in my childhood memories.) I climbed through the staff room window and out onto the lawn beyond, risking damaging the nasturtiums which bordered rankly against the wall. 'And Hang Marking!' I said as loudly as I dared. The Head's study was nearby.

'You should be careful where you say that kind of thing.'

I turned round with a start. It was Geoffrey, sitting with his back to the wall and holding a small book which he stuffed hastily into the pocket of his flannels as I approached.

'I've got a free period. I can hang anyone or anything I like! What're you up to, anyway? Have 3B gone down with the measles?'

'Yes,' said Geoffrey with a satisfied grin. 'They're sick unto death; every last one of the little beasts. I've packed them all off to the San.'

'Good idea!' I said, but felt an inner disquiet all the same. This was not the man I knew – conscientious and scholarly. What could have happened?

'Was there any particular reason why you decided to strike them down with the plague?'

'They weren't listening to me. Why should I talk to them? And look!' Geoffrey waved his hand. 'Who'd want to stay inside on a day like this?'

'Won't they fall behind with their work?'

'No more than your marking will fall behind. Go on, Jack! Sit down.'

I sat down. Geoffrey turned to me with a mock-serious look on his face. 'That's better. Take it easy for a while. Admit it – don't you sometimes find yourself thinking there must be more to all this than... all this? Don't you know what I mean?'

'I'm not sure that I do.'

'I mean books and chalk dust and horrible smelly little boys and blackboards and endless, endless talking. We don't listen enough; do you know that, Jack?'

'We talk, they listen. That's the way it is.'

'But there's so much to hear. If we would only learn to be silent for once and *listen*, we'd be able to hear so much more. We've forgotten that.'

I said nothing. I wondered what books he had been reading that had made him talk like this. What was in the volume he had slipped so surreptitiously into his trousers when he saw me approach? Surely it could be nothing improper. I could not believe that Geoffrey would ever consider reading anything that was smutty or inappropriate.

We sat comfortably side by side letting the sun warm us, not speaking but listening as Geoffrey had suggested. After a while, I began to see what he had meant. Now that the sounds of our voices had ceased, there were other things to hear – a distant car climbing the hill out of Wantage, the whirr of Haynes' mower, the patter of Cuthbert's paws on the new paving slabs outside Fields' House (Cuthbert was the school dog), birdsong, the gentle susurration of the leaves of the plane trees which bordered Cricket Bigside. I was, to be honest, dozing off and so, I am sure, was Geoffrey when our joint reverie was disturbed by Muriel Richards, the new Matron of Fields' House, who was passing with a load of laundry in her arms.

'Hey, you two lazybones! Don't you have any work to do?'

'No!'

'Then you can help me fold these sheets. Come on!'

We climbed to our feet reluctantly, but perhaps not very much so. 'Damn pretty girl,' said Geoffrey under his breath and I was forced to agree with him. Sister Muriel Richards was a very pretty girl indeed. How could it be that I hadn't noticed it before?

Later in the staff room, and only after a certain amount of chaffing, Geoffrey showed me the book that he had been reading.

'*The Poetical Works of Keats*! Good heavens! You must be going mad,' I guffawed, uncomfortably aware even as I mocked Geoffrey for his adolescent taste in poetry how much like that oaf Harries I sounded.

'Yes. Why not?' He looked offended. 'It's glorious stuff. I never read it properly before. I've not read any of the Romantic poets properly.'

What could I say? I'd heard him refer to the Lakeland Poets, the Georgians and even the Metaphysicals as fly-by-nights, kid's stuff, silly nonsense, only the previous term when he was trying to persuade me that nothing later than Chaucer was worth reading, let alone teaching.

'It all ended with *Beowulf*,' he had said. 'Nothing really worthwhile's been written since then, you know.'

'Shakespeare?' I'd responded, with the air of one who has just trumped his opponent with an especially splendid card.

'"Upstart Crow",' he'd replied, and that was just about that. If Geoffrey was reading the poetry of John Keats and enjoying it, then there was something going on that was very odd indeed.

I did not mean to spy on Geoffrey, but as I have said before, a boarding school is a closely bounded community and it is not easy to keep secrets here. We both had rooms in the Masters' Lodge, where the younger and unmarried members of staff lived rent-free in bedroom-*cum*-studies and our movements could be easily heard in the uncarpeted corridors and staircases. We were not kept under lock and key, of course. Once we had done our share of extracurricular duties we were as free to come and go as if we had been accountants or motor mechanics. Nevertheless, it was considered unusual for a junior master to stay out late by himself. Forays to the *Stag at Bay* or the *Green Man* or any of the other public houses in Wantage were not uncommon, naturally, but we tended to go in groups rather than solitarily.

I was lying in bed – it must have been about half-past-eleven – reading *Busman's Honeymoon*, by Dorothy L. Sayers. I've always enjoyed mysteries and this was not the first time I'd read this particular story, even though it was, in my opinion, far from being the best of the Wimsey novels. Perhaps it was the fact that Wimsey was married to Harriet Vane by the time the story took place that had spoiled it for me. The original purity had been lost. But now… now it was different and I found that my mind kept straying away from the story to considerations of Muriel Richards. That would never do. She was a colleague, nothing more, and I had no doubt that someone as attractive as her would be sure to have a sweetheart of her own. She would certainly not be interested in a prematurely middle-aged history master with chalk-dust under his fingernails and worn leather patches on the elbows of his sports jacket. I reined in my errant thoughts and returned to my book.

I was disturbed a little later by a loud creak outside my bedroom door. Was it Williams returning from the gym, where he liked to spend his evenings engaged in vigorous exercises with the Indian Clubs? No, the footsteps were going to, rather than from, the staircase which led down to the ground floor. Somebody was going out, then, either from my floor or from the floor above me. That was odd. As it was a weekday the pubs would be closed by now and the boys would be locked into their Houses. I could imagine no reason for any master to be anywhere other than safely ensconced in his study or tucked up in bed.

Consumed with curiosity, I got out of bed, crossed to the door of my bedroom and turned out the light. Then I positioned myself by the window and pulled back the curtain a little, so that I could see who it was that was slipping out of the Lodge so late in the evening. My bedroom was located directly over the front door of the building, so that it was not difficult for me to watch people come and go if I chose.

The door creaked open, and a figure stepped out. It was Geoffrey. I was not surprised that it was him, even though he was not the kind of person whom I would previously have considered to be fond of midnight excursions. It was a time when queer things happened, you see. The moon was shining brightly; a waxing crescent, and the last of the day still lingered on the western horizon. I suppressed the impulse to call out. In fact, I felt rather ashamed of myself. What was I doing, peering out of windows and following the comings and going of my friends? I'd be taking notes next and reporting Geoffrey to the authorities, and then some little Hitler would come and ask us horrible and embarrassing questions. Only a few years ago we'd fought a terrible war just so we wouldn't have to live under such conditions now. I turned away, determined to mind my own business, and went back to bed.

Sleep did not come easily. I was waiting, I confess, for Geoffrey's return. What would I do when I heard his feet on the stairs? Open my door and confront him in the passageway? Demand to know what he was up to? Or ignore him and pretend that nothing was happening? After all, if Geoffrey had found himself a lady friend and was making nocturnal visits to her then it was absolutely nothing whatsoever to do with me. I never admitted to myself that I might be jealous. 'Good luck to him!' I'd have said if Harries had suggested it, and slapped on the back; both of us good fellows and men of the world.

So I never knew it when I did finally drift off, and it was not until the next morning, when the sun crept past the curtain that I had carelessly replaced the previous evening and shone directly into my eyes, that I even realised that I had been asleep. It was still very early – about twenty past five by my bedside clock – and I was annoyed to be awake so soon. I climbed out of bed and went to the window, determined to pull the curtain fully closed and give myself the opportunity of another hour or two's rest. As I tugged at the faded blue velvet of which the curtain was made, I looked out of the window and saw Geoffrey closing the garden gate of the Lodge and he, catching the movement of the fabric out of the corner of his eye, saw me looking at him. *Damn. That's torn it*, I thought. Even though Geoffrey didn't know that I had seen him leave the night before, he most certainly knew that I had seen him return this morning.

I felt most infernally awkward. What should I do? Pretend that nothing had happened? Pass Geoffrey the marmalade at the breakfast table and make my usual remark about the solidity of the boiled eggs which, it being Thursday, would be waiting, clad in knitted egg-cosies, by our tea-cups? I should have known my friend better than that.

Less than a minute later there was a knock on my door and Geoffrey came in, as was his way, without waiting for my "come in". His face was flushed and his hair was in a state of considerable disarray. I put on my dressing gown and sat at my desk. Geoffrey flung himself into my old armchair.

'Geoffrey,' I said, feeling more as if I were addressing a pupil than a master, 'before you say anything, please let me state that you are under no obligation to justify your actions to me, of all people.' Good heavens, why was I speaking in such a foolish stuck-up way?

Geoffrey sat back and ran his fingers through his hair, disarraying it still further. I noticed that his eyes were very bright and that they had turned an extraordinary shade of green. That was funny – what colour were Geoffrey's eyes, anyway?

'Oh don't be daft, Jack. Put the kettle on, there's a good chap. I'm parched.'

There was no question of my going back to bed this morning, I could see. I lit the gas ring, boiled some water, and made tea for us both. I passed a mug over to Geoffrey, who drunk half of it in one gulp despite its being scalding hot.

'Ah! That's better!' He sighed gratefully and sat back in the chair.

'Now, I suppose you want to know where I've been and what I've been up to.'

'Only if you want to tell me. It's nothing to do with me, what you get up to. So long as it's legal, anyway.'

'I promise you, Jack, that I've not been out breaking into peoples' houses, if that's what you mean. Or stealing clothes off their washing lines.'

'No sack of swag concealed in the Second Eleven's pavilion, then.'

'No!' Geoffrey grinned.

'Geoffrey... if you're seeing somebody...'

'Ha! Like that odious little man Harries thinks, you mean?'

'Well... yes, I suppose so.'

'The answer to that is yes. And no.' Geoffrey leaned forward. He spoke softly, so that I had to lean forward too in order to hear him clearly.

'What do you mean?'

'I mean that yes; I have been seeing somebody, or something, and no; it's not the way that Harries thinks it is.'

I had a sudden thought. 'Geoffrey; you've not joined the Freemasons, have you?'

He laughed out loud. 'Jack, you idiot! Of course I've not joined the blasted Freemasons! Can you see me with an apron and trowel?'

'No, I can't. Is it the Hellfire Club, then?'

'Now you're being silly. I happen to know they're not accepting new members. No, you're going to have to find out for yourself.'

'What?'

'Come with me and see.'

I hesitated. This all sounded very queer indeed. Whatever it was that Geoffrey had got himself involved with, it was having a powerful effect on him. He was strangely excited, constantly shifting his position in the chair and unable to keep still for very long at a time. His eyes, although they had lost their green lustre, were still dilated and glistening with an unusual brightness.

Drugs, you say, and I cannot say I'm surprised to hear it. Drug abuse was not the problem it was to become in later years, but I was not so naïve that I had not heard of cocaine, heroin and marijuana and I was beginning to suspect that Geoffrey might be dabbling in their use. If so, he was skating on very thin ice indeed.

There were two things I could do. I could report him to the Head, or to the police, and all those unpleasant things I had thought about the night before – arrest, interrogation, trial, sentence and incarceration – might happen to him. Or I could go along with him and find out for myself what was going on. What I could not do was to leave things as they were. My duty was plain – I had to do something.

'Yes, all right. When?'

'Saturday. We'll go there Saturday night.' Geoffrey leapt to his feet. 'Thanks for the tea.'

His shoes left grass stains and chalky smears on my carpet.

If anything, the languorous atmosphere which overhung the school intensified over the next couple of days. It was becoming quite impossible for any of us – masters or boys – to concentrate on our work. At any normal time we would have been very concerned about this. The Vale School prides itself on its ability to get the very best out of the boys who live and study here. This does not happen by itself, but as the result of hard work done by us all. I felt that I was, with my lapses of attention, in some way letting down the boys who were entrusted to my care. But… somehow I could not bring myself to believe that it mattered, and neither did anybody else; so ensorcelled were we.

I sat with my Middle Sixth class on a grassy bank overlooking the cricket nets, feeling more like an Greek philosopher surrounded by his acolytes in an Athenian *lyceum* of the ancient times than a history master at an English boarding school in 1953. We spoke of this and that, a little history, a little religion, what were England's chances in the third Test Match, who was the greater historian – Trevelyan or Macaulay. Some of the boys joined in the discussion, some lay back and stared at the sky, some were engaged in earnest *sotto voce* conversations with one another. To this day I cannot say whether we were wasting time that should have been devoted to serious study or whether we were discovering the true meaning of education. I would like to think that we learned things that Friday afternoon which would have eluded us in the dry confines of the classroom. What I mean is… what Geoffrey said. We schoolmasters spent too much of our time standing at the front of classrooms giving out knowledge, but never taking it back, never listening to anything but our pupils' answers and then only so we could correct them. Perhaps even the dullest boy could come up with some new insight and say something worth hearing.

So I listened for a change, and we talked as I have described and eventually our informal class came to an end as the sound of the school bell drifted lazily over the grounds, staying with us just long enough to let us know that our period of study was over before meandering its way beyond the row of lime trees that marked the perimeter and dissipating into the open country beyond. 'That's it, boys,' I said, letting them go to their Houses and games and recreations. They wandered off, in ones and twos and threes, still talking quietly among themselves. I gathered up my books and began to walk back to the Masters' Lodge and my study-bedroom. Perhaps I would get my bicycle out later and go for a spin along the lanes which ran up and down the length of the Vale of White Horse. The weather was warm, but not too much so, and the exercise would be good for me.

It was not the shortest way back to the Lodge, but nevertheless I found myself passing by the side of Fields' House. I believe I was intending to look at the notice board which was affixed to the wall just outside the Junior Dining Room. Something to do with an archaeological field trip I was trying to organise for the post-exam fortnight, probably.

'Jack!' The voice came out of a ground floor window.

'Matron?' I recognised Sister Richards' voice.

'Are you busy?' Muriel leaned out of the window, her elbows resting on the white-painted sill.

'Not especially. Why; have you got some ironing for me to do? More sheets to fold?'

'No! Don't be silly!'

'What is it, then?' I must have sounded annoyed – actually I was caught on the hop, as it were.

'Oh, it's just that... no, don't worry. It's nothing at all, really.'

'Nothing?'

'Nothing special. I'm sure you must have lots of terribly important things to do, like marking or revising or whatever it is you masters like to do in your spare time. Never mind. Off you go, now.'

'Oh, all right. Goodbye, then,' I said to the back of her head.

I rode my bicycle furiously up and down the roads of south Oxfordshire all that afternoon and worked up a terrific sweat, but it did me no good. No good at all.

Saturday was a half-day, so once I had finished lunch my time was my own. I would not be required again until Sunday morning at ten o'clock, for Chapel. I was eager to discover what it was that Geoffrey wanted to show me, so I hunted him down. It took a while, but following a suggestion from Higgs, one of the under-gardeners, I found him in the Music School, sitting in a circle of fifth-formers who were listening to the gramophone. It was playing Ralph Vaughan Williams' *Fantasia on a Theme by Thomas Tallis*, as I recall.

Not now. Later, he mouthed. *Tonight. It has to be tonight.*

So it had to be tonight, then. That left me with ten hours or so to fill in some way or another.

I spent them in re-reading some of my collection of mystery stories. Of course, when you revisit a story which has been designed to be a puzzle you look at it more critically than you did when you first read it. Once you are no longer caught up in the excitement of the storytelling you can take the time to look more closely at what the writer was doing when he composed the plot. Often, detached from your interest in the characters – and even so-called "detective stories" have interesting characters; the better ones anyway – the red herrings and various other devices that the author may have used can appear rather unconvincing and artificial. As I sat in the garden outside the Lodge, and tried not to ruminate on my *faux pas* with Muriel Richards the day before, I found myself thinking *I could do this. I could write something just as good as this, if I had the time and a few good ideas.*

Why I thought this, I cannot say. My previous attempts at story-writing – at school or University – had been stiff, awkward affairs. "Literate, grammatical, cold and uninvolving" was how they had been described by the friends I had been so unwise as to show them to. My tutor had told me bluntly not to waste my time on something to I was so clearly unsuited. He was a man I greatly respected, so I had taken his advice.

I had a pad of foolscap paper on my lap, and as I sat and read I made notes; ideas for stories of my own. I knew that they would come to nothing, naturally, but the intellectual exercise was stimulating and the time passed more quickly than I had expected. If I'm being completely frank I'll have to admit that I dozed for a few hours. The sun was warm and the air was balmy and it was yet another perfect day in that perfect June.

I knocked on Geoffrey's door at a quarter to eleven. He opened it immediately, as if he had been waiting behind it, ready for my call. 'Ready, Jack? Right-o.'

We tiptoed down the stairs and out of the front door, closing it silently behind us. Our bicycles were kept in a shed behind the squash courts; a short walk across moonlit lawns.

The moon… It was at the full that night, a huge presence hanging in the southern sky, extraordinarily bright. The sky was absolutely cloudless, but we could not see the stars, so intense was the light of that moon. If some astronomer had told me that the moon had left its orbit, which they say is a quarter of a million miles distant from us, and had descended until it was only a few thousand feet above our heads, I would have believed him. I would never otherwise have credited that I would one day find myself being *dazzled* by moonlight. But it was far from being the strangest light that Geoffrey and I were to see that night.

I was not surprised when Geoffrey, who was riding ahead of me, turned westwards as we left the school gates. Whatever it was that he had seen, whatever it was that had affected him so greatly, whatever it was that was entrancing the whole school, it had to be something to do with the ancient places which lie to the west of Wantage, in the Vale of White Horse. Sparsholt and Kingston Lisle we passed, as the road dipped and rose on its way through the rolling countryside of Oxfordshire. Neither of our bicycles carried lights. Usually that would have earned us a wigging from the local constabulary, but the illumination from the moon which shone from our left was so intense that we could have claimed in court that lights were unnecessary. And there was another thing – we saw no people or cars that night. Not one.

After a few leaf-speckled miles of country road, Geoffrey turned left and started to pedal harder. We were riding up a narrow lane now, and instead of following the valley side we were going up the side of it. Our bicycles were old bone-shakers, without gears, and I had to put my head down and raise myself from the saddle in order to pump the pedals hard enough to keep up with my friend. He, in his turn, seemed to be accelerating, as if he were under a compulsion to reach his destination as soon as possible. Or, it was *pulling* him towards it.

If it had not been that the lane we were going up was so steep, I am sure that we would have been blinded by the moonlight shining in our faces. We were now proceeding directly south, past Dragon Hill towards Uffington Castle and the White Horse itself.

White Horses are a common feature of the kind of chalky downland country where The Vale School is situated. They have been cut in the hillsides for many centuries and although they are transient things, for the grass grows over them if they are not kept scoured, they are ancient too. Our White Horse – if I can be so arrogant as to claim ownership of it – is a stylised rather than a realistic representation but it is extraordinarily expressive. The Horse seems to be galloping across the hill into which it is cut, as if the East Wind had gone hunting, and there was quarry to be found in the West. White Horse Hill is a favourite spot for picnickers, kite-flyers and model aircraft enthusiasts, who regard its mystery as an everyday thing.

The nearby Castle is an Iron Age hill fort – now just a set of circular earth ramparts. The wooden stake fence which once surmounted it and protected those who sought shelter within it is gone, and will never be replaced. It also has counterparts in southern England, notably Maiden Castle in Dorset.

Was the Castle to be our objective that night? I wondered what could be happening there and had a brief mental vision of the interior of the earthworks; a silver dish in which incantations might be said, and spells be woven. 'Which way now?' I called out to Geoffrey. He made no answer, but dismounted from his bicycle, leaving it in a hedge by the side of the lane. We were not far from the place where the day-trippers usually left their cars, judging by the scuffed and pockmarked nature of the ground nearby.

'Upwards! And Westwards!' Geoffrey replied. I left my bicycle next to his and scrambled through the hedge into the open field beyond. Slantwise light washed over us, leaving long shadows in our wake.

We were both pretty fit back then and so we climbed the hill at a fair rate, skidding on the turf beneath our feet in our haste and leaving the White Horse and the Castle on our left, until we crossed a ditch and encountered a six foot wide white streak in the ground, surrounded on both sides by farmers' fences. Ah... This was the Ridgeway, an old path and sometime drover's road. I had a shrewd suspicion of where Geoffrey was taking us.

I should say that all around us, although the air itself was still, could be heard a myriad of small sounds – a miniature cacophony. The countryside was alive with movement. The trees were at rest, naturally, but the call of the night-birds and the rustle of small creatures in the grass and the hedgerows to both sides gave an air of busyness that was as far from the general idea of a summer's night as being a calm, hushed and peaceful time as can possibly be imagined. Millions of small lives were being lived and lost with every breath we took. I pointed to the right, and Geoffrey nodded his head.

We walked about a mile westwards along the Ridgeway and my suspicion slowly grew to a certainty. Ahead of us, invisible to begin with, drowned in the moonlight, but growing stronger with every step we took, a dome of pale green radiance hovered over the ground, partially obscured by a grove of trees. Geoffrey was walking ever more quickly and it was only with difficulty that I was able to keep up with him. We crossed another path, heading north-south. It would not be very far now, I was sure.

'Is that it?' I pointed toward the light. 'Is that where we are going?'

Geoffrey stopped and turned. Even though he was facing towards me and away from the glowing source in front of us, his eyes were glittering emerald-bright. 'Can you doubt it?' he replied.

I could not. There could not be the slightest doubt left in my mind.

I caught up with Geoffrey and together we walked the last hundred yards to the grove of trees from which the light was flowing; cast about in streamers and threads of ghostly brilliance. We both felt it now – a force pulling us bodily forwards, compelling us to walk faster and faster until we were almost at a run and our feet hardly seemed to be in contact with the earth below. The sky was alive with the flutter of wings, the grass in the fields to our left and right was bowed to the west and the trees of the grove were rustling and swaying. But, as I have said, there was no wind that night. The air was utterly still.

At last we came to a halt. We stood in a gap in the circle of trees, surrounded by constant life and movement. Before us, a vortex of verdant luminosity, swirling and tumbling above the holy ground below. We were come to the place which is called Wayland's Smithy.

I tell my fourth-formers about the Neolithic barrow, or burial mound, that lies behind the guardian trees. How it is at least six thousand years old, and how it has been revered as a sacred burial ground by the peoples of the Vale since its first building and, who can say (for this is an ancient place), perhaps before then as well; as far back as the beginning of time itself. I tell them of the Sarcen stones which support the burial chamber, of the bodies which have been found there, and carefully replaced.

Simply to tell them is not enough. I take them too, on a quiet afternoon in early Spring or late Autumn, when the crowds are elsewhere, and we sit inside the grove and are silent for a while, considering the meaning of Time. Then, when even the noisiest boy has stopped talking, and the atmosphere of the place has taken hold of our imaginations and we are ready to listen, I tell them of Wayland, the Saxon god of metal-working, also known as Weland, Volund or

Volundr, who may have come originally of the Elven race. I relate the story of greedy King Niduth, who sought to enslave the great smith, and of Wayland's terrible revenge on the King, his sons and his daughter. I tell them of the legend; how if you leave a horse and a silver piece by the Smithy, and go forth without looking back, you will, if you have left good coin and not attempted to observe what happens within the grove, return to find that your horse has been shod and your money has gone. Then we go into the chamber with candles, one or two at a time, and look about ourselves, touching history. And then we go home for tea.

The mystery of the grove – the crystallisation of Time around the stones of the tomb which lies at its heart – never fails to make an impression on even the rowdiest of classes.

Geoffrey and I stood on the threshold of the enclosure. It seemed to us that we had reached a turning-point in our lives. We could turn away, and go, and not return. That was inconceivable to me. We could stand where we stood now and watch; watch the light scintillating before us and feel its gentle touch on our faces. Or we could go forward and embrace it. We had been standing side by side, but now I turned to face Geoffrey.

'This is a fearful place. How can you bear it?'

'It has been calling me – you know that, don't you, Jack?'

'Yes, I know. How many times have you been here before?'

'Twice. Once last week and once when you saw me, Thursday night.'

'Was it as it is now?'

'It was… like this, but not so bright, not so intense. Not so… *vital.*'

I shuddered. 'Do you not fear it?'

'Yes. I fear it greatly. But… you felt it too, didn't you? You felt it tugging at you. You have seen its influence over the school – we all have. How could you possibly not seek it out and find it?'

'Are we the only ones who have ever come here?'

'I am sure that we are not. But we are the only ones who are here now.'

I took a deep breath. 'Have you been inside?'

'Inside the tree-circle? No, not before now. I have been afraid to go in there alone, lest I never return.'

'You are not alone now, Geoffrey.' I did what I had never done before; I took Geoffrey's hand in mine and together, like two little children, we stepped hand-in-hand into the tree-pillared temple of light and left the world of Men behind.

Immediately the pulsing, vibrating force of the light entered our bodies. It was as if the longings and yearnings that I had been experiencing for the past few weeks had been amplified a thousand-fold. The sensation was so overwhelming as to be almost beyond endurance – one of gladness, and revelation and desire. I looked at Geoffrey. His thin face was lifted to the stars above, the stars which now shone directly down onto us, at the centre of a whirlpool of whizzing, humming, singing (for the light had a sound associated with it) sparks of pale green luminosity.

I found the words to speak, although speech was superfluous, 'It is something too old and too strong, too rich and too strange for we mortals to endure for very long.'

'It is killing us with a surfeit of delight,' Geoffrey replied.

The life-force splashed over us again and again. Still holding hands, we walked slowly over to the mound which stood in the middle of the ring of guardian trees. This hump of grassy earth was the focus of the energies which filled the air around us. It drew me to itself with an irresistible force.

'Shall we go in?' I asked. 'Is it allowed?'

'I do not know. I afraid of it; more afraid than I have ever been in my life.'

'So am I.' But I was exhilarated too. I knew that, although the opening to the chamber was the opening to a grave, and that it might be my grave, I could not turn away from it now.

'Will you not come with me?'

'No,' Geoffrey replied. 'I think that I would have gone there before, the other times I was here, if it had been right for me to do so. I will wait for you outside, and I will pray for you.'

I took both Geoffrey's hands in my own. 'Pray well, old chap, for I believe that I am placing my immortal soul in great peril. But I *must* go in there. There is a secret to be discovered that I must find out. I think that it has been waiting for me all my life.'

'I know.' We clasped each other tightly, and we embraced as men do who go into battle, not knowing whether they will see one another again. Then I ducked my head and stepped into the entrance to the chamber. The light followed me.

It was as I remembered it, dank and musty, earth-smelling and chilly, and for a moment I suffered acute disappointment. Was this it – was the secret I sought nothing more than a commonplace matter of soil underfoot and damp stones to either side? Looking behind me, I saw Geoffrey, briefly silhouetted against the swaying tree-tops. I edged further forward into the chamber.

As my eyes adapted to the darkness, and the sounds outside receded behind me, I became aware of a pressure bearing down on me. I am not claustrophobic, so it was not the knowledge that tons of earth and rock were arching directly over my head that was affecting me so, but something else. Also, I was seeing bright pinpoints of silvery light ahead. I rubbed my eyes and blinked, but they were still there.

There was another thing. It is no more than ten feet from the entrance to the chamber to its back wall but I had, I am sure, already walked further than that without coming into contact with it. In addition, the passage appeared to have widened around me, so that I seemed to be standing in a sizeable cavern, rather than the narrow space into which, as I knew from my visits with my classes, you could not fit more than four or five people. I stopped and turned slowly to each side, reaching out with my fingertips, trying to touch the walls and failing. My hands fell to my side.

I did not know what I should do. I did not know where I was, even though I had, or so I thought, been here many times before. The certainty which had driven me to this place now seemed to me to be a very foolish thing, an illusion, based on nothing but dreams and my own credulousness. Why had I followed Geoffrey to the Smithy? Why had I not had the sense to stay outside the barrow, as he had?

As I stood there, trying to decide whether I should turn and run back to the surface (if that were possible) or stay where I was, the cavern slowly grew lighter, and I saw that it was full of shapes – shapes which I cannot describe; except to say that they were alive, and moved, and spoke in a soft tongue that I could not understand. I thought of H.G. Wells' Time Traveller, and the evil Morlocks who dwelt underground and feasted on the decadent Eloi from the sunlit lands above. Was I to meet a similar fate? I wished that I carried a weapon – a knife, or a gun, or even a box of matches.

I was not to be left in a state of indecision for very long, for two of the figures – they were no more than three feet tall – came to me and whispered to me in their rustling speech. 'What do you want?' I asked one of them, but he did not understand me. Instead, he pointed with a blunt finger towards the darkness before us. It seemed that we were to go in that direction. My nerve failed me briefly, and I turned swiftly and looked behind me, expecting to see some trace of light from the world above, but there was nothing there but a blank wall of rock. Wherever it was that I was now, it was not the country I knew, but somewhere separate from it. I would not be able to return to the surface by simply retracing the steps that I had already taken.

'What do you want?' I asked again, but this time there was no reply. They took me by the hands and led me forward. Unsure of their intentions and very afraid, I let them take me with them, pushing my fear to the back of my mind as best I could. There was to be no going back now. I had committed myself to this adventure when I entered the barrow, though I had not known then what form it might take. The darkness closed in around us as we walked and I held tightly to my guides' hands, not wishing to stray from the right path and be lost in the dark.

I have no idea how long the tunnel was. It might have been as short as fifty yards, or very much longer than that. Common sense tells me that it should have sloped downwards, otherwise it would soon have emerged from the side of the hill, but it was completely level except for the occasional step or low wall which my silent guides took care that I should not trip over. There was light to see by – a quiet light, green-tinged as the light had been in the world above – but I cannot say where it came from. My companions carried no lanterns, nor were there torches fixed to the walls of the passage or skylights in its roof. There was silence, broken only by the sound of my breathing and the soft pad of our footsteps. From time to time the passageway opened out into a wider space and I would feel a sense of great relief even though, as I have said, I am not particularly inclined to claustrophobia.

We proceeded in this manner for a long time, passing from one cavern to another through low passages where I had to duck my head and, at one point, go down on all fours. The fear, which I had thought I had suppressed, came back to me now more terribly than ever. I was being led into a trap, far beneath the surface of the earth. I would never return; I would be buried here for ever with these grey shuffling creatures in their dimly-lit underworld. I had a heartfelt longing for open skies, moving air and brilliant colours.

Eventually we entered an open space far greater than any we had been in so far, illuminated by a copper-coloured light which emanated from the walls. It was set out rather like a church, or an auditorium. There were semicircular rows of stone benches on which were sitting many more of the small people who had led me here. Now that there was more light to see by, I could make out their faces – strange faces, half-formed and indistinct, with huge eyes. Each of these people was dressed in a green jerkin and wore a soft cap and slippers.

The walls of this great underground hall gave forth a red-gold light, as I have said. It seemed to come from translucent panels, arched and patterned with arboreal shapes of stem, branch and leaf. Between these panels, standing in deep alcoves, were carved figures whose shapes were not easy to discern against the luminescence next to them. They were not human; of that I am sure.

The roof of the hall reminded me of a great cathedral, stone-vaulted and high, studded with ornamental bosses of jewelled colours, shining down on us like the planets in the night sky of our own world. I knew now that the distance between this place and my home could not be measured in ordinary miles, feet or inches.

But I must move on in my story, and tell you of the encounter which I had in that hall, and which has shaped the course of my life ever since.

At the focus of the semicircle stood a daïs, and on that daïs were set two thrones, carved out of dusky lignite. And what am I to say of the Two who sat upon those thrones, and held dominion in their subterranean realm? It would be no more than the truth to say that they were beautiful. But their beauty was, as it were, an irrelevance. It affected me, of course. I cannot deny it, nor would I wish to do so, but I believe that even if they had been appallingly ugly, they would still have inspired my reverence. As I approached them, I saw that their solemn brows were bound about with chaplets of bright stars.

The two creatures who had led me here left my side and took their seats in the benches. I was left alone to meet the rulers of this place.

They were a Lord and a Lady; and the Lord was strong and the Lady was grave. He embodied Justice, she Wisdom. I knelt at the foot of the steps which led to their thrones and paid them worship.

'Where is the other one?' The Lord's voice was deep and resonant, forged from the iron bones of the earth.

'My Lord, he has stayed outside.' The Lady spoke with the voice of all living things, quick and bright.

'Does he fear us so very much?'

I found my voice. 'Yes, my Lady, he does. I fear you also.'

'Look at us, Man. Are we to be feared?'

I raised my eyes slowly. 'Yes, my Lady. You are greatly to be feared. It is fitting that I should tremble in your presence, even as I adore you and your Lord.'

'This is a courteous one, is it not?'

'It is wise for him to be so. Do you not know, Man, that we could un-make you with a glance, or a small movement of our hands?'

'I know it very well, my Lord.'

'Tell me then, and be careful to let courtesy guide your speech; why have you come here?'

'I have come, my Lord, my Lady, because my friend brought me here. But also, because I have a great longing within me, and I think that you know of this longing and whence it comes.'

'You mean that we have engendered these feelings within you.'

'Yes, my Lady. Why is this? Why have you visited this yearning ache upon me, and upon the children who have been entrusted to me?'

'You dare to ask us questions?'

'My Lord, I must.' I did not want to arouse the wrath of the god to whom I spoke, but the truth drove me onwards. 'You know what it is to have responsibility for those in your care. Are these not your people? And do you not love and cherish them? Is that not the meaning of kingship?' I waved my right arm in a wide arc, encompassing the space around us, indicating the benches and the people who sat expectantly upon them, watching us closely.

The Lord rose to his feet and lifted his right hand. 'You speak to me of kingship? You, common mortal, talk to me of responsibility?' His face was full of anger, his eyes flashed cold fire.

The Lady raised her hand also. 'Cease, my Lord. Does a little honesty upset you so much? This is a fallible human creature, animated dust. He does not deserve your ire, but rather your understanding.' The Lord took his seat again, and rested his chin upon his hand.

'Know, little Man…'

'I am called Jack, my Lady.'

'Know then, Jack, that we rule here, as your lords and masters rule in their own country – your country. Know also that the borders of your country and ours are not fixed, but ebb and flow, so that sometimes your world of fire and iron invades our quiet lands and sometimes our world of mists and silence overlays yours. Has it not happened before; that myths and legends – as you call them – have strode across your wide hills and green fields, sword-girt and mystical? Do you not know of Arthur and Excalibur? Or of Joseph of Arimethaea and the Isle of Avalon? Or of cunning Odysseus and the sacking of Troy?'

'We call them stories. Sometimes we believe them and sometimes we do not.'

'Nevertheless there is truth in them, would you not say?'

'Yes, my Lady. We call it a higher truth, or a deeper one.'

'You are wise to do so.'

'My Lady!' I cried out. 'Speak to me not of wisdom! I am a shallow, hollow thing.' And I wept, for I saw myself to be a being of very little worth.

The Lady stepped down from her throne and joined me where I knelt at the foot of the daïs. 'Jack. Look at me. Look in my eyes.'

I had not dared to do so before. 'Your world is a hard place; a hard practical place full of hard men and hard choices. It is not as this world is. I know that you are a teacher. We honour teachers very much; for are not my Lord and I the Teachers of all these souls here?' She meant the small people who clustered around us, giving obeisance to their King and Queen.

'We know that your pupils need all the help that you can give them if they are to be happy and successful in the world that you have created. But if their learning consists only of hard facts then they will grow up hard too; and hard men are brittle, and break easily. They need what we have been giving them, these last few days while our world has spilled over into yours.'

'Will you stay with us?'

'No, we cannot – even now the tide of which I have spoken to you is flowing back. Before this night is over, my Lord and I and our people will have receded beyond your reach. I do not think that we shall meet again on these shores.'

I was desolate. 'No, my Lady?' I wept again.

'Courage, Jack! Though you need no such gift from us, I think. Not many men would have stepped through the Portal as you did this night.'

'My Lady.' It was the King. 'The time is fast approaching when we must return this Man to his own place, or take him with us for ever.'

I was filled with a wild hope. 'My Lady?'

She smiled. 'No, Jack. You have a full life to lead, and work to do which cannot be done here. You would hate it in our world.'

'But I would be with you!'

'That cannot be; for I am my Lord's and he is mine, and we are very jealous of each other. Do not be sad; I do not mean that you shall be alone for the rest of your life. There is someone waiting for you in your own land; you only need to ask her and she is yours. That knowledge is my second gift to you. The first gift, you have already received.'

'What is it?'

'You will find out soon enough. Consider; were not my Lord and I known to you already, even before you came here?'

'I do not know.'

'Look in your heart, and you *will* know. We are Legend, my Lord and I.'

I bowed my head. 'My Lady.'

'And lastly, because these things go in threes in all the best stories,' she smiled again,' I have a third gift for you, which you may choose to accept or not, as you wish.'

'What is it?'

'It is the gift of Lethe; of forgetfulness. You can choose to forget the events of this night, remembering them only as a dream which faded with the morning sun. Or you can remember them all, in which case you will never be fully content with your life, for you will be left with the yearnings which brought you here, and they cannot be assuaged while you dwell on these shores.'

I thought for a short while. 'My Lady, you offer me a choice which is no choice at all, for how could I choose to forget you, whatever the cost to me? Give your gift to another. Let me remember.'

'You choose as your heart directs, Jack. I think that you have chosen well, for yours is a spirit that will never be content with the ordinary and the everyday. It has brought you to us, has it not? Let the memory of this short hour we have spent together guide you through your life, until we meet again on the farther shore. Farewell!' And she lifted me up in both of her arms and kissed me on the lips.

At once a mist interposed itself between me and the Lady, and I saw no more of her or her Lord, nor heard any more than a last 'Farewell!' from them both, nor felt any more than the touch of the Lady's lips upon my cheek and the King's strong arm upon my shoulder.

* * *

It may be that I slept, or that time had passed at a different rate while I was in the other world, for when I could see clearly again I found that I was lying next to Geoffrey, both of us propped up against the burial mound. It was a clear summer's morning with a light dew-fall, and the birds were singing loudly in the trees above our heads. I prodded Geoffrey, who was snoring loudly. 'Look!' I said, as we staggered to our feet. 'It's just like in Keats' *La Belle Dame Sans Merci:'*

And I awoke and found me here,
On the cold hill's side.

'Keats!' said Geoffrey. 'What are you doing quoting that blithering childish nonsense to me for? You know I can't stand him! What the hell are we doing here, anyway? Did we get very drunk last night?'

The enchantment under which the school had lain evaporated overnight and everything returned to grim normality. You may think that I am overstating it, but normality, the world of Harries and his kind, appeared very grim to me then, beguiled as I was by memories of the Lord and the Lady and their underground land. For others, who were not blessed or cursed like me, it may have been different.

I wonder still about Geoffrey – poor Geoffrey, as I sometimes think of him now. I have long since abandoned the idea that you can, by looking at a man, or even after knowing him for a considerable number of years, tell what he will do when faced with the unknown. I do not think that I am a very brave man, nor is Geoffrey a coward, but when it came to it I went onwards into the burial chamber and he did not. And so I met the Lord and Lady, and received their gifts and the very great joys which they have given me, and Geoffrey received nothing, except for the gift of forgetfulness which I passed on to him. He does not know what he might have gained had he gone with me that night and I will never tell him, for I do not think that I shall ever pass beyond the ken of the Other Realm and it behoves me to be careful in what I do and say.

I am sure that I saw very little of the country which the Lord and Lady ruled and I cannot believe that it was limited only to the dark places under the earth. Unless, and this thought disturbs me, they live there now and not out in the sun and air with us, because the tide between the worlds has forced them to retreat there. Has our busy world of doing, and making, and fighting, and getting, and spending grown too strong for them, and is what happened to Geoffrey and me in the summer of 1953 in the Vale of White Horse the last we shall ever see of them? Or are they, as I hope, only waiting for us to realise our mistakes, and open the way for them to join us?

For they are there still, and they are puissant and strange, and they keep their promises. I know this to be so, for they have kept their promises to me – all of them. But what if I had provoked the Lord to an anger which his Lady could not soothe? What dreadful oath would he have sworn then, and what awful powers would he have unleashed upon us? Can Dream always keep Nightmare in check, will Wisdom always temper Power?

For the sake of us all – of our world and the realm which lies beyond the fields we know, I hope so. I truly hope so.

The Familiars

Hazel :
My Friend Hilary

Hazel: My Friend Hilary

NOW THEN CHILDREN! LET'S ALL GATHER AT THE FRONT OF THE classroom, shall we, and I'll tell you a story. Come along now! Put the toys in the boxes. Eleanor, why don't you help Rosie tidy up the books? Dawn. Dawn? Dawn! Do wake up, dear. It's story time! You can play with your abacus later. Put it away for now, there's a good girl.

'Peter... Don't do that.

'Jaya! Leave Duncan alone! Sit at the front where I can see you better. That's right. Are we all ready? Are you all sitting comfortably? Then I'll begin.'

I reached into my desk for that old standby *Stig of the Dump* but it wasn't in its usual place in the right-hand drawer and I remembered that I had taken it home with me the night before. I'd been on baby-sitting duty at my sister's. I say baby-sitting, but actually Heather's James is very grown-up for a six-year-old. He had shown no sign of the restlessness that was affecting my class. Anyway there was no problem; the book would be in the pocket of my coat, which was hanging in the lobby.

'Ian, I'm making you class monitor for a couple of minutes. Children, you must all sit quietly for a moment while I pop out to fetch something.'

I was gone for thirty seconds, that's all. But when I returned all was screaming pandemonium.

Again.

Every teacher, especially one who works in a primary school like Ascot Road Infants, knows that there are some days when the children just won't settle. I'm not talking about individuals here. It's part of our job to keep a weather eye open for unexpected or sudden changes in a child's behaviour. A garrulous boy who becomes quiet, a sweet-natured girl who starts to scratch and bite, someone who refuses to take off their jumper even when it's boiling hot; these are the warning signs we're trained to look out for and which make our hearts sink when we notice them.

Usually it's nothing. Nothing serious, anyway. A child may be extra sensitive to adults' concerns. A piece of bad news on the television may have assumed a disproportionate significance in the child's mind. Usually a little talk is all it takes to set everyone's minds at rest.

Actually, bad news can upset a whole class, especially if it involves a child. Really big events, like the London bombings, bring out what I call group anxiety. Six- and seven-year-olds can't distinguish between local dangers – like traffic – and remote ones, like being blown up by terrorists. This needs careful handling. As a teacher you mustn't lull them into a sense of false security, but neither should you frighten them into the kind of state where they retreat into themselves.

And then there are the things you can do nothing about. Rain, for instance. It makes a distracting noise and prevents the children from going outside to play. Even worse is a high wind. The rushing sound and the visual distraction of trees swaying outside can turn the most well-planned lesson into a farce. This is when I generally reach for *Stig of the Dump*.

But there was no wind today and it hadn't rained for nearly a week. Something else was going on.

We used to be able to light up in the Staff Room but that's banned now, of course, and the rumours of the existence of a gin bottle in Miss Hedges' locker are just that – rumours. The kids would spot it on our breath straight away. In fact we can't even smoke outside when the wind is in the wrong direction as it either drifts across the playground or back into the school via the girls' toilets. All that's left now is a lingering smell of stale Old Holborn by the front porch which will doubtless disappear when the school is eventually redecorated or, more likely, demolished. We share a site with the next school up, Ascot Road Juniors, and the local politicos are always going on about amalgamating the two schools in the name of efficiency and something called "stakeholder value", whatever that might be.

In the meantime the schools are separated by a wire fence stretched across the joint playground area, and a good thing too. Some of those Year Sixes are pretty big and tough and Mary Taylor's entry class consists of little more than toddlers. I stood by the dividing fence at break time and chatted with Mary, while keeping an eye out for cross-border incidents. I told her about my problems with keeping Year Two in order.

'You think you've got it bad,' she replied. 'It's been absolute blasted chaos for the past fortnight. Look over there!' She pointed to the far corner where a minor whirlwind of Year Ones was occupying the climbing frame. 'They're just the same in class. I'm petrified that Trudi's going to come in on us.'

'She probably knows what's going on already,' I pointed out. Mary nodded. Our Head, Trudi Webber, is a smart cookie. Her husband's involved with the Council and they're both on all kinds of public committees. 'Let's see how it's going next door. Jerry!'

A tall figure detached himself from the corner post of Ascot Road Juniors' adventure playground. He strolled over to the fence. 'Yes, Hazel?'

'How's it going over there with the great big boys and girls? Everything all right?'

'Sheer bloody hell, of course.'

'So no change, then.'

'None whatsoever. Tots playing up?'

'Rather.'

'You have my deepest sympathy, dear ladies. Now, if you don't mind...'

We were dismissed.

I popped into Waitrose after school to pick up a thing or two for later. It costs a bit more to shop there, but it's more civilised than the Tesco's down the road. A better class of shopper, as a rule. Look, I'm not being snobbish. It's just that I prefer it, and it's local to me. I'd have to take the car if I went to Tesco. How green is that?

Anyway, Waitrose is usually blessedly free of rampaging children and yelling babies and that's the real reason I go there. I get quite enough rampaging and yelling during the school day, thank you very much.

And today was much the same. There was no screaming to speak of, but every push-chair I passed had something odd about it. Whether it was the intent expression on the face of the boy or girl, or the harassed air that hung over the parents... I didn't know. Of course all parents of small children are harassed, that's a given. But there was something different, something I find hard to put into words. Something strange, other-worldly. Something that affected me curiously, as if I had an appointment coming up that I was apprehensive about, like a job interview or a check-up at the dentist. Not worrying, exactly but – disturbing. We were all disturbed, all of us; parents, teachers and small children. Even the teenagers – sullen or boisterous, dressed in uniform black – sitting on the benches by the supermarket car park had seemed preoccupied in a way that had little to do with unbalanced hormones. We were all, though we couldn't see it clearly at the time, in a state of nervous anticipation.

I bought a few essentials, queued, paid and walked the hundred yards to my first-floor flat. It was only after I had put the milk in the fridge and the bread in the cupboard and had sat down in front of *Neighbours* with a cigarette, a cup of tea and a plate of digestive biscuits that I finally realised what had been so strange about the babies and infants I'd seen in Waitrose. Each child had been staring with fierce concentration at his or her hands. And those hands had been *blurred*.

Mrs Webber called an impromptu staff meeting in the following morning's break. She told us that a number of parents had noticed their children behaving unusually and had asked if we had seen anything similar in school. The unspoken implication, as ever, was that it was somehow the school's fault. 'I've had a word with Jane Manners over at Foxglove Primary,' Mrs Webber said, 'and they're having just the same issues that we are, so I'm happy we're doing nothing wrong. Even so...' and she outlined some changes in our routine. Mostly this meant less formal teaching and more pastoral work. We were to try to interact more closely with our pupils and see if we could get an idea of what was going on.

'Pump the little blighters, she means,' said Mary during our lunchtime no-smoking break. 'It'll all blow over in a couple of days, you'll see.'

But it didn't.

I wonder – did you have an imaginary friend when you were young? I did. Her name was Hilary, the same as my rag doll. I think that was because I didn't want anyone to find out about her. Possibly I thought I would betray myself inadvertently by vocalising my side of our conversations. But I could always have said I was talking to my favourite doll and my parents would have smiled and nodded. Even then I knew with a child's certainty that I was an odd, quiet little thing, and that I was not turning out quite as my mother and father had expected or hoped. There had been no brother or sister for me. I never found out why.

Best not to be caught talking to myself then, or to a fictional playmate.

Hilary had been my best friend for fifteen years by the time I went to University. Exuberant where I was restrained, chatty where I was taciturn, adventurous where I was cautious, she was the cause of the scrapes I got into from time to time; escapades that would make my parents and teachers shake their heads and declare that they were surprised, and whatever could have got into Hazel to make her behave like that?

Hilary was the pretty girl who got all the boys; I was the plain friend who relied on her for introductions. It was Hilary who tried vodka, who smoked her first spliff in my company, who was discovered at the back of the gym with Craig Machin in a state of mutual undress.

But it was Hazel who got the necessary A-level grades to get into Durham and read English and Hazel who fully expected when she went in for teacher training that she'd end up expounding on the work of the Brontë sisters to a classroom full of enthralled Sixth formers. Somewhere along the line, though, I think Hilary took over and I ended up with primary school kids.

Who often had secret friends of their own.

That was what I was seeing now, amongst my Year Twos. Every one of them, almost without exception, seemed to be engaged in a continuous secret conversation with an invisible partner. Even the noisiest of them – Ian Chambers – was quietly whispering to himself and looking down into his cupped hands throughout the school day. Nothing I or any of the other members of staff did had the power of distracting the children for more than a few minutes at a time. To add to the strangeness of the situation this preoccupation was spreading steadily up through the year groups. I wandered into Year Three's room one morning to find them as distracted as my year had been a week previously. And Mary's tinies were looking like the babies in the supermarket. They were completely locked into themselves and their hands had that same blurred quality I had first noticed in Waitrose.

Somehow we carried on. There was, after all, a curriculum to follow, targets to be attained and educational value to be added.

It was a week or two later that I woke up suddenly in the middle of the night and knocked the alarm clock off the bedside table. It fell to the floor with a muffled *ting*. I muttered something under my breath and was reaching for the light switch when a voice came out of the darkness.

'Leave it Hazel. It doesn't matter. Tomorrow's Saturday.'

'What?'

'Leave it.'

I realised with a sudden clarity that I was dreaming. I was not awake at all. Anyway, I recognised the voice.

'Hilary?'

'Hi.'

'What the hell are you doing here?'

'It's nice to see you too.'

This was ridiculous – literally so. I laughed. 'Hello. Long time, no see.' That was true enough. I hadn't spoken to Hilary for years. Months, at least. But it was nice to hear her again, even if it were only in a dream. 'What have you been up to, Hil? Trouble?'

'No, not at all. I'm a reformed character. Look – do you mind if I snuggle up?'

'Go ahead.'

If I had been the kind of person who keeps pets, what happened next would have been no surprise to me. But I was startled when a soft, warm, furry presence slipped next to me in bed, climbed onto my left arm and nuzzled my neck with a moist tongue. My first thought was that downstairs' cat had somehow got into my flat. But cats don't talk, do they? And this one most certainly did. In my dream, anyway.

'You're a very fortunate lady, you know,' the creature said. Its voice was soft and slightly buzzy in my ear. 'Not everyone has someone like me. Not yet.'

'Not yet?'

'The children have. The babies definitely have. You must have noticed by now.'

'A friend, you mean?'

'Yes, more or less.'

'Are you saying that the children are running around like madmen, or lying curled up like catatonics, because they've all had dreams about mysterious animals getting into bed with them? And watch where you put that tail!'

This was the most lucid dream I had ever had. I mean, how often have you been *tickled* in a dream?

'Dreams? Surely you don't think this is a dream?' Furry laughter. 'See you again soon.'

And then, just like that, I fell asleep – or doubly asleep – and when I awoke the alarm clock was lying on the floor next to my bed. There was no animal presence in my flat, all the windows were closed and the door was locked on the deadbolt, as usual. I was alone once more.

I spent the following day in a state of mild distraction. It was fortunate that the children paid me very little attention, absorbed as they were in their private worlds, gazing fixedly into their cupped hands, their mouths and lips moving in silent conversation. The only thing that disturbed our routine was the appearance in the early afternoon of a council van. It had come from the Community Hygiene Department. A rat, or some similar small mammal, had been seen in the Year One classroom. Several, in fact, together with an assortment of birds, butterflies and amphibians.

'Nature Study?' I asked. Perhaps the mites thought they'd been asked to hunt for some mini-beasts and bring them into school. But no.

I had been half expecting it, so it was no surprise when Hilary came to me again that night, as I lay snuggled up under my solitary duvet. I think I would have been disappointed if she had not. We chatted about old times and I asked her what she'd been up to and it was... oddly thrilling. As before, she left suddenly and I fell into a deeper sleep immediately afterwards.

The invasion – or infestation as Mrs Webber called it – continued. Word reached us on the teachers' grapevine that we were far from being the only affected school. The problem was national – international, even –

although there was little about it on the television, except for an admonitory feature on *Newsround* about the responsibilities involved in keeping pets. We soldiered on like the troupers we were, even though the children – and it was all the children throughout the school now – mostly ignored us.

And then this morning, after another vivid nocturnal meeting with Hilary, I woke to find a tabby cat lying on the bed next to me. It looked directly into my eyes as I sat up in bed, then followed me closely as I got up, put on my slippers and walked into the kitchen. Its presence was strange, yet utterly familiar. I had no fear of it. Perhaps its mouth moved as I put the kettle on. Perhaps I heard it speak. I think I might know its name.

Something great, something extraordinary, something that will change everybody's lives is about to happen, I just know it. I wonder what it will be?

Mike:
Your day of change

Mike: Your Day of Change

HAS EVERYONE GOT A COFFEE? YES? THEN LET ME TELL YOU ALL about how it was for me on my own personal Special Day...

Fuck me! But I was feeling rough that morning. All my own fault? Night on the sauce? Well actually, sir or madam, I think you'll find there was blame on all sides. And we had something to celebrate, didn't we?

So. It was half-six. Sun just starting to show through the blinds of my nice little loft. And me feeling rough. No surprise there. Not unfamiliar at all. But I wasn't expecting to hear voices. I hadn't had any more to drink than usual and I'd stayed off the white stuff, like a good boy.

At first I thought it was my phone. The way I worked it out, I'd left it on silent the night before. It must have fallen into the bed next to me. Believe it; I sleep next to my phone. It's life and death to me. Or more important than that. It must have gone off in dildo mode and woken me up and I must have hit answer automatically. That made perfect sense. And if it had been my mate Bigsy on the horn I'd have understood perfectly why it was telling lazy sod – i.e. me – to get his arse out of bed and into the office.

Only it wasn't my phone talking. It was something my bleary eyes registered as small, squidgy-soft and brownish-green. Which my phone most definitely wasn't. And the voice was female. Which Bigsy most certainly wasn't. What the fuck was happening?

OK. Let's go back a couple of months to when I first noticed there was something funny going on. Back to my old job at Twyford, Armitage and Shanks. It was like this – we'd all had a crack at number 23a Blenheim Ave. Me first, because I was the senior negotiator and I was fucking good. Three months and nothing. No interest at all. So the guvnor gave it to Nisha, the new girl. Give her a chance, he said. Earn her spurs.

'Spurs?' I said. 'Fuck off! Like she cares!'

Shanks looked at me sideways. 'What d'you mean?'

'She doesn't like football?'

'No, you plank! Spurs. Horses. Knights in armour. Not football.'

I sighed. 'Yes boss. But she won't shift it. Not even if she was Joan of Bleedin' Arc. Are we done?'

'Yes. Piss off.'

Nisha didn't shift number 23a, Blenheim Ave. She tried, I'll admit that. She rewrote the prop des ten times. It was a work of art by the time she'd finished. But there was one problem. No, make that two. First, the place was a shithole. No doubt about it. Do you like the smell of rotting garbage? Good, because the main bedroom overlooked next door's compost heap. Enjoy the quiet life? Unlucky you, seeing as how there was a club full of long-haired Norwegian death metal fans doing their grungy thing just two doors down. Got a nice motor? Not for long, if you left it parked outside.

Two reasons, I said. The other one? The vendor wanted one and a half mill and wasn't going to budge. 'Rising market,' she said, on an echoey line from Paraguay or Argentina or wherever it was she'd holed up. 'Do you take me for stupid?' she said. 'Sell me short, would you? You're all crooks, the lot of you.'

Which I won't deny.

So Nisha worked her cute little tail off and got nowhere.

Which suited me just fine. Let me explain.

It came every time – every time I was at some little drinks-and-a-few-nibbles thing in North Finchley, East Barnet or bleedin' Crouch 'Practically Hampstead' End. I'd meet this babe or this dude with the useful-sounding contacts and we'd talk about the weather and have a moan at Blair and we'd be getting along nicely and I'd get them a couple of drinks and some spanner'd put fucking Coldplay on the stereo. Good stuff, eh? And good for business, whether pounds, shillings and pence or some horizontal hoopla. And then the babe or the guy in the Dockers would ask the question. 'So Mike, and what do you do?'

Over the years I'd tried every spin I could on this one. I was an entrepreneur, a negotiator, a dealer, a consultant. I was a placement specialist. And it never worked. 'Oh, you're an *estate agent*,' they'd say, and their eyes'd drift sideways and they'd have to go to the loo or they'd just spotted old Charlie who they'd not seen for absolute bloody yonkers. And that was it, mate No Charlie for you tonight.

So we tended to stick together. Fucking incestuous, us. Which is why I was keeping my eye on Nisha, who was, no doubt at all, extremely tasty.

She'd had number 23a on her books for six weeks before I made my move. Of course I'd been raising my profile with her, but not so much as to put her off. Just little things – a favour here and there, let her drop me a tip or two. You know, professional but friends. Have a drink or two after work but don't make no move, boy.

So when I asked her about 23a one slow afternoon she gave me that sad smile I liked so much and told me there was nothing doing and we might be going to lose the exclusive. As if I didn't know. I suggested we go round and take a look. Maybe it smelled funny. Perhaps the cleaners had been doing shit instead of moving it. Or we could check out its Feng Shui.

We checked out its Feng Shui (I'd bought a book the day before). Nope, it was all perfectly aligned. We sniffed for smells in the kitchen. Nope, everything was squeaky-clean. I rubbed my thumb on top of the fridge to make certain. Sure enough, it squeaked. Ditto the bathroom. Ditto the living room. Even the stash of echhi behind the aspidistra (freshly watered) was clean, if you take my meaning.

Guest bedroom? Check. Second bedroom? Double-check. Master bedroom? Now that required more attention. Much more attention. Attention which cute little Nisha with her cute little butt and her cute not-so-little tits was happy to help me out with. Happier than I'd expected, to be honest. And I'm always honest.

We gave that master bedroom a close examination, one way and another. Nisha's enthusiasm for her job was most gratifying. 'You're an energetic lad,' she said, buttoning up her blouse. 'You bet,' I said, unbuttoning it again and throwing her back on the bed for a second viewing and a full structural survey.

I think I'd have applied for a mortgage there and then, only a sudden wave of tiredness swept over me and I flaked out on the bed just where I was. I hope I didn't squash my colleague too much. But as I zoned in and out the way you do after an especially vigorous workout I thought I heard a voice. A male voice. And mixed up with the buzzing in my head was the thought, *Oh fuck, we've been caught. There's someone coming up the stairs and we're fucking shagged.* But that made no sense, because it was next to me on the bed and what it said was, 'You silly, silly girl.' Which didn't sound much like the vendor or her agent, did it?

I pretended I hadn't heard it and gave her another one. And then we went back to the office, grinning and smelling of sex. At least, I was. Grinning, that is. Nisha looked less sure of herself but that didn't stop us going back the next day. And the day after that.

It wasn't long after that first viewing that old man Shanks got a cat. Like we needed one. And fuck only knows why *he* needed one. But there it was, sat in his office, by his chair or on his desk. And him fucking *stroking* it, like your Nan does. I started wondering whether he'd lost his marbles; and if he had, what about a partnership for me? My name over the door. My share of the profits.

Look, I know what you say about estate agents. Parasite is the least of it. But I say it's business. And business is tough. Business is looking for chinks in your competitors' armour and slipping in the knife. Business is getting the best deal for yourself. Business is looking after Number One. You don't agree? Well fuck you, you hypocrite. Look in the mirror.

So I kept my eyes open. I did business. I checked Shanks for signs of early senility. I shagged Nisha whenever the opportunity came up. Still – in those cosy post-coital moments I kept on hearing that voice, again and again, saying the same old thing. *Silly little tart. What are you doing with that slimeball? Dump him now, why don't you.* Polite, eh?

And I couldn't see how a sparrow could've got into the flat, unless the cleaners were leaving the windows open.

I walked into the office bright and early a day or two later. Early worm gets the bird, see? I wasn't the first, though. No, there was Bigsy my ol' drinking buddy (and handy in Lettings) sitting at his desk with an idiot grin on his face with some kind of rat on his left arm. Fuck me if he wasn't stroking it, just like the guvnor and his moggy.

'You hold it and I'll whack it,' I said, grabbing a ruler and advancing on him with malice aforethought. Fuck me again if Bigboy didn't hide the animal in the pocket of his Burtons.

'Clear off, Mike,' he says with some strange expression I've never seen on his face before. As if he was *sorry* for me, the bastard. And it was weird, because there seemed to be more animals around the place. In shops and pubs, and nobody minded. Sitting next to drivers in their cars. I saw a copper petting a squirrel in East Finchley, just as I was about to shift a dampish purpose-built to a nice young couple with cash-rich parents and no sense.

And then it was *that* morning. Nisha had been losing interest in me, so we hadn't tested the master suite in 23a for a week or two. In other words I woke up alone. I was at home in my own bed, though fuck knows how I'd got there.

She'd only shifted it after all, the sly bint. Number 23a. To some Russian or Arab or something. For the full asking price. And I'd smiled and said well done and hinted that I might be up for some additional congratulations if she wanted. And she'd given me the sad smile and hadn't we moved on? Shit. I supposed we had.

I slipped out of bed, shaved, showered and shat and got myself out the door. I still didn't know, you see.

Bus to the office. Shanks didn't trust us to take the office cars home, though he convinced us he was doing us a favour, not making us liable for tax. He was a salesman too, right? So two stops on the bus; though fucking mobile zoo would have been a better description of it. The place was seething. Wings, jaws, claws and paws. And people everywhere with stupid fucking grins on their faces.

Of course the office was no better. Everyone had got in before me. Every desk had a smiling cretin sitting at it and an animal standing, crouching or perching on it.

'Go on then, Mike, you old wanker,' said Bigsy, waving some kind of rodent in my general direction. 'I've shown you mine. Now you show us yours!'

'My what?'

'Your familiar, you dick!'

'My what?'

'I think he means me,' said a small voice from my coat pocket. And something with a slimy-green face jumped out and oozed its way up my sleeve.

'What the fuck are you?' I swept the disgusting thing off my clothes. It landed on a desk and at the same time I felt a funny twinge, like a toothache that's not quite happening yet but is going to give you fucking screaming hell before very much longer.

The creature drew itself up on its four legs. 'I,' it said, 'am a Great Crested Newt.' I looked at it.

'Where's your great crest then, you ugly fucker?'

'I am a *female* Great Crested Newt. Therefore I have no crest. I do, however, have an attractive pattern on my underside. Look.' It rose up on its hind legs and showed me a sort of yellow splodge on its belly.

'Christ, you're ugl…' And then it struck me. I was talking to some kind of lizard, sitting on a negotiator's desk in Twyford, Armitage and Shanks' main office. And it – she – was talking back to me. Clearly the triple Sangrias I'd knocked back the night before were still running around inside my head.

'What's her name?' asked Shanks, coming out of his goldfish-bowl office with that cat in his arms. 'Mine's called Marietta,' he added, as if I gave a toss.

One more stupid question that morning wouldn't have made any difference so I asked it, right to the revolting creature's face. 'What're you called, then?' But before it could answer, Bigsy jumped up.

'Asbo! Her name's Asbo! After what you got up to last night, my son, you fucking need one!'

That did it. I spun on my heel – bad move – and made it like offski. I was out of it, and that Great Crested Newt could throw itself into the fucking toilet for all I fucking cared.

I got nearly as far as the kerb before it hit me.

Perhaps it was the booze addling what was left of my brain. Perhaps I wasn't as smart as I thought I was. After they got me into Shanks' office and I stopped screaming and they took the pencil out from between my teeth they explained how it was – that Asbo and I were bound together by a link that couldn't be broken. They handed the reptile over to me and told me to hang on to her, literally for dear life. After a while I stood up, lurched over to the door with the animal in my pocket and caught the Northern Line to Waterloo. I was buggered if I was going to walk around with a fucking lizard hanging round my neck. I'd show them.

No. The bastards at T, A and S showed *me*. They followed me onto the Tube and they *let* me throw Asbo off Waterloo Bridge. They didn't stop me jumping into the river after her. Anyone would think they didn't like me, though I suppose they did call for help. After a while.

I must say the river police were quick. There'd been a lot of cases like mine, the frogman said, clutching his dolphin-familiar. Quite a few deaths. Nasty way to go. Standing orders to watch the railways, bridges, high buildings, that sort of thing.

I soon discovered that your familiar's form said something about you. Big shots got big impressive familiars. Policemen, soldiers and the like got dogs. Ordinary people got cats, birds, whatever. Bigsy got a rat. There was still some justice in the world, then.

But slimy little amphibians? No. They were rare. And the funny thing – the fucking bollock-crunching thing – about it was that whenever I tried to move a bit of property after that day the punters would take one look at Asbo and laugh in my face.

'Why don't you wear a sign round your neck?' said one bloke, leaving me standing on the kerb like a twat. 'It could say Greasy Lying Bastard on it.' Ha-fucking-ha.

So that was that. All the sales jobs went to people with nice cuddly friendly familiars with nice fur and cute fucking whiskers, not stinking pond-life reptiles like mine. I left T, A and S the following week. And for a while it was rough.

I probably don't have to tell you this, but there's a fine line between doing very nicely thank you and being totally fucked. I was totally fucked. No job meant no commission. No commission meant no mortgage payments. And that special deal Shanks had set up for me so I could screw down the vendor on my nice little loft wasn't so special if I couldn't keep up my end of it. I was on the street within a month. Me and fucking Asbo pond-life Great Crested Arsehole.

It was bad enough that she was repulsive to look at and smelled of stagnant ditch-water. But that wasn't enough. She had to *talk* as well. And not just ordinary look-out-you're-about-to-step-under-a-bus-let's-go-for-a-pint talk. Nothing so useful. No. She bloody *lectured* me. Like she was the fucking Voice Of God. Morality was her speciality. Being nice to people so they'll be nice to you. Or just for the sake of it, because it's the right and proper thing to do. Spread the good karma around. I've told you already what I thought of that. And if it was true that looking out for me and fuck-you was the only way to get by when I was in work it was even more so when I was dog-eat-dog out of it.

I had it hard. I had pain. I had fear. I had despair. Like you. I tried to kill myself several times. I even had to sell my iPhone to buy food. That's how bad it got.

Just like it was for you good people here. When I started you off on this course last week I told you that total honesty is the only way you're going to make any progress, and it's true.

Today I've told you the total honest truth about myself and my familiar. You're all sitting here in front of me today because you've been referred by your doctor or Social Services. All of you face being sectioned or being put on the risk register. All of you have dysfunctional familiar relationships. All of you had a Day Of Change that ruined your lives. You're living in the pit.

I've climbed out of that pit.

This is your very last chance, ladies and gentlemen, boys and girls. *The Twelve-Step Plan to a Fabulous Familiar*. And I'm here to tell you – to show you – that it *can* be done. You see, whatever it is you face – humiliation, disgust, rejection – you can be sure I've faced it too. And I'm living proof that you can survive it. I'm a survivor. I've come back from nothing to running my own counselling business, which, I'll have you know, is doing pretty darn well. So can you, if you try. Your lives are stretched out in front of you like an open road.

Are you ready to take the first step along that road? It won't be easy, but it will be worthwhile, I promise you. Yes? OK, take out your familiar. Hold him or her in front of your face. Yes, that's it. Now, let's take Step One. Ask the First Question. We'll all do it together. Don't be afraid. I'll lead you.

Right. I'll go first. Here we go. 'I'm Mike. Who are you?'

You see, everyone? She has a name. The day I learned and accepted my familiar's true name was the day my life turned itself around. I firmly believe that today is going to be that day for *your* life. Now let's all say the names of our familiars – our darlings – in turn. I'll lead off…

Barbara:
Inseparable

Barbara: Inseparable

THIS IS HOW IT WAS FOR ME:

It was the end of another fabulous, busy day. One of those non-stop days when everything you do goes so well that, despite it making you feel so worn-out you could just curl up on the sofa and sleep for a couple of days, you wish it would never end.

We kicked off with a breakfast meeting at oh-six-thirty hours. Me, Lynn, Jacob, Henry and, once he'd shifted his sorry arse into gear, Simon. I so like to get started well ahead of time. It gets the whole day's work off to a flying start.

There were three jobs, all afternoons. I put Lynn in charge of the Culrose / Wargraves and assigned Jacob to the MacDonald / Trumans. I had planned to let Simon handle the Timms / Shakesby do but he didn't look very with-it that morning so I decided to look after it myself. Probably I'd always meant to, as the alternative was to do nothing – as if – or spend the afternoon in the office. Which is not my idea of fun at all. Simon looked a little pissed-off when I sent him back home. Too bad. You're either in play or on the bench. It was starting to look as if Simon might turn out not to be one of us after all.

So then while Lynn and Jacob got on the phone and gathered their forces, I grabbed hold of Henry and briefed him on his duties. He'd only been with us six months and he wasn't ready yet to oversee a big job like the Timms / Shakesbys all by his little self. He scuttled off, checklist in one hand and phone in the other and got to work. *Go on,* I thought. *Impress me.*

All three operations started at fifteen hundred hours, but to say 'start' is misleading. In fact, I'd been working hard on these three jobs –

and several others – for the past six months. This afternoon's work was the culmination of many hours' careful, painstaking preparation on the part of me and my team. It was also the point at which we earned the greatest share of our revenue. Not that we didn't bill earlier, of course, but most of that money went straight to our subs.

Once I was sure that Henry was on top of things I set off on my rounds. You simply cannot do too much oversight is my motto but, even more importantly, you must *communicate*. Everyone needs me. I'm needed on site – to reassure everyone while doing some discreet chasing-up. I'm needed back at base to nip logistical problems in the bud. Even now I'll happily get in a vehicle and shuttle stores if that's what it takes. Do the face-to-face work. And talk, talk, talk. Talking, persuading, getting to know people, earning their trust and respect. That's what I do best. People like me and I like them. That's what makes me happy. That's what's made me successful. That; and delivering on my promises. Word of mouth is the way you get on. It can make or break you.

The day passed in an organised whirl. Everything worked; or when it didn't one of my lieutenants or I dealt with it discreetly and invisibly. Discretion's our watchword. I'd put it on the letterhead if it didn't make us look like a dodgy escort agency.

And at oh-three-hundred hours the following morning I finally locked the office door, rattled the padlock on the loading-bay gate and set the alarm combination. We were done. Another fabulous, busy day.

I love my job. Nobody – *nobody* – does it as well as me.

George was fast asleep and snoring by the time I got home. No matter. I still needed to wind down, so I took a shower in my bathroom, wrapped myself in a nice fresh towel, poured a drink – first of the day – and watched some mindless telly in the drawing-room. It was oh-four-thirty by the time I slipped into bed. I dropped off straight away.

It was George's job to organise Sunday breakfast. He'd got quite good over the years at gauging the right time to bring the wake-up cuppa and when I was ready for grapefruit, or a fresh fig or a bowl of apricots and yogurt or whatever he guessed I'd like. He wasn't bad at guessing either. The main, the most important, rule was that I got to listen to the omnibus edition of *The Archers* over breakfast, so I had to be awake by ten.

The rest of Sunday was flexible. It was much too soon to make follow-up calls for the previous day's jobs, although it's not unknown for me to be rung up in the middle of the day – or the evening – with expressions of interest from guests. I prefer not to get too involved with business matters on Sunday, but work is work and a contract is a contract and there's nothing like a personal recommendation for bypassing that nasty old sales funnel, is there?

Normally I'd be spark-out after such a busy Saturday but this time, for whatever reason, I woke before George. Perhaps it was the voice that did it.

My first thought was that the radio alarm clock had come on by accident. Perhaps there'd been a power cut and the clock had got itself confused. But it didn't sound like a radio voice; it didn't have that radio way of speaking. It sounded like a real person talking to another real person. I say real; but it wasn't exactly. It had a peculiar timbre that I couldn't quite place.

The voice was speaking very softly and, so far as I could tell, it was coming from somewhere in the bed. The room was dim and I couldn't see anything so I reached for the bedside light. I was just about to flick it on when the voice stopped and another spoke in answer.

I had no trouble identifying it. I should know my own husband by now. The sound of his voice, indistinct but unmistakably male, gave me something of a shock. Although I hadn't considered it up until then I now realised that the first voice was undeniably female.

George stopped speaking and the first voice – the strange woman's voice – started again. That did it. Although I understood nothing of what was going on, unless I was hearing things and going gaga my husband was having a conversation with another woman and, to pile insult on injury, was doing it in our bed while I was still in it. I turned on the light.

'George! What are you up to?'

My husband sat up and rubbed his eyes. I looked at the indentation in the pillow where his head had been. No. No sign of a handset. He hadn't been enjoying a spot of telephone sex on the side, then.

'Sorry. What?' It's an annoying habit of George's that he begins every conversation with me by apologising. It's not at all necessary.

'You were talking to somebody.'

'In my sleep, you mean?' George ran his hand through his not unattractively tousled hair. 'I must have been dreaming.'

'Who were you talking to?'

'In my dream?'

'Yes.'

'Lord. I don't know.' He swung his legs over the side of the bed. 'Cup of tea, love?'

And that was where I left it. I'm not a madwoman.

Linda, Michael and the boys came round for Sunday dinner. After that I put in an hour or two on the web and made some social calls. There was an alumni get-together in a week or two and it was one of my jobs to round up the troops. Then over to the other side of the village for drinks at Jeremy's. I chatted to Rikki and swapped a recipe or two with her, we watched a DVD of their holiday in Moscow (again!) and got home just before eleven. A typical Sunday, then, and no more funny voices. George must have taken the hint.

On Monday morning I was first into the office, as usual. The beginning of the working week is usually a bit quieter and I like to take advantage of the lull to do some strategic thinking. You see, although the firm's called Epithalamion (*For your Day of Days*) we do much more than just organising society weddings. Or, at least, we plan to. It's always the same in business, I find. You get a great idea, you market and execute it well and you make money. Great. But then all the me-too boys come along and start undercutting you and the next thing you know your nice cash cow is buckling at the knees and foaming at the mouth. So what do you do? You franchise out your good idea and think up another one. That's what Mondays are for. I'd already thought of one or two stonking new opportunities (which I'm certainly not going to tell *you* about) that previous week. All I had to do now was work out how to monetise them. Oh all right, I'll tell you. One of them was to launch a mid-market version of Epithalamion called, say, Nuptial Delights. That would look good in the *Daily Mail,* I thought. Just so long as there was margin in it we'd clean up – people have so little time these days. It's nice to able to help them out.

Later on I had the underperforming Simon in and challenged him to amaze me with his achievements over the next month. He got the message that his job was on the line and ran off to be a busy little bunny-rabbit. At least, I think he did. It was hard to tell as he still seemed rather... detached.

The rest of the day was marketing meetings, client calls and some retail therapy. By the time I got home around twenty-hundred I was ready to put my feet up, have something nice to eat and drink, and unwind on the sofa with George.

That was the plan. But George didn't respond to my cry of 'Hi honey, I'm home!' and when I finally tracked him down to his lair in the upstairs study he was *talking* to somebody.

That was enough. I sent him to the guest suite.

Over the next week it seemed the whole world was drifting off to la-la-land. Nobody could concentrate any more. They all walked about in a dream-state with foolish smiles on their faces or with their lips moving as if they were on their Bluetooths or chewing gum. It's very bad management practice to lose your temper with staff but I came as close as makes nearly no difference that week. The worst thing about it was the way they looked at me; as if they were offering me their *sympathy*. Anyway, everything went completely to pot. And just to make it worse, it wasn't just my staff who'd been carried off by the fairies. My clients were just as bad. Nobody returned my calls, invoices didn't get paid, nobody wanted to talk to me. That really hurt. I'm a people person, you know? But wherever I looked, whoever I spoke to, everyone was completely self-absorbed and, mostly, their lips were moving. Sometimes you could hear them speak; often it was silent, like a slow reader using his finger to follow the words across the page.

Of course now we all know – *you* know – what was happening. But back then it was as if Christmas had come early and there were presents for everybody. A sword for Peter, a horn for Susan and a bow for Lucy.

But nothing for me. Nothing at all.

And then, once everything had settled down and we were getting used to the new way of things, the awful realisation that I was different to over ninety-nine percent of my fellow human beings came near to crushing the life out of me. I still couldn't bear to let George back into our bedroom. 'I am not sharing our bed with that... thing!' I told him, and he looked hurt and replied that he and his Clarinda were still the same old George; and that his familiar was the same part of him that she had always been. It was just that now she was physically incorporate. I knew he was right, but it made no difference to me. Not to the way I felt.

I looked inside myself – of course I did. I sought that presence within me – that part of myself that should by rights have taken an external form; but he was not there. Or, if he was, he was so much a part of me that he could not be split off. That's what one counsellor told me, anyway. It was, I think, supposed to make me feel better – this idea that I had such a well-integrated personality that my familiar was physically inseparable from me.

But George still pitied me, I could see that in his eyes and the way they couldn't help looking away from me. It was quite unbearable – to have my own husband feeling sorry for me. I went to a man who ran group sessions, hoping to find others like myself, but it turned out that he was mainly interested in helping people who couldn't get along with their familiar's forms. His familiar was, I must say, remarkably ugly. I let him take my £250 and say he was sorry, but he probably wasn't going to be able to do much for me.

So to all of you my friends on the Unfamiliarity forum, that's my story. Thank heavens for the Internet, that's all I can say. I'm not going to carry a pet or a doll and pretend he's my familiar as one of you – Notawitch, I think – suggested. Firstly, I think that would be cheating and secondly I honestly don't think it would work. If my fellow humans didn't spot the masquerade, their familiars would.

Perhaps – just perhaps – he will appear one day. Maybe he's just being a little slow (although as it's been almost a year since most people got their familiars I'm starting to wonder). Meanwhile, work and life go on and it's not turned out quite as badly as I thought it would. The kids still talk to me; my people still do what I tell them. I use the phone rather more than I used to and I tend to avoid face-to-face meetings. I remember the way I used to look – or not look – at disabled people and I feel ashamed of myself. For that is what I am now; disabled. No doubt I'll get as used to it – or not used to it – as someone who is blind or deaf or in a wheelchair.

No, that's going too far. I shouldn't be such a drama queen. I've not been changed or harmed in any way. I'm no different from the way I was a year ago. It's the world that's been shaken up, not me. But please God, or whoever it was who made me this way, would it really be too much to ask for me to have a familiar of my very own? Just so I can rejoin the human race?

Please?

Mousie:
In the garden

Mousie: In the Garden

T HE NURSES HERE ARE VERY NICE, BUT THEY DO KEEP CHANGING. No, not their clothes, silly, them. I never know who's going to come when I press my button. That shouldn't bother me by now, but it does. Maria's my favourite nurse. She hardly ever changes.

It's quite boring here a lot of the time and there isn't very much to do. I'd like to read some books if I could, but by the time they reach me they're all messed up. The pages are wrinkled and the covers are bent and the colours have run like washing. Mum says that's because of the autowhatsit thing they have to put them through to get rid of the germs.

Mum comes to see me nearly every day. Dad doesn't come as often, but he has important business to go to. Sometimes he's here after teatime and he's still wearing his suit from work.

There's a television at the foot of my bed and I've got a remote for it. It's gone a bit melted from going through the autothingy but it still works if I press the buttons right. The telly picture's not very clear through the plastic the tent's made of. I wish it could be inside here with me.

Mum calls me Mousie, which isn't my real name. If I went to proper school she'd probably have called me Mousie when she picked me up at going-home time and all the other kids would have made fun of me over it.

Let me tell you about my room. It's quite big but most of the space is taken up by my special bed. There are lots of boxes on stands with flashing lights and bleeping buzzers on them and they flash and bleep all the time. They used to keep me awake but they don't any more. I hardly notice them; only when the bleeps or the lights change, or a new one starts, and then all the doctors and nurses rush in and look very serious and important. Usually they fiddle with my tubes a bit and go away again. Mum is a lot more smiley when that happens and quite often Dad turns up with her, even though his job is so busy. He calls me Graham, which is my real name.

Mum can't kiss me when she has to leave because of all the plastic. Instead there's a kind of glove attached to a tube she can put her arm in and stroke me or fluffle me that way. She always says she loves me when she says goodbye. It's a kind of magic spell to keep me from harm.

Look; I was talking about my room. Apart from the telly and the big bed with the plastic tent all around it and the bleeping flashing boxes there's a door with a little window in it. The door leads into a corridor and if I'm feeling well enough to sit up and lean over I can see the doctors and nurses and sometimes the other kids going backwards and forwards. None of the other kids can come and see me in case they do something wrong to the flashing-light boxes and break them.

I haven't been in a bed in a tent in a room in a hospital all my life. It's only been since my tenth birthday. No, that's wrong, I was here a lot when I was six. Mum says I was in a preemie unit when I was born. She says I came too early.

There's something else in my room. I nearly forgot to tell you. There's a window. I can't see out of it very well as it's too high up, which makes me sad, but Mum says it doesn't matter because it only looks out on another building in the block. It's not as if you can see mountains or the ocean or people through it. Mum's always trying to cheer me up like that but I still wish I could look out of it. You never know, there might be something interesting out there. More interesting than clouds or sky which are all I can see through it.

I don't mind it when Maria calls me Mousie even though she's not my Mum.

The telly's all right, but I'd like a change.

I've asked Mum to get me some books. I don't care if the autowhatever messes them up. I want books about gardens. Why gardens? Mum asks. I say it's because I like gardens. When I wasn't in hospital I used to play in the garden at home and I liked it when we went to Cornwall on holiday and I could go to see the big gardens that are in an enormous plastic tent like mine, only my tent isn't enormous.

If it *was* enormous I'd be able to walk about in it instead of being stuck in bed. I could run around. Sing. Shout. They get worried by shouting here so I don't do it and my singing is terrible, so I don't do that either.

It's not soppy, me liking gardens, is it?

It's very boring here. Did I say that already? I often wonder when I'll be able to go home again. I've got lots of friends at home. Some of them are real and some of them are on the Internet. I talk more to the Internet ones than the real ones because the real ones don't come round very much. I don't know why. Perhaps it's because they're afraid they'll catch what I've got, even though you can't. No really. It's in my blood, what I've got. Don't worry. You'd have to drink it, like a vampire, if you wanted to catch what I've got. Of course you don't want to catch it, because if you did you'd end up living in a tent in a hospital like me.

Oh. Maybe it's because they don't want to hurt me and kill me by mistake or in an accident. That's what Mum said when I asked her. I like to believe what Mum tells me and I usually do, but I didn't believe this one because it's rubbish. Why should anybody want to kill me, even in an accident?

There are other children in the hospital but I don't see them because I'm in a tent and they've got germs. I wish I could have my computer in here with me so I could talk to my internet friends, but the autothing would melt it and anyway they say it would stop the bleeping flashing boxes working properly.

I think they're making that up.

Mum has finally brought me in some books! *Gardening* books! With pictures of forks and spades and trowels in them. I told her I didn't want books on how to *make* a garden, I wanted books about *being* in gardens. I don't know if she understood me. Grown-ups can be terrifically dense sometimes. I'll carry on watching the telly and being bored instead, I suppose.

I've been sleeping a lot more than usual recently and having funny dreams. They have to wake me up in the morning now, I'm so dozy. Usually I'm all ready for them when they come in. I wonder if they've been giving me stuff to make me sleep more. I asked Maria about it but she only smiled and told me not to worry.

That's what she always says. She's pretty and she's nice and I like her a lot but she never says anything much. She never answers questions properly, but none of the grown-ups do that. They never have. They keep secrets from me.

Those dreams. They're... bothering me. I'm running in them, or I'm flying all by myself or I'm swimming under water without running out of air and talking to the fishes and the crabs and the prawns and the lobsters and singing to the whales. Shouting, even.

So to stop me from being bothered by the dreams I'm reading the crinkled-up garden books. They bother me too; only differently.

There's this programme on the telly just after teatime. It's for little kids really but I like it. It gives me a funny feeling, like the dreams do. This boy with a funny blue head goes by boat to a garden full of friends and funny creatures. Nobody's ever sad or cross there and at the end the birds sing a song and they all go to sleep in their beds. There's a nice man with a kind voice who talks to the characters, but you never see him. The music is nice and gentle. I'd love it if I could go for a walk in that garden.

Of course it's not the only thing I watch. I like *Tracy Beaker* and *My Parents Are Aliens* and *Judge Judy* and *Blue Peter* and *Ninja Turtles* and the *Chuckle Brothers* and *Jeremy Kyle* and the *News*. And *Home And Away* and *Neighbours*. And *Coronation Street*, though that's on a bit late for me.

Nobody seriously believed he would be going home again, not even his mother and father. Not this time.

Mum brought me some new storybooks yesterday. They're much more like it. There's one about a boy who wakes up in the middle of the night and goes into a garden and meets a girl there. I like that book a lot. Then there's another where a boy is very ill and there's a garden that's hidden behind a wall and when a girl finds it she stops being bad-tempered and he becomes well so he doesn't have to be pushed about in a wheelchair any more.

Both those books make me feel happy-sad, especially the second one. I don't like to cry when Mum or Dad are here, so I do it after they've gone home. It'd be smashing if I was one of those boys in those books.

I'm reading the books over and over again. I think I prefer the other one now, the one where the clock has to strike thirteen before the boy can go into the garden and see the girl. There's an ill boy in that book too, only he's not part of the story.

I'm still having the dreams where I'm swimming or flying or running with the creatures. They're getting stronger every day.

There's one special creature in my dreams. She's a girl, like the girl in *Tom's Midnight Garden*, only she's not. I mean she's not a human girl. She's an animal, but she can talk. She talks to me all the time in the dreams. We have adventures together and we help each other. Her name is Mousie, just like me. I told her my real name is Graham Hugo Dreyford and asked her what her real name was but she said no, it's Mousie, really it is. I laughed a lot at that. It's fantastic having her around. We like each other so much I'm sorry when it's time to wake up and say goodbye. When I wake up it's back in the tent in the hospital.

I've got my Mousie every night now. I think I know what the books mean when they talk about people falling in love. I think it's like this.

Something wonderful has happened! Mousie has come true! She's here with me during the day now as well as when I'm asleep. One lovely morning she didn't go away when the dreams stopped. I have to hide her under the pillow or beneath the sheets so nobody can see her. I talk to her all the time. I wonder if I'm going bonkers. It might be the pills doing it. That's happened before with pills. I saw some amazing things. You've no idea how happy I'm feeling now. Mousie and me; we tell each other the most fantastic stories.

Graham's mother and father noticed the change straight away. After all, it was the same change that had been taking place all across the world. First in babies, then in toddlers, then older children, then adolescents and now in adults. But they had wondered whether, given the desperate nature of Mousie's condition, the great change would manifest itself in him.

They stood, hands clasped, watching the pair through the translucent walls of the tent. Would their brave boy's familiar be able to save him or was her end approaching as relentlessly as his?

The Boy

* * *

I don't bother hiding her now. Nobody seems to worry about my Mousie, even when she turns into a mouse or a rat. She's not dirty and she's not got any germs on her, has she? I asked the doctor this morning and he said there's nothing to worry about, it's all perfectly natural, you're doing very well, we're all very proud of you. Which is what he always says.

I like it best when Mousie's a bird. It's a shame she can't fly up in the real sky with the real birds – only she's real too, as real as could be – but she says she doesn't want to fly very far away from me and if she did it would hurt both of us very much.

Her feathers are very soft when I stroke them. I love to be with her, loving her, doing nothing but just being together.

Nothing…

But, I say to her, there is *one* thing she could do. One special thing. It's that window up high in the wall. If she could fly up to the window and look out of it she might be able to look down and see what's outside. You see, I remember when I came here before there were gardens in the gaps between the buildings. It would be great if she could see one of those gardens for me – I'm sure there's one there. Perhaps she'd be able to go down into it and explore it and come back and tell me all about it.

Mousie? Would you go and look at that garden for me? Find it, I mean, and then come back and tell me where it is and what it looks like? I'd love to see it. I bet there's a real garden down there, with real flowers growing in it and a bench to sit on and drink orange squash and eat a Mars bar like they used to let me do at home sometimes. Wouldn't you like to see it? Wouldn't that make us extra specially happy? Don't you think?

Go on Mousie! Don't wait! Off you go! Fly for me!

A gap in time; immeasurable by any clock.

Wings beat. An aspiration of flight, an ascension of dreams.

There is no fear now; even in this place that is so very full of fear. Instead, nothing but an effortless yearning reaching for a place beyond.

There is no pain.

Muscles that tense and relax, tense and relax, tense and relax while the world turns very, very slowly.

Gravity is defeated – it is, after all, the weakest of all forces. Why should it hold any of us down, let alone such as they?

Freedom calls. Who could possibly resist it?

And a great, joyous peace.

Staff Nurse Maria Stokes was the first to reach Graham's bedside when the crash call went off. She was as quick as she possibly could have been, but she was still too late.

The torn edges of the tent fluttered in the escaping oxygen. Maria turned off the gas valve; there was a fire risk. Then she walked slowly around the bed to where Graham's body – small, much too small for his age – lay. The boy lay unmoving on his front, his head resting on the floor, his feet caught up on the side of his bed, facing the window. His arms were outstretched, like wings. There was no sign of his familiar.

'Poor little chap,' said Bene, Maria's fox-familiar. 'Do you think he...'

'No,' Maria replied. 'I don't think...' but then she had to pause and help the ward sister get Graham back into bed and tidy away the broken catheters and torn dressings.

'No,' she said again, later, when she had closed the door behind the boy's parents and left them alone with their son. 'I don't think he reached the window.'

'But?'

'But, of course,' said Maria, holding Bene next to her cheek. 'I'm sure *she* did...'

Outside the window, in the garden, the flowers nodded to one another in the gentle afternoon breeze.

Deirdre's House

The Study Window

WATCH OUT!'

'Sorry.' My response was instinctive, born of good manners rather than genuine regret. Or, more likely, cowardice. Not wanting to make a scene, or accuse the other party first.

Because it wasn't my fault. The young woman's pushchair took up the whole width of the pavement. What was I supposed to do? Step out into the road and let her by? Not likely – it was crammed bumper-to-bumper with eastbound commuter traffic, glare-blinded by the morning sun.

Twins. There were twins in the pushchair, sitting side-by-side and wearing identical artificial fleece suits in yellow and blue. Each had a bobble hat pushed down on his – or her, I couldn't tell – head. Each wore a sulky expression, not unlike their mother's.

'Go on then! Get out of the way! You blind? Can't you see I've got kids?'

Yes, I could see that; and I supposed their needs would override mine, by the simple virtue of their being children. I slowly turned my back on them and prepared to retrace my steps.

'Eh! Where're you going now?' the woman said.

I pointed up the road. A few tens of yards away the galvanised iron railings which divided the pavement from a car dealer's premises were interrupted by a gate. 'You can get past me there,' I said, half over my shoulder.

Ever since the accident I have walked with a limp, so I made slow progress. I could feel the woman's annoyance burning into the back of my neck. There was nothing I could do about it but remember to let my left leg take its own time on the forward swing and make sure that it was firmly planted on the ground before I tried to move my right, as I had been taught.

It must have taken me a whole minute to reach the gate. All the time I could hear the woman muttering and swearing behind me, the way they do these days. I expected she had a job to go to and was in a hurry. The twins; they would go into a nursery or a childminder's – day-care, as it was called. I wondered if she had a husband or so-called "partner" at home and whether he was going out to work too. Most couples had to leave home during the day, I had read, so they could pay the mortgage on their expensive little houses.

I reached the gateway and turned to rest my back against the railings. 'You can pass now,' I said, not loudly as my leg was aching badly.

'About bloody time too.' She had bleached hair tied up on the top of her head, smudged-panda eye makeup and a scarlet slash of lipstick for a mouth. I didn't know whether to despise her or pity her. Perhaps I wasn't thinking about her in those terms. Probably I was wondering about her name. Was she a Sharon or a Dawn? A Wendy or a Karen? A Chloe or a Samantha? My mind often runs off along such lines.

She pushed past me, but as she went one of the wheels of the oversized pushchair caught against my right foot, dislodging it and throwing all my weight onto the weak side. I put out my hand to steady myself. A hiss of breath escaped my lips.

'Sorry,' she said. 'You all right?'

'I think so,' I said, but as I spoke my left leg buckled under the strain and I fell forward at a sideways angle. At the same time a red sports car, driven by a young man with a baseball cap pushed back on his head, came screeching out of the yard. It swerved to avoid the pushchair and struck me a glancing blow on the hip.

'You blind?' the man shouted. Even as I was thrown back against the railings by the force of the car's impact the thought ran through my head that I ought to buy a white stick and a pair of dark glasses to stop people asking about the state of my eyesight. Perhaps I smiled.

'Stupid old tosser!' the youth yelled back at me as he barged his way into the traffic. 'Stay at home, granddad!'

The twins must have picked up the bad temper in the air, because they both began to wail loudly. Their mother knelt down in front of the pushchair. 'Now, Ashley, shush. It's all right, Mitchell. Nasty man's gone now.' They must have had dummies hanging around their necks on pieces of ribbon. I noticed when she turned the pushchair around that both the twins' little mouths were chewing furiously on latex rubber.

'Bastard,' she said. 'They don't care, do they?'

'No. They're in much too much of a hurry,' I replied.

'Are you going to be all right? Did he hit you hard?'

'No, not very hard. I think it's only bruised. I'll be black and blue in the morning. Go on – you'll be late for work.'

'I will, at that. You sure you're OK?'

'Yes, I'm sure.' She took hold of the handles of the pushchair and kicked off its footbrake. I gingerly leaned forward away from the railings and took a step. That went quite well, so I swung my leg and took another. That was good too. It looked as if I was not as badly hurt as I had thought. 'See?'

'Yes. Bye, then.'

'Bye.'

She thrust against the pushchair – which must have weighed a fair bit, loaded down with bags and toys and babies as it was – and headed off. I took another step. That was satisfactory, and the next, and the next, but then something seemed to give and my left leg slipped and wouldn't support me and with a groan I slumped down onto the concrete of the pavement.

'Help!' I cried, and it was meant to be a great, desperate howl of pain, but it only came out as an old man's asthmatic croak. It was enough, though, despite the noise of the passing cars. The young woman turned and saw me.

'Oh, god,' she said. 'You're not all right, are you?'

'No,' I said, 'I don't think I am. Do you have a, what do you call it, mobile? Could you call me an ambulance?'

The girl applied the pushchair's footbrake once more. Another pedestrian shoved past us, nearly stepping on my outstretched left foot. He muttered something, too. 'No, sorry. It was robbed off me last week. Look – do you want to go over there?' She pointed to a café on the other side of the road. 'Have a sit-down? Cup of tea?'

'I don't think I can get across the road.' There were four lanes of traffic; two heading east into Camberley, and two going west to Blackbushe and Hartley Wintney. All of them were crammed full.

The young woman shook her head. 'No. You don't look at all well.

You'd better come home with me.'

What did I think I would find in her house? Not that I expected it actually to be a house. I had already formed a mental image of where she lived – a set of expectations. There would be a concrete staircase and a broken lift. Or if the lift worked, it would smell of urine and be covered in graffiti. The doors would grate and creak. Her flat – it would be a council flat – would have a front door that opened out onto a walkway. There would be wrought-iron grilles fixed across the windows and thrown-away syringes scattered among last autumn's un-swept leaves.

I was preparing myself for these horrors as we made our way slowly along the pavement. I wouldn't mind, I told myself. I wouldn't be such a terrible snob. This girl, for all her hurry, had taken pity on me and was helping me. She would be late for work; maybe have her pay docked. It was fundamentally her fault, but still... she was being kind to me in her own way and I ought to be capable, even now, of showing my gratitude to her in a graceful manner. I should not try to load a burden of guilt on her shoulders. She probably carried enough worries and cares already.

Our progress along the pavement was slow, despite my determination not to hold her up. The babies grizzled. They would be fretful at having their day's routine upset. 'Is it much further?' I asked. 'Only...'

'Here we are,' she replied. I blinked. We were standing in front of a neat double-fronted Victorian villa of polychrome brick with stone lintels and a half-glazed front door on which hung a polished brass knocker. Fully-lined curtains hung in the windows and there was a boot-scraper in the form of a cat with an arched back by the side of the quarry-tiled garden path. She unlatched the gate. 'After you.'

I didn't understand. I had walked up and down the side of the A30 many times and I had never seen this house before. Never spotted it sitting comfortably back from the main road, a safe distance from the torrent of thrumming Fords, Vauxhalls, Fiats and Hondas. I was sure that if I had seen it I would have remembered it, even if I had not summoned up the nerve to open the front gate and enter the garden so I could examine the house more closely. What number was it? I looked at the front door again. A small enamel plaque told me that the house's name was *Bide-A-While* and that it was number 288. The house to the left – a Seventies construction of brick and wood cladding – was number 286. The discount carpet shop which abutted it to the right was number 290. So. This house had always been here. It was I who had been unobservant all these years, I who had missed it.

The girl – she was only a girl, really – parked the pushchair on the grass and took a large iron key out of her shoulder bag. She unlocked the front door and pushed it back. 'In you go now.' she said. 'Kitchen's at the end of the passage.' She looked straight at me. 'Enter of your own free will.'

Her name was Deirdre, she told me. I said I was Mister Hobbs, which seemed to satisfy her. She installed Ashley and Mitchell in a pair of high chairs and busied herself with kettle and tea-caddy while I sat down carefully on a Windsor chair and had a look around.

The best way I can describe Deirdre's kitchen is to say that it reminded me of home. Not home with Margaret, but before that. Home with Mum and Dad. Everything, from the row of mugs hanging under the painted wood shelf by the larder to the vintage twin-tub washing machine and the black enamel Aga was old-fashioned but, at the same time, new; by which I mean that they hadn't seen many years' service. The mugs weren't chipped, the cooker knobs had yet to lose their indicator numbers. The paint was fresh, but of a curious buttery shade rather than the brilliant white that is general these days. The kitchen table was made of solid wood and covered with the kind of shiny floral-patterned cloth you find in French country cottages, and the kettle, although it was electric, was of a traditional design rather than being jug-shaped. Set into the back wall was a wood-framed window overlooking a lawn which ran down towards a hedge. I could just make out a vegetable patch set out with stakes and lines for runner beans.

Deirdre gave the twins a plastic cup of orange juice each. 'Milk and sugar?' she asked me.

'Just milk, please.'

She poured two cups of tea and placed a willow-pattern plate of shortbread biscuits in the middle of the table. After checking that the twins were still happy she sat down across the corner of the table from me.

'This is most terribly kind of you,' I said. 'I'm sorry if I've messed up your day.'

'That's all right. I didn't have much on. What about you?'

'I'm feeling much better now, thank you.'

We fell silent. I have never been much for small-talk. And besides, I was preoccupied. Something was wrong. Well, not *wrong* exactly, nothing you would tell the police about, for example. But something didn't quite fit. Deirdre, for a start. She didn't match this house. I could see no way that the kind of job I supposed she did – care nurse, shop girl, office assistant or receptionist – could pay for this place. There were a number of other possibilities, of course. Perhaps she rented an attic room from the house's real owners. Or she shared the rent with a number of others. Or it belonged to her parents. Or she was married to a comparatively well-off man. (I checked her left hand for a wedding ring. Nothing.) Or was she his mistress? Was she the type of girl to become a man's mistress? I knew little of such things.

'You're wondering what I'm doing here.'

'N-no.'

'Yes, you are.' She smiled.

'It's none of my business.' I took a sip of tea to hide my confusion.

'You're right enough there.' She smiled again, enjoying my discomfiture. I have never been confident in the company of attractive young persons, so I got to my feet and, using the table-top to steady myself, went over to say hello to Ashley and Mitchell.

'How old are they?'

'Nine months.'

I pulled silly faces and growled at them, which they liked, grinning and gurgling and spraying orange juice over my jacket.

'Children!' Deirdre jumped up and dabbed at the juice-spots with a kitchen cloth. Her touch was gentle yet firm, her perfume unexpectedly light and subtle.

'It doesn't matter,' I said. 'It won't show. But... may I? I mean...'

'You want the little boys' room?'

'Yes, please.'

'It's down there, second on the left.' She frowned as I turned around to face the kitchen door, one slow foot at a time. 'Shouldn't you be using a stick or something?'

'I'd rather not. It's...'

'None of my business. You're right.'

She held the kitchen door for me and I stepped out into the passage. 'On the left,' Deirdre said again.

'Thank you,' I replied.

The passageway had seemed quite short when I first entered the house – no longer than you might expect it to be, given the apparent size of the place. But now, even though I had rested and taken refreshment, it stretched out before me like a hospital corridor with the glazed front door a distant square of light. I was still rather unsteady on my feet so I let my left hand run along the wall, risking marking it or dislodging one of the pictures which hung from the rail above. And so, when I passed the first door on the left I couldn't help pressing against it a little. It opened a few inches and, losing my balance as I had lost it in the road outside, I fell hard against the door and my weight pushed it fully open. I nearly fell into the room beyond.

It was a study, or small library, equipped with a filing cabinet, bookshelves, a large wooden desk and a swivel-chair. The desk faced toward me and on its surface stood a very up-to-date looking computer. It was the first modern, 21st-century, object I had seen in that house. Behind the desk and chair was a sash window, shaded by a blind drawn half-way down. I could see green grass and a flowerbed through the gap between the bottom of the blind and the windowsill.

These were my immediate impressions of the room. I instantly realised, of course, that I was in the wrong place and, not wishing to abuse my hostess's hospitality I turned to leave. But…

That window… The passageway ran from the back of the house to the front door. The study was on the right of the house as seen from the front. But there was a shop right next to that side of the house. There could be no window behind the desk, only a solid wall.

Strange… but hang on, wait. I was being silly. The house was set well back from the main road. We were *behind* the carpet shop, not next to it. The lawns I could see must also be behind it. The house must have been built long before the adjoining properties and when the land to either side was sold for redevelopment the owners would have wanted to keep the gardens for themselves.

There was an easy way to find out. I crossed the floor of the study, walked around the back of the desk, leaned against the sill and looked through the window.

I saw new-mown lawns under blue skies. Beyond them, a hedge of woven yew. Beyond that, rising ground on which I could see fields of wheat. At the top of the slope, a grove of oak trees, moving slightly in a light breeze. No carpet shop. No road. No traffic. And, although I was facing eastwards, no sign of the busy towns of Camberley and Sandhurst.

I did not hear the study door close behind me.

It seemed to me that I would very much like to explore the garden beyond the window, so I snapped back the catch and raised the bottom sash. It was nicely-fitting and well-counterbalanced and lifted very easily under my hand. The gap was now wide enough for me to get though, so I swung first my right and then my left foot over the ledge, ducked under the window and dropped lightly to the ground outside. I stood up straight and took a deep breath. The air was clean and fresh and perfectly poised between warmth and coolness. Gravel crunched grittily beneath my feet as I walked away from the house and onto the silent-padded grass of the lawn. I reached the hedge and turned back to face the way I had come.

The house stood before me, four-square and slate-roofed as I had expected, surrounded by the gravel path I had just left and the grass on which I now stood. Ivy hugged its walls and curled around its windows. I knew that if I went round to the back and looked in I would see Deirdre and little Ashley and Mitchell sitting in their kitchen, drinking tea and sipping orange juice.

I wouldn't do that just yet. After all, I was not meant to be here. I had not been invited into this perfect garden with its immaculate lawns and flowerbeds. I should return to the house immediately and use the lavatory before I was missed. Suppose Deirdre was banging on the door right now, worried that I had fallen again and hurt myself?

But then I looked in the other direction, towards the field of grain and the woods and the sky, and I knew that if I turned back now I would regret it for ever. So I walked along the hedge until I found a gap – actually, it was a gate of grey-weathered elm – and stepped through it into the field. As is common, it was bordered by an unsown strip of ground and I was able to walk around it until I found a pathway, slightly sunken and shaded by a line of trees, which led up the hill towards its crest. I wondered if I would be able to reach the top of the slope, me with my gammy leg and all, but found to my delight that I was striding with ever-increasing vigour up the path and that my old injury gave me no trouble whatsoever.

I had taken off my overcoat upon entering Deirdre's house. Now I removed my jacket as well and slung it over my shoulder, loosening my tie with my free hand. When I reached the top of the hill and was standing on the fringes of the wood I put my jacket on the ground and sat on it. I wanted to look out over the countryside below. I hardly noticed – it seemed only natural – that I was not at all short of breath, despite my climb.

The crown of the hill was three hundred feet or so above the house, which stood like the pool in the centre of an oasis, surrounded on all four sides by its well-kept gardens. There was, as I had noticed before, a vegetable patch and an herbaceous border behind the kitchen and an all-encompassing hedge. At the front, where the A30 road ran in the world I knew, was a narrow lane. It snaked off into the distance in two directions, winding its way around the field boundaries. It would not be a fast road to drive down – in fact there were no signs of motorised vehicles of any kind.

The fields varied in colour and shape. Some were full of wheat, like the field I had passed on my way up the hill; others appeared to be lying fallow. Yet others were meadows, running down to streams whose only indicators were rows of trees and the muddy trails of cattle. Further off in the distance, the air hazed and blurred the outlines of the countryside and I guessed at, rather than saw, the blue-grey outlines of village, church and town. The sky overhead was scattered with slow-moving clouds casting moving shadows on the ground below.

The air… it was like electricity in my lungs, sizzling and sparking. It was a simple joy to breathe it in, to feel it charging me with new life and strength. As I sat and watched the birds soar above and below me, and absorbed this world and its living air, I felt my old pains and worries fall away from me, to be replaced by new energy and freedom.

Reinvigorated and wanting to see what the rest of this land looked like, I rose to my feet and walked around the wood for perhaps two hundred yards until I returned to my starting point. In every direction the landscape was like the one I had already seen, except that I caught the glint of a distant sea to the south and a darker patch to the east suggested the presence of a large town. I sat down again and looked towards at the house. I really should return. How long had I been away? Five minutes? Ten?

More like two hours, a voice inside my head told me. I stood up in a panic. I must go back now! But the voice spoke again. *What about the wood?* it said. *You haven't been in there yet.* And the same logic which had told me that I could not return to the house without exploring the garden would not let me leave the wood behind either. So I turned my back on the sunlit world around me and entered the cool, green shade under the trees. They swiftly enveloped me.

How big was the wood? How far across? I did the sums in my head. I had walked more or less two hundred yards or so around the top of the hill. Pretend it was circular. Then it would be two hundred yards divided by three across. That was two hundred feet. Sixty yards. Not far, not even through trees and undergrowth. Not far at all. I set out with renewed confidence. I would reach the other side of the hill-top in only a few minutes.

But woodland is deceptive. Paths fail, or do not lead straight. The sun is hidden, and the rustle of leaves, branches and undergrowth betrays the ear. I do not know if I walked in circles or retraced my steps many times. It is possible, though I can think of no particular reason why it should be, that the wood was much larger inside than its exterior dimensions suggested. I do know that I grew more and more disoriented and that my initial pleasure in the brusque strength of the oak-trees, the delicacy of the flowers and ferns that grew around their roots and the song of the birds that nested in their branches, slowly gave way to anxiety. It was high time I got back to the house; but which way should I go? I had no clear idea of direction any more and foolishly, instead of stopping to get my bearings, I walked until I was too tired to go any further or think sensibly. I was close to panic.

As time had passed, my anxiety had developed teeth and claws and become *fear*.

I did not know what to do next. I was hopelessly lost in this ever-different, always the same, wood. I realised that if I gave way to my fear I would probably get myself into even deeper trouble. And then the blessed thought struck me that that if I waited until sunset I would see the sun as a scarlet beacon blazing through the tree-trunks, guiding me westwards to Deirdre's house. So I sat down next to a birch-tree, putting my jacket back on as the air had become cooler, and waited. And presently I slept.

And I dreamed. It must have been a dream, for it had a dream's sharp reality. I dreamed that Margaret was with me once more. She was as she had been when I first met her; young, sparkling, raven-haired and green-eyed, bubbling with mischief and fun. She ran up to me, took hold of my hand and pulled me to my feet. 'What're you doing here, Ted? Come on! Let's get out of this dark, dingy old wood!'

'It's a very nice wood,' I protested, but there was a look – *that* look – in Margaret's eyes that would not be gainsaid. I never could resist her when she was in that wild mood. So I let her tug me along the path, and her hair whipped back in the wind of our passage and brushed against my face. I breathed in its scent and sighed for the pleasure of it.

I had thought the fragrance of this land's air enough for me, but this; this was far greater and more delightful. I wondered if I might not become delirious with joy and I shouted out as we ran, 'Hoi, Eloi!' and listened for the echo.

To the edge of the wood we pelted hand in hand; down the hill to the house and its garden, and round the back to the side I had not yet seen – the west side of the house which abutted number 286. There was a conservatory built on there, and inside it was a bamboo and wickerwork sofa and next to it a table on which stood a tray, laden with teacakes and scones and blackcurrant jam and Dundee cake and a silver bowl filled to the brim with golden clotted cream. 'I'll be Mother,' said Margaret, and poured the tea, as Deirdre had done a few hours earlier. Although we had dashed though the door and flung ourselves willy-nilly down onto the sofa, neither of us was out of breath for very long.

We ate our tea and talked and talked, and it was like the old days when we were first married and she was my darling Gretel once more. And when I looked at the back of my right hand all the standing-out veins were gone and the liver-spots which had covered it were vanished too. And when our tea was finished we found that we had, all of a sudden, run out of words to say and that we wanted to move beyond speech altogether; and we made love on the sofa while the sun swam slowly through the sky and blossomed crimson in the west. Afterwards we fell asleep in one another's arms.

And then I was on my feet with my left arm bracing myself against the wall, in the little downstairs cloakroom in Deirdre's house, bereft. I knew I should not stay here long, so I did myself up, washed my hands and dried them on the roller-towel. Then I gritted my teeth and walked back down the passageway and into the kitchen. I wondered what I should say. Would Deirdre and the twins still be there? Or would it be the police, wanting to know what was going on here, sir?

Deirdre looked up as I entered the kitchen. I must have looked very odd. I *felt* odd – I had been through so many strange experiences in the last, how many they were, hours. But... Ashley and Mitchell were still sitting in their highchairs, still slurping noisily on their juice. I picked up my teacup. It was half-full and still warm.

'Was everything all right? Are you OK now?' Deirdre looked concerned.

'Yes, thank you.' I drew a deep breath. If she thought everything was normal, then I must behave as if it were, despite all that I had just been through. 'Very well. But I mustn't detain you any longer. You'll have things to do. Shopping. Housework. Your job.'

'So I do. It was very nice of you to call on us.'

'I enjoyed my visit very much. Thank you for the tea and biscuits.'

'My pleasure. My great pleasure. I'll see you out. Say goodbye to the nice man.'

'Bye-bye, bye-bye.' The twins each waved a podgy, messy hand at me. I waved back.

'Goodbye, Ashley. Goodbye Mitchell.' *See you again soon?*

Deirdre handed me my overcoat and helped me down the passageway to the front entrance. As we passed the study door, I couldn't help turning and looking longingly towards it. The girl saw my involuntary movement and smiled enchantingly.

'That's my favourite room, I think,' she said. 'They're all nice, though.'

'I'm quite sure they are,' I replied. My bad leg dragged painfully as I forced myself to walk the rest of the way down the passage, towards the front of the house and the world beyond. I let myself rest against the wall while Deirdre took out her iron key and unlocked the door. She opened it and I passed reluctantly through. There was the garden path, and there, only a few yards away, the rushing main road.

'Would you like to come back and see us again another day, Ted?' the girl asked, holding the garden gate open for me. The morning sun was shining oppressively into my eyes and the heavy air was disturbed only by the passage of cars, buses and lorries up and down Blackwater High Street. My leg was hurting pretty badly now.

'Yes I would,' I said, admiring her long, jet-black, wind-ruffled hair and deep, sea-green eyes. 'I should like that very much indeed.'

The Nursery

IT IS SOMEWHERE IN ENGLAND – AND IN FRANCE AND AMERICA AND Russia and, for all I know, in every country in the world. Somewhere in a town near you; perhaps your town. Down an ordinary street, next to the shopping centre or in the middle of a row of Victorian cottages or on the top floor of a tower block in a housing estate. Anywhere, really, just around the corner in the most ordinary, everyday places.

A little way off the High Street, next to the Thai restaurant and the fire station, round the back of the bookshop or overlooking Tesco's loading bay, there is a house. A *special* house. You may never need to find such a house yourself, but if you do it will be there waiting for you. You may find it or it may find you. And when its front door opens and you go in you will discover…

What?

The knife slipped in Deirdre's hand while she was slicing the cheese for the twins' teatime Welsh rarebit. It made a nasty nick in her left thumb.

'Oh, f-f-fiddle,' she said in exasperation. It was already half-past three and soon Ashley and Mitchell would be awake and calling for their tea. They were always so hungry these days. Toddlers were like that, she knew. They were probably due another growth spurt. Hey-ho, new clothes, new shoes. Another trip to Mothercare.

It was only a tiny cut, but deep all the same. So she sat on one of the kitchen chairs and waited and watched her thumb. And, slowly at first, then faster, like a time-lapse film, the skin knitted itself together and the two sides of the cut joined up. Five minutes later it was healed, with no trace that anything had happened – not even a little scar tissue.

Deirdre smiled to herself. There were a number of advantages to being a witch and this was not the least of them. She picked up the knife once more.

They parked the silver SL500 in a side street about a quarter of a mile away. It was not that they couldn't have parked it closer, for they could. Nobody would have noticed. Nobody would have minded. Any traffic warden who had come across it in the course of his duty would have made a note of its presence, but somehow forgotten about it so that later, if his patrol brought him back to where it stood, it would have struck him as something new, even if only an hour or two had passed since he last saw it. It had its own kind of invisibility.

They did not leave the car so far from Deirdre's house because they cared about clogging up the traffic in Blackwater High Street nor because they wanted to avoid getting a parking ticket. It was simply that, as the elder one said, you needed a bit of a break before making a visit. You needed to get your mind into gear, he said, and his junior colleague agreed with him, as well he should. He was young and inexperienced, but not without ambition.

As ever, the traffic in the Blackwater-Camberley area was dense and slow. The Thames Valley is still a prosperous place and popular among those who work in the well-paid IT industries. They can afford cars, lots of them, and what use is a car if you do not drive it? And so, although these cars were shiny and new and equipped with the latest pollution-reducing devices, the air was heavy with exhaust fumes, diesel smoke and sulphur. The younger of the two breathed it in deeply. The elder smiled to see such enthusiasm in his protégé.

Deirdre finished slicing the cheese and put it back in the fridge. She had been making bread earlier and it stood by the side of the Aga, cooling slowly on a wire rack. Cheese, toast, a little Worcestershire sauce. Apple juice. Maybe an orange each if they'd agree to eat it. The twins were at a funny age, as ever.

On another day, she might have been putting something together for one of her visitors. Henry, Al, Eloise, Joe, Mary, Ted, Tim, Christine, Cyril, James, Charlotte, Frank, Ian, Tosie, Mike, Imran, Benjamin…. The list went on for ever. On any normal day, one or another of her friends might come to her door and knock – diffidently or peremptorily as was their individual way – and she would invite them in with a smile. They would chat; exchanging news, talking about their lives, the weather, their children, their wives or husbands, what was on the television, what bargains were to be had at Blackbushe Market... And if, afterwards, a visitor might not be able to put his finger very precisely on what she had said; well that was in the nature of gossip, was it not?

Then, by intention or contrived accident, each guest would go to that part of the house where his dreams waited for him. Deirdre's house, despite its modest external proportions, had many rooms, each suited to a different kind of person and his needs. Some visitors never left the kitchen, but stayed there talking to Deirdre until it was time for them to go. For those who wished to investigate a little further there were libraries, studies, boudoirs, drawing-rooms, billiard-rooms, still-rooms, bathrooms and mysterious dusty attics at the top of narrow uncarpeted stairs. Others left the house altogether and explored the fields and woods, or city, or river, or lake, or desert, or jungle, or wide savannah, or whatever new and compelling world they looked to find beyond its walls.

One travelling man, old and footsore, brought his washing every fortnight and sat quiet-eyed while she ran it through the Hotpoint. A few wanted nothing more than to go with Deirdre to her bedroom and make love to her. They were not disappointed. Nobody who entered Deirdre's house with an open heart was ever disappointed.

Today, as it happened, the house was empty except for Deirdre and the twins. Perhaps the two in the Mercedes knew that. Perhaps they did not. It is unlikely that they cared very much either way.

Deirdre turned on the wireless. The sound of Joe Loss and his orchestra filled the kitchen; quietly at first but becoming louder and brasher as the set's valves warmed up. 'Dum, da-dum, da-dum-dum, dum-da-dum-dum,' sang the witch as she took a turn around the table. 'Dee-dee, deedee-dee, deedee-dee, dee-dee,' picking up a dish-cloth. 'Dada-da, da-dum!'

She was drawing breath to launch into the third verse of "Wheels" when the front door bell rang. Deirdre was used to interruptions – they were in the nature of her calling – so she put the dishcloth back on the draining board, took off her apron, patted down her auburn hair and went into the hall to answer the door.

There were two of them, which was rather unusual. Deirdre's people were mostly solitary. That was one of the main reasons they came to her, or she found them.

Were they Mormons? Certainly they were dressed alike, in matching brown trilbies, nondescript grey suits, blue shirts and patterned ties. Still, she would find out soon enough. It was clear they hadn't come to read the gas meter.

'Come in,' Deirdre said, standing to one side of the doorway. 'Enter of your own free will.'

'Thank you, miss,' said the elder of the pair. He removed his hat and his younger companion did the same. They entered the house and closed the door behind them, shutting out the fumes and noise of the High Street.

'I expect you'd like a cuppa,' said Deirdre, leading them down the passageway to the kitchen. She pointed to the table. 'Sit yourselves down. The kettle's on the hob.'

They each took a chair and sat in silence while Deirdre brought the water up to the boil and made a pot of tea.

'Milk? Sugar?'

'No milk, four sugars, please,' said the younger. The elder shook his head. 'No milk, no sugar.'

Deirdre smiled and poured two mugs of tea. She handed them over and sat back. She would let them drink their tea and wait for them to tell her what they needed in their own way and their own time. There was no particular rush. Ashley and Mitchell were still fast asleep, if the absence of sound from upstairs was any kind of clue. The whole house was very quiet and still. Good.

The elder guest sipped at his tea and nodded. It was evidently hot enough and strong enough for him. The same must have been true for his younger colleague for he suddenly lifted his mug and threw its scalding contents directly into Deirdre's eyes. It splashed over her face and splattered across the range behind her, hissing and spitting like an angry cat. She screamed and fell back against the brass rail of the Aga, raising her hands – too late! – to cover her face.

The younger flung his mug down onto the kitchen floor with a splintering crash. He leapt to his feet and took hold of Deirdre's hands, pulling them behind her back and lifting them up to her shoulders so that she screamed again and bent over forwards. Her forehead hit the kitchen table with a dull thud.

'Neatly done,' said the elder approvingly. The younger felt a warm glow of satisfaction. He had made a good start.

'Put her in the chair.'

The younger kept hold of Deirdre with one hand while with the other he pulled out a spare chair from under the table. He forced her to sit down and, aware that the witch would soon recover from the initial shock and pain of the attack and start to struggle, took four black plastic cable ties from his pocket. With them he fastened her arms and legs securely to the chair. The tough nylon of which the ties were made cut brutally into Deirdre's skin. Lastly he looped her long, dark-red hair around the top rail of the chair and knotted it so that her head was pulled back and up and her throat was left exposed and vulnerable.

'Good. Very good,' said the elder to the younger. 'Now come over here and watch.'

The younger resumed his place at the table.

'Look at her face.'

He did as he was told. Deirdre's eyes were tightly closed and her skin was blotched and peeling. The tea, undiluted with milk, had been close to boiling and the sugar had made it stick to her skin like napalm. She groaned, but whether it was from the pain of her burns or from fearful anticipation of what might be going to happen to her next was uncertain. But slowly, just as had happened with her thumb only a few minutes earlier when she had cut herself, she started to mend. Her scalded face began to heal itself. The livid redness faded and the swollen blisters slowly subsided and after only five minutes her skin was as clear and unblemished as it had always been. She opened her eyes; they were as limpid green and belladonna-sparkled as ever. The kitchen clock stood at a quarter to five.

'Excellent!' said the elder. 'We have established two important facts. What is the first?'

'She's a witch. An encompacted practitioner of the Secret Arts. That is witnessed by her swift restoration.'

'Correct. Any ordinary person would have been very badly scarred by your little bit of fun. Scarred for life. She would be yelling the place down. Instead; look! She is perfectly well. Once upon a time we might have put her in the ducking-stool and she would have floated instead of sinking. That would have told us what we need to know. Of course there are no ducking-stools left outside museums in these... enlightened times, but the principle remains sound. What else have we learned?'

'Er...'

The elder smiled; an expression to make his acolyte blench.

'We have also discovered this; that whatever we may do to this one, whatever tortures we may administer to her, however much we may harm her, we cannot damage her permanently. That is good, is it not?'

'Is it? I don't understand.'

The elder shook his head. These youngsters had so much to learn!

'It is this; there is no limit to the pain we can inflict on her. She can escape us by fainting for a few moments. She may occasionally require a little longer than that to recover from some of the more... extensive excruciations. But she will always come back to us just as good as new. And then we will be able to start on her all over again. It will be as it is elsewhere; where the flame is not quenched and the worm does not die. Is that not true, bitch?'

Deirdre looked up. 'Yes, it is all perfectly true.' Her eyes were tinged with a strange melancholy. 'I could choose to die, though.'

'You could try, but I do not think you have the strength of mind. Your body will repair itself, whether you permit it or not. It would take a greater will than yours to prevent it. Is that not so?'

'Yes,' said Deirdre with a sigh. 'I suppose it is.'

'Good. So now we know where we stand. I will tell you presently why my impulsive young friend and I have come to visit you today. Firstly, however, I think we should establish – in some clear, simple, practical way – quite unmistakably in your mind exactly who is in charge of this situation.'

'I will tell you something in your turn, for you must know it. It is this; that whatever you do to me today I will always love you. That is unalterable. It is permanent and final.'

The younger laughed and spat, and his spittle landed on the floor and ate out a sizzling crater of corrosion. 'Can we get on with it now?' he said.

'Yes,' said the elder. 'Let us begin.'

The younger picked up the steaming kettle from the stove. He pulled the neck of Deirdre's blouse forward and slowly poured the kettle's contents down her front making sure that her breasts and belly received their full share of the boiling hot water. The witch shrieked in agony and the legs of her chair beat a wild tattoo on the flagstones of the kitchen floor.

The two watched and waited as the water cooled down and Deirdre recovered. 'Of all the rooms in a present-day house, the kitchen offers by far the most scope for our operations,' the elder observed. 'So few cellars or dungeons, these days, but this is every bit as good. For example, look at all those knives on the rack over there. Knives for cleaning. Knives for filleting. Knives for skinning. A cleaver for heavier work, such as chopping. And that splendid cooker. A four-oven Aga, no less. Always kept nice and hot, even in summer. So many possibilities there...'

The elder put his elbows on the table and leaned forward, so that his face was no than eighteen inches from Deirdre's. Not so very close, it is true, but near enough that a rancid gust of ancient decay blew from his mouth into her nostrils with every word he spoke.

'What else have we? Oh yes, the sink. A fine, deep, butler-style sink. How long could you hold your breath if we compelled you to bend over in front of it with your head underwater? Thirty seconds? A minute? Surely no more than a minute and a half, even if you had the chance to draw breath in advance. And look over your head! What's that for? That rack? Oh, yes, it's for drying clothes. You can lower it with those ropes there, peg the wet things to it and then pull the whole contrivance back up to the ceiling. How ingenious! And how useful as a restraint! The wrists could be tied *there* and *there* and the subject suspended freely in the air for our ready convenience. What else can we see? Oh yes. What fun! Meat hooks. What more do I need to say?'

The cable ties were pulled up to their maximum tension. She did not attempt to free herself, nor did she waste any of her strength in struggling. Such a *male* thing that would have been; to fight back thoughtlessly, even when there was no possibility of overcoming one's captor. A gesture; meaningless, nugatory, vain. Merely a last desperate claim on a man's self-respect. It was not for her. Her strength, such as it was, lay elsewhere.

The elder took a leather strap from his coat pocket and laid it hard across Deirdre's face, leaving a broad red stripe like war paint.

'Why do you do it?' he asked. 'Why do you take them in – these worthless people? These discards, no-hopers, losers, wasters and rejects. Why do you pamper them so? Don't you know they're *our* property? Don't you realise you've been stealing from us? This has to stop. You know that.'

'If she's a thief,' said the younger, 'we should cut off her hands.'

'Too much shock, not enough pain,' said the elder. 'But a nice traditional thought, just the same. "Let the punishment fit the crime", eh?

'You know we deal in pain.' He slapped Deirdre's face once more. 'What about you? How do you feel about it? Have you ever wondered about it? How you would stand up to it?

'Perhaps you fear it. You should, you know. But,' and he gave her three more vicious, cutting blows across the face with the strap, 'perhaps you have had other thoughts. Perhaps you have imagined yourself tied as you are tied now. Maybe you have considered how it might feel to give yourself in helpless submission to your master. Do you ever get a little excited, a little *moist*, when you read about the punishments that we administered to the women of your kind in the centuries that are gone? Do you stroke yourself? How about it now? Will you be bound naked in thongs, and writhe and moan under the lashes of my whip? Will you count the blows at my command? And will the ceaseless pain and the soaring ecstasy of your surrender become one and indistinguishable? Will you bow down before me then, open yourself to me and acknowledge me to be your Saviour and your Death? Is that not your true desire? Will you not yearn to proffer me your absolute obedience? Will you kiss the leather that binds the rattan of my riding-crop and beg me to mark you with it?

'This is my promise. I will come here every day and every day I will whip you; whip you until your blood runs down on to the ground, whip you to delirium. And you will obey me, either because you dread the lash and wish to please me in the hope that my hand will fall on you with less force, or because you yearn for it and seek to embrace it totally, yield to it, wrap yourself in its toils. It may be that when I stop to rest you will plead with me to start again, only harder and faster.'

Deirdre looked up. Her face was flawless and clear once more and her eyes were brimming over with sorrow. 'You are lost,' she said. 'You are lost and sad and alone and I wish I could help you as I try to help everyone who comes through my door. I would, you know, if only you would let me.'

'I do not think that you are in a position to help me in any way.' The elder's face twisted into a sneer. 'Do you think I am one of those helpless, pathetic creatures you... entertain? I know what you do for them. You are a common whore, do you know that?'

'I give them what they need. I could do the same for you, you poor, forsaken thing. Listen to me. Try to remember – were you always like this? So hard and cruel? I cannot believe that you are happy now. You had dreams once, I am sure, but I think you have kept them hidden away too long. They have festered and gone bad in the darkness. Think back. Tell me there was a time in your life you remember with joy. There must have been such a time, even for someone like you. Let me show it to you. Let me take you to it, so that you can see clearly what you have become.'

She looked deep into her tormenter's eyes. 'There is still hope for you. Don't give up on yourself. I won't give up on you. I can rescue you. It's what I do. Please let me…'

The elder looked away and, just for a moment, there was a different look in his eyes, as if Deirdre's words had awakened something that had been asleep for many long years of men's lives. But then…

'Shut up!' cried the younger. 'Don't talk to my master like that.' He leapt to his feet and applied the kettle and the palette knife and the flat-iron and the electrical flex repeatedly to the witch. Several minutes passed.

'I think,' said the elder to the younger, 'that you should, rather than going all-out on the subject with your, I must say, commendable enthusiasm, pay more attention to the, er, light and shade of the art of torment. Simply bludgeoning the subject like that may give you some immediate gratification but I think you will find it rather more *in*effective than otherwise. Calm yourself. And *sit down.*' The air congealed around his words.

'Yes. Master,' said the younger, chastened. He sat down.

'Now then. Are you awake?' The elder slapped Deirdre's face lightly with the back of his hand. Her eyes flickered open. 'Ah, yes.' He sat back.

'This is beginning to pall, you know. Much as my young friend is enjoying his part in his first real punishment detail, it is becoming rather boring for me, despite your attempts at persuading me otherwise. Now, I will ask you for the first and last time; will you close your door and keep it closed?'

'No, I will not.' The witch's voice was scarcely audible.

'Even if I keep my promise to inflict daily, continual pain on you? Unbearable pain?'

'I cannot leave my post.'

'Spoken like a true soldier in the Army of Righteousness!' The elder laughed, and his apprentice joined in.

'Very well. We will move on, then.' He turned to the younger. 'I have pointed out most of the salient features of this room, such as they relate to our operations today. But there is one or, rather, there are two items that I have omitted. What are they?'

The younger looked around. 'Um, the boots by the door? The Welsh dressers? The curtains?'

'Nearly. What do you see in the corner?'

The younger looked. 'A broom, an ironing board, a... oh...'

'Very good! Well spotted! We will make something of you yet! Yes,' and the elder turned back to Deirdre who was sitting up straight in her bonds with a look of horror in her eyes which the elder could not fail to notice.

'Oh yes! A palpable hit! High chairs – two of them. It is my experience that where there are high chairs there are young children. And where there are children there must be a mother. He leaned forward once more. Again, gusts of corruption blew into Deirdre's face. 'Somewhere in this house, in a prettily decorated nursery in the attic no doubt, there are children. They are *your* children, are they not? You are their mother.' He smiled with a grin like a throat-cut.

A desperate horror flooded Deirdre's mind. 'Please, no,' she said, 'I beg of you. Do not go there. The twins...' Her voice died away. She knew that the situation had passed its crisis point. From here on nothing that anybody could do would make any difference to the ultimate outcome. There was – there could be – no further hope. Knowing that, she wept. Her tears mingled with the blood and spew on the tabletop.

'Do you see?' the elder said to his colleague. 'Do you see how it all turns out? How ridiculously vulnerable she is?'

'Yes, I do. We shall always win, while they are so weak and we are so strong.'

'How foolish you creatures are! You give yourselves to us so freely, so innocently. You tie your ankles together with bonds of morality so you cannot run from us; and so we catch you. You despise the weapons we bear; and so we wound you. You will not learn to fight as we fight; and so we defeat you utterly. You will not hate as we hate; and so we damn you for ever.'

'We cannot kill you, as you know, although we can and will come back here repeatedly and hurt you again and again if you do not comply with our requirements. The only way you can prevent our return is to close your door and keep it closed. For the very last time, will you do as you are told? Or are we to go and visit your children?'

Deirdre shook her head. 'No. I cannot do as you ask.' She continued weeping.

'Then know that you have brought what is about to happen on yourself. You could have prevented it. Come on!' They rose to their feet and left the kitchen. As he left the younger gave Deirdre one last skull-cracking blow across the back of the head with a rolling pin. She slumped forward in the chair. Blessed unconsciousness came, so that she did not hear the slow footsteps climbing the stairs, nor the opening of the nursery door, nor the voices; quiet at first, then increasingly louder and higher in pitch.

She did not hear the screams; the endless shredding of the air in the attic room. She was spared that agony, although had the elder considered the mercy which the younger had unintentionally granted her he might have felt it necessary to impose sanctions of his own upon the stupid fool.

Time passed, and the garden beyond the kitchen window began to glow with the light of evening. Deirdre crawled back to consciousness. She lifted her eyes and looked around. The kitchen was empty and silent. There was no sound to be heard anywhere in the house. They were gone, then.

For a while she sat completely still, gathering her strength for the ordeal to come. She breathed deeply, and as she exhaled the bonds on her wrists melted, her hair unknotted itself from the back of the chair and fell away, and she was free. She stood up slowly and looked down. Her body was unmarked and perfect. Even the pools of blood and vomit which had stained the table, floor and wall of the kitchen had disappeared. She adjusted her clothing. There were some rips and tears which she would have to mend later. But now… now she must go upstairs and deal with what she knew she would find there. She felt sick.

She had failed; failed badly. Could she not have tried a little harder to avert the calamity that she knew had taken place in the nursery? For what was pain? – a minor inconvenience, surely, in the wider scheme of things. She should not have let it distract her from her purpose. And now… now there were consequences to be faced, better sooner than later.

With her heart weighed down with dread she trudged up the stairs to the first floor of her house, rounded the landing and ascended the narrow flight leading to the nursery. She pushed the door open.

Inside was a scene of the most terrible carnage. The air was soaked with a gagging faecal stench and there was no surface in the room that was not covered in bloody filth. Deirdre turned her face away and drew a deep breath. Where were they? The twins? Under the splintered cots? Or inside the wardrobes, white-painted with a stencilled pattern of kites and balloons? Where? No… ahh! Deirdre drew herself up to her full height.

'Come out of there! Come on – I know where you are. Out! Now! Ashley! Mitchell! I am not pleased with you. Not pleased at all.'

The twins emerged from behind the playpen. One was holding a stuffed panda which had somehow escaped the massacre unscathed. The other had a toy gun, which he dropped. To their credit, they both had the grace to look a little sheepish. Ashley had his thumb jammed in his mouth while Mitchell shuffled his feet and looked down at the carpet.

'Just look at this mess! All over the walls. And the windows. And the ceiling. It's dripping! I thought I had made it perfectly clear before now. You must, must, must tidy your room up before bed-time.'

'Sorry, mummy,' they said in turn. Deirdre's expression softened a little. 'I know, children. I know. They were very wicked men. But you can't possibly go to bed in all this chaos. You'd better come down to the kitchen and have something to eat. We'll tidy all this up tomorrow morning. Tonight you can sleep with me.'

'Thank you!' they said in unison.

Deirdre smiled. They were *good* children really, and it wasn't fair to expect them to show adult levels of self-restraint. She was lucky to have them. And her joy in them helped to overcome the regret that she had not been able to save her visitors from the ruin they had wrought upon themselves. Could she have saved them, despite everything? She would never know.

'Deirdre, old girl,' she said to herself later, while the twins tucked into their pizza and chips, 'never mind. We'll watch an old film tonight and try to forget about all this nastiness. And tomorrow – tomorrow is another day!'

On the Town

DEIRDRE WAS FEELING OLD. ESPECIALLY SO TODAY, ALTHOUGH there was no reason she could put her finger on why today should be any different from yesterday or, for that matter, tomorrow. The pain was no different from usual.

Nevertheless, and despite her daily immersion in the metaphysics of cosmic Time and Space, Deirdre felt, when she woke that morning, that Time had tricked her and had not left her as untouched as it had always said it would. She rolled back the candystripe sheets and Witney blankets of her bed, stepped into the woollen slippers that were neatly placed next to it, stood up, stretched her arms and yawned.

'Ouch!' There was an unexpected twinge in her left shoulder and an unaccustomed stiffness in her legs. Neither had been there when she had gone to bed the previous night. Nor – she looked down – had her legs shown such prominent veins or her belly protruded so.

If you or I were to wake up one morning to discover that we had aged twenty years overnight I should imagine our first reaction would be one of screaming panic, even though such an event is not uncommon with the onset of middle age. We always think of ourselves as being younger than our years, even as the stiffness of our limbs and the progressive fossilisation of our minds give us the lie.

But for Deirdre greying hair, thick legs, sagging breasts and a tired face meant something more. For her to wake up in a bodily form that was so unwelcome must have a meaning beyond the simple passage of time. She would have to do something about it, but not just yet. She had to put the children first, and that meant giving them their breakfast. Deirdre sighed, put on her dressing gown, and prepared to chase the twins downstairs to the kitchen.

* * *

'Ashley. Mitchell. Pay attention now.' The children looked up from their high chairs. Ashley was clearly annoyed at being distracted from his porridge. Mitchell simply looked to one side. 'I'm going out for an hour or two.'

'Where?' asked Ashley.

'Why?' asked Mitchell.

'I'm going to see a friend. An old friend. I won't be long.'

'How long?' asked Ashley.

'A piece of string long. Do you two want to watch the telly while I'm out? I'll put a film on if you like. What would you like to watch? *Five Children and It*? *Dougal and the Blue Cat*? *Flubber*? *Herbie goes Bananas*?'

'*Spartacus*,' the twins said.

Deirdre sighed. 'Again? Really?' The twins nodded. 'Oh, all right, you two, if you must. *Spartacus* it is.' She waited while the boys finished their breakfast. Then she helped them down from their high chairs, took each of them by the hand and led them up the two flights of stairs to the nursery.

It had recently been redecorated and remodelled. Gone were the kites and balloons on the walls, steam trains and Spitfires on the curtains, cots and changing table on the floor. Deirdre was not the only one in her house who was changing with the passage of time and although neither of the twins appeared to be any older than eighteen months, she knew that they would soon be ready to leave baby things behind them.

Still, it was a pity they had decided they wanted to be Goths. All that black and purple! Not only was it ridiculously, stereotypically witchy, it made the place so gloomy she kept bumping into things. Never mind. They'd grow out of it – but into what?

Despite her misgivings Deirdre had yielded to the boys' demands for a television of their own. A sixty-inch plasma screen dominated one wall of the nursery and the speakers of a surround-sound system had been fitted to every corner. The noise they made would be quite horrendous, she knew, once the film got into its stride.

She took the DVD out of its box and slotted it into the player. The screen lit up. This was where the fun began. Each twin wanted sole use of the remote control and she was double-dashed if she was going to try to arbitrate between them. Especially today, when she was feeling so *old*. 'Goodbye, Ashley. Goodbye, Mitchell,' she said, closing the nursery door behind her. They paid her no attention whatsoever.

Eileen lived a few doors down from Deirdre. Not as mortals count doors, of course. They – you and I, that is – could only gain access to the front door of Deirdre's house from the pavement of Blackwater High Street in Surrey. Deirdre's house had many other doors but they did not open out onto our world.

Most of Eileen's visitors believed that she lived on the twelfth floor of a high-rise council block in Liverpool's Scotland Road. Deirdre rapped twice on the cat-knocker of a door that had once been painted green but was now covered by an unsightly security grille of rusted and graffiti-spattered iron. She stepped back into the lift lobby so that the CCTV cameras could see her clearly. There were footsteps in the stairwell behind the broken firedoor. They seemed to be coming nearer. She hoped that Eileen would open up before they got very much closer.

There was no response from behind the grille. Surely Eileen was in? Deirdre banged again on the knocker. 'Anybody home?' she called, not too loudly. No point in calling unnecessary attention to her exposed position. 'Hey, Eileen!'

'All right, all right. I'm coming! Can't you wait?' A rough voice blared from a speaker fixed high up in the door.

'Eileen, it's me. Let me in, please. Hurry.'

'Deirdre! Just a mo.' There was a slap of carpet slippers on linoleum and a rattling of keys from behind the grille.

'Dust and Stars!' Eileen said as she opened the door and unbarred the grille and caught her first sight of Deirdre. 'You've let yourself go a bit! Come in, love, come in. Enter of your own free will.'

Deirdre passed through to the hallway and waited while Eileen refitted the grille and slotted the door-chains back into their sockets. 'Come along. Kettle's on. You look parched.' She shook her head sadly. 'There you go, love. Into the lounge. I'll be round with a cuppa in a jiffy.'

'Thank you, Eileen,' said Deirdre, giving a sigh of relief.

Eileen's lounge window faced east across New York's Central Park. Many of her visitors recognised the Dakota Building through the springtime trees. It acted as what Eileen called a grounding point; a fixed place where they could attach themselves if the strangeness of the adventure they had found themselves involved with became too much for them. Eileen would say, yes that's where John Lennon lived with Yoko Ono until he was murdered. 'Murdered?' some of them would say in astonishment, and Eileen would have to bring them up to date with an event that had not yet happened in their lifetimes. Then they'd talk about the Beatles and Eileen would tell them about the times George Harrison had been to see her and the places she had taken him. 'To India, to see the Maharishi?' they'd often ask.

'Yes, sometimes,' she'd reply, 'but more often somewhere else.'

'Where?'

'That's for me to know,' she'd say and wink and change the subject, often without them noticing.

Eileen sat down, poured the tea, and opened a packet of chocolate digestive biscuits. 'Not that you deserve any, the state you're in,' she said with a wink and a smile. They drank their tea and chatted about inconsequential things – people they knew, places they remembered. From time to time there was a rap on the front door and Eileen got up and let a visitor in. Deirdre could hear them talking in the hallway. Then a door opened and closed and Eileen returned and sat down again with a happy smile on her face.

After the third interruption Eileen came back to find Deirdre standing by the picture window looking out over Central Park. It was late in the afternoon now and the buildings around her were casting long shadows across the grass and up to the first floors of the apartment blocks opposite. The westering sun coloured the spaces between the shadows with a warm orange-red haze. Deirdre opened the window and the sounds of the city came into the room; taxis and buses in the avenues below, aircraft in the skies overhead and – blanketing all – a susurration of voices. The voices of trees and grass in the gentle wind, of people in streets, offices and subway stations; the breath of the living city.

Deirdre looked out and drew the city's air into her lungs. Its air and its life. Eileen stood next to her and took hold of her hand.

'Would you like to go out there for a while?'

Deirdre turned to face the older witch. 'No, I can't. My house, my visitors, the twins... I should be going back to them.'

'Don't worry about them. They'll be fine. Especially your two. If anybody can look after themselves, it's them!' She laughed and Deirdre joined her.

'I suppose you're right.'

'Of course I am. Now come along.'

A fire escape led from a landing next to the window down to the second floor level. Deidre followed Eileen and waited while she unlatched the ladder at the bottom and dropped it down to the sidewalk below. She climbed down and waited while Eileen pulled the ladder back up.

'Go on!' said Eileen. 'Take as long as you like!'

'Thank you.'

Eileen had changed Deidre's form for her on the way down the fire escape and she now appeared to be a tall black woman wearing smart grey business clothes and an ethnic bracelet rattling against the gold wristwatch on her wrist. Anyone who saw her would assume that she was a rising young professional; a lawyer or a marketing executive perhaps.

Which way to go? Left? Right? Uptown or down? Harlem or SoHo? The Village? Deirdre didn't know. This town was strange to her, known only through films and books So, not wishing to get lost in the financial district on one hand or the wilderness of north Manhattan on the other, she faced forward, crossed the taxi-clogged street and passed through the gates into Central Park.

Immediately a grove of trees closed around her and the streetlights and noise of the city faded into the deep background. The transition from urban bustle to sylvan peace was startlingly abrupt. So startling that Deirdre stopped to look around. Behind her, the park entrance and the busy sidewalks of New York. Ahead and to both sides, the mystery of the wood, swathed in a green so dark that it was almost black. The path beneath her feet was covered in last autumn's leaves – but this was spring. Surely the Parks Department would have swept them up by now?

Forward, said a voice from between her ears. *See what you can find*. So Deirdre, who was a good girl, did as she was told. Besides, she had an inkling of what was happening to her. So she followed the path, hardly noticing when its concrete turned to earth and the fallen leaves changed from umber to emerald, from crisp to soft. The midnight air grew warmer and the sky lighter. Every step she took was bringing her closer to summer, it seemed.

The wood, which had been silent when she first entered it, was coming to noisy life. Although Deirdre's footsteps were muffled by the soft ground underneath, that only served to bring into clearer focus the rustle, patter and scrape of the creatures which lived there. Deirdre looked from side to side as she slowly walked along and now and then she caught sight of a flashing eye or the flick of a tail in the undergrowth. The moon was up and shining brightly through the overhanging branches. She held out her hands and marvelled to see them so fabulously lit, silver on black.

Deirdre walked. She was content to do so, because of the peace that surrounded her and the way that peace was seeping into her soul. She knew that the animal sounds which enveloped her were not the sound of hunters and hunted. There were no squeals of fear, no hurried scurries to the safety of underground dens, only purposeful gathering, nurturing and mating. And because of this knowledge, and the fact that she understood its nature as many others would have not, she felt a little separated from herself. She was enjoying the night-time magic of the wood, but she could not completely believe in it, despite the fact that her city clothes had melted away and she was clad in a long dress of white muslin, clasped at the neck with gold.

And so, when a man sprang out from behind a beech tree and stood before her with his arms outstretched and a wide smile on her face she did not start, for she was not particularly surprised, even though he wore nothing but a breechclout and a necklace of green acorns.

Deirdre put her hands on her hips. 'Hello, Eileen,' she said.

The man smiled wider. 'Eileen? What are you talking about?' he said, and his voice was as rich and warm as his ebony skin. 'I'm Andrew. Who's Eileen?'

'You are. Come on, don't you think I know what this is? The Enchanted Wood? Where you will lead me to a well, beneath which lies a princess who has been sleeping under a spell for five hundred years, and whom we will awaken with a kiss, and who will take us on a ship with a hull made of cedar logs and sails woven of young girls' dreams to the Isle of Sage where our destiny lies. And there we will conquer a fiery monster, and afterwards there will be a tapestried, firelit room with a richly hung bed of damask silk and you will embrace me and I will surrender myself to you and we, who have earned one another by feat of arms, will make strong passionate dragon-love all night and part forever in the morning!'

She crossed her arms over her chest. 'I know this world,' she said. 'You get to it from the first landing of my house, through the linen press. It's beautiful, it's one of my favourites, but it's not what I want right now.'

The man shrugged. 'Okay,' he said. 'What *do* you want?'

'This,' said Deirdre, and clicked her fingers twice.

She was standing in Battery Park. Her companion from the wood was standing next to her, dressed in a sharp suit and Italian shoes. She was wearing a cocktail frock under a light coat. Her dark glossy hair was swept back from her face and tightly knotted at the nape of her neck. He was dashing and handsome, she lively and very pretty.

'We have two choices,' Deirdre said. 'Back to your apartment right now…'

'Or?'

'Hit the town!'

'And then?'

Deirdre grinned. 'Then we go back to your apartment!'

'You're on, baby!'

'Baby? Oh, pulease!'

'Taxi!'

They saw a Broadway show and danced to the music and nobody stopped them. They found a little subterranean bar, where a young man stood with his back pressed hard against the nicotine-stained wall and an electric guitar in his hand and sang torch songs from Ethiopia and Paris in the voice of a disturbed angel. They drank Old Fashioneds and listened intently. The men in the bar looked at Deirdre, until their women slapped their faces or took them away from temptation. The girls behind the bar looked at Deirdre's friend and rehearsed what they would say about him to their friends the next day.

They walked the streets unmolested, laughing, happy. They rode the subway uptown. They stood under a marquee and kissed invisibly.

There was a cocktail party, in an apartment so far above the ground that it was not overlooked by even the highest towers, where you could walk through the salon windows onto a roof terrace and float above the city as if airborne. The 3am city, still threaded with red and white car lights, where the sounds from below reverberated from glass walls and asphalt streets to the stars above. Deirdre stood with her hands on the railing, chatting to the up-and-coming actress to her left, praising her performance, drinking in the view, feeling Andrew's strong arm on her slender waist. Feeling *young*. They should go soon, she knew. This evening, this wonderful evening of warmth and people should end, as all things end. But not until… She looked at Andrew.

'Can we…?'

'Yes.' He clicked his fingers twice. And he was gone.

She was sitting on a leatherette chair by the window in Eileen's lounge in Eileen's flat in Liverpool's Scotland Road. Eileen was on the sofa, smiling. Nobody spoke. Then Deirdre, as if a signal had flashed in the room, got up from her chair and fell to her knees in front of Eileen. She bowed her head. 'Mistress…' she said. She could not express her feelings. The night – that wonderful night – had evaporated away, like dew on a summer's morning. And nothing had changed. It had not been enough. She was still too tired, too scarred. She could still not face going back to Blackwater where men came out of the treacherous daylight to inflict pain on her.

'My child,' said Eileen and leaned forward to the younger witch. Tears were streaming down her cheeks. 'My child.'

'Oh Eileen!' sobbed Deirdre. 'They hurt me so badly. And I could have… I could have hit back. I still don't know if I should have or not. I could have saved them so easily. I didn't know. I didn't know it had got so bad, until… until…'

'Until you found out how it used to be. When those men came to your door. I know, my sweet. It can be most dreadfully sudden, when it happens. The irons, the stake, the fire. They haven't gone away, those men. The witchfinders. They still want to hunt us down. They still want to torture and rape us. They are our adversaries and they come when we don't expect them to and they turn our hospitality against us. They want misery and pain as much as we want happiness and joy. They are cruel and ugly and they want to make the world in their image and its people their slaves. They wanted to blight you with anger. They wanted you to hit back at them, to legitimise their own hate. They wanted you to be as foul as them. And you such a pretty one…'

'Pretty? Me?' said Deirdre, looking up. Her cheeks were blotched red and white and streaked with salt trails. Her hair hung in lank rat's-tails.

'The prettiest of my children. Come to me.' She patted her lap and Deirdre got up from the ground and sat on the older witch's lap. She put her head on Eileen's shoulder.

'You are tired,' said Eileen. 'Aren't you, my lovely?'

'Yes, Mistress. I didn't realise…'

'Not Mistress. Don't call me that. Not here. Not today.' The air in the room had become warm and sweet-scented. The light had faded to an amber dimness.

'Mother...'

'Yes,' said Eileen soothingly. She undid the top buttons of her floral housecoat and lifted up her cotton blouse. 'Here, my beautiful one. Here you are.'

'Oh, Mummy,' said Deirdre in a soft voice, 'Oh, Mummy...' She leaned forward and took Eileen's proffered breast in her mouth, rolling the nipple between her lips and sucking gently on it until the milk flowed freely. Its taste was sweet on her tongue, its warmth comforting and satisfying in her throat and belly. She sighed in profound happiness and Eileen echoed her. It was all very quiet and still and private and joyful. The two witches lay together, naked now, arms wrapped around one another in the dim twilight of the room while Deirdre drew sustenance first from Eileen's right breast and then from her left. It may be that at one point suckling gave way to love-making, or it may not.

Later, Eileen made a casserole of bacon and celery. Deirdre stood next to her in the kitchen and helped with cutting up the vegetables and laying the table. At one point the doorbell rang and Eileen let in a boy of no more than 14 years old. He was silent, thin and wiry, and his eyes spoke of dealing and street-corner fights and the belt-buckle his stepfather wore. Eileen showed him into the broom-cupboard off the kitchen and he, seeing not mops and bristles but a long beach of soft white sand under a moonlit sky, cried out in delight and ran forward until his feet raised phosphorescent trails in the quiet waves and he fell forward into the creamy waters of the bay.

'It is worth it, isn't it?' said Deirdre with a smile, closing the cupboard door behind him. 'When it's like that. When they love it so much, when it's so easy to help them. It does them so much good and it takes so little out of us in return.'

'It's always worth it,' Eileen replied. 'But especially...'

'When it's hard. I know. But what about when it's hard and it doesn't work? What about that? Oh Eileen, I've been so *hurt*!'

It still wasn't enough. For all its delight, this brief stay at Eileen's had only named her wounds. It hadn't cured them. More drastic measures would be necessary. She made her mind up even as she wished Eileen goodbye.

A day or two later, Deirdre knocked again at Eileen's door. The elder witch answered and seeing the wicked grin on Deirdre's face, looked down. *Oh*, she thought.

'Now then Ashley, Mitchell,' said Deirdre. 'This is your Nana Eileen and you're going to be staying with her for a week or two. Promise you'll be good.'

'Yes, Mummy.'

'Yes, Mummy.'

'Good boys. There you are, Eileen. Everything's going to be just fine.'

'But... but why have you brought them here?'

Deirdre pushed the toddlers through the door and into Eileen's hallway. 'Because I'm going to do what I really need to do. Take a break. Go away for a while. Go on... you'll enjoy it as much as they will. You'll have fun.'

The twins looked at Eileen. Eileen regarded the twins. 'Oh yes,' she gulped. 'I'm sure we will.'

Happy Highways

THE HOUSE WAS UNNERVINGLY QUIET. DEIRDRE STOOD IN THE HALL, with her door-key in her hand, and listened to the silence. The traffic noise from outside had ceased immediately she shut the front door. All the sounds that every ordinary house makes were stilled. No creaking of floorboards, no hissing of pipes, no rattling of windows, no whirring of computer fans, no swooshing of washing-machine or dishwasher. No distant radio or television. Not even the underlying hum of mains electricity pulsing in conduits and sockets.

That silence demanded respect. 'Deirdre, old girl,' the witch said to herself. 'I don't think we're wanted here.'

It was as if, with the twins Ashley and Mitchell staying with their Nana Eileen in Liverpool, the house wanted to be left alone for a while. It had nothing against Deirdre; there was nothing personal in it. It just needed – its own space. Deirdre giggled at the thought of her house appearing on a daytime TV show, talking to Oprah or Jeremy about how its needs weren't being met by its occupants. *How does that make you feel, Bide-A-While?*

'Sorry,' she said. 'I'm going in a minute. Just let me pack, eh?'

Deirdre liked to use public transport as much as possible; in the mortal world at least. She was perfectly happy to take a bus to the Meadows shopping centre or a train to Guildford. But generally she used different ways of getting around, involving the use of doors other than the one which opened out onto Blackwater High Street. And so although she had a car it was rarely used. Most of the time it sat in a timber garage at the bottom of the garden, where the oil drained from its cylinder head and its tyres slowly went flat. She was neglecting the poor thing.

The rusty padlock securing the garage doors didn't give up without a fight. Deirdre coaxed it apart, pulled the doors wide open, and looked at the car. Its dusty headlights looked reproachfully back at her. Perhaps they blinked in the unaccustomed sunlight. Deirdre started the car, drove it out of the garage and parked it by the back door. She went back into the house and collected her things. There wasn't much to pick up – just a holdall, three-quarters full. Returning to the car, she put her bag in the boot, got back in the driver's seat, shut the door, slotted the key into the ignition... And stopped. Something was wrong. She got out and looked at the car once more.

There was absolutely nothing the matter with it. It was compact, fuel-efficient, reasonably comfortable, fast enough for her needs. Its MOT was up to date, it was comprehensively insured, she had had it serviced only six months ago. There it stood, four-square on its wheels, painted a not unattractive shade of metallic green, waiting for her to jump in and set off.

Set off on what?

Adventures. That was what. She was going off on adventures and a mid-range five-door hatchback was not exactly an adventurous choice of transport, was it?

'What would you like to be?' Deirdre asked the car. 'A limousine? A Land Rover? A Morris Minor? How about a Bugatti? That'd be something, wouldn't it?'

What kind of petrol-steel-oil-and-rubber dreams did this child of Swindon enjoy? The freedom of the roads? The companionship of the car park? The voluptuous caress of the polishing mitt? How would they be related to human dreams? Or to *her* dreams? Was that the key to her question? Were her needs and the car's needs connected in some way she had not considered before?

Deirdre rested her chin in her hand and thought. 'I think... I think you should be a... a...' Yes! Of course! There wouldn't be much space for her luggage, but wasn't that the whole point of the exercise? To travel light? Deirdre looked at the car in a *particular* way and moved her right hand *just so*.

The growl of the bike's exhaust followed Deirdre down the A30 as she sliced through the morning commuter traffic and headed westward. It seemed to her that it was in the west that she would find the adventures she sought.

* * *

Westward... Across the sunlit southern counties of England Deirdre sped, at one with the machine that carried her. She was aware of the admiring glances from the men she passed; half of them for her and half for the vintage motorcycle she rode.

She could have made it as far as Land's End if she had kept going until the end of the day, but she was in no particular hurry and the sun was getting in her eyes. So she stopped outside a pub somewhere in Devon, put the bike on its side-stand, took off her helmet, and walked into the bar. It was six o'clock, and the room was almost empty.

'Have you got any rooms for the night?' she asked, putting the helmet on a table.

The man behind the bar put aside the glass he was polishing. He looked Deirdre up and down.

'Are you a biker?' he asked.

'Yes... I mean no, I'm not a biker, but I am riding a bike.'

'We don't care much for bikers around here.' He turned and shouted into the gloom behind the bar.

'Doris!'

A heavy-set, middle-aged woman appeared, presumably the landlady. She also looked Deirdre up and down.

'Yes?'

'Young lady wants a room.'

'Please,' said Deirdre. 'I'm tired and a little hungry.'

The woman crossed her arms. 'Come far?'

'I've come from Camberley. It's near London.'

'Anyone with you?'

'No. I'm all by myself.'

The woman paused for thought. She obviously had her doubts about this attractive, unaccompanied young woman. Deirdre was tempted to reach into her mind to help her decide, but no. That would not be fair.

'What are you riding?' the barman asked.

'A Vincent,' Deirdre replied.

The man's face lit up. 'A Black Shadow?'

'Black Lightning, actually.'

'You are? You're having me on! It's outside?'

'Yes.'

'Can I... I mean...'

'Yes, of course you may.'

The man turned to the woman. 'She's staying.' And then to Deirdre, 'Come on, then. What are we waiting for?' He led the way out into the yard.

It was all engine, wheels, pipes, spokes and tubing. Built in 1951 and capable of nearly 150 miles per hour in standard road-going trim it had been, in its time, the fastest production motorcycle you could buy and even now it was a formidable machine. The man whistled as he saw it. He walked up to it slowly. 'This is yours?' he asked, shaking his head in disbelief.

'All mine.'

The man rested his hand on the tank's gleaming paintwork. The engine was still hot, and it was making little ticking sounds as it cooled down. The exhaust pipes were blued by the fires that had burned inside them.

'My dad had one of these. A Black Shadow it was, actually. He loved it more than... more than anything.' He shook his head again. 'He used to take me for rides – up to Exeter, down to Bideford. It was like flying, only faster. Do you think I could...?'

'Yes, go on.'

He sat on the bike and pushed it upright with his left leg. The side-stand retracted. He gave Deirdre a strange, yearning look and she nodded. 'It's all right. I don't mind.' She had guessed what he wanted.

Later, Deirdre sat in the saloon bar and ate mutton pie and mash. She had changed out of her riding kit and was wearing an unexceptionable outfit of cotton skirt, t-shirt and cord jacket. The woman's suspicions had been quieted by her husband's evident delight after he returned from his ride around the nearby lanes. Deirdre could hear him now, in the public bar, talking about it.

'Tell me something,' said the woman, bringing Deidre a cup of Irish coffee. 'Are you famous?'

'No, not so far as I know.'

'But you must have a lot of money, to own a bike like that.'

'I've got enough.'

'Hmmm. I hope you don't mind my asking, but why did you let George borrow your bike? How did you know he'd bring it back? He might have stolen it, taken it anywhere.'

'Oh, that was easy.' Deirdre gave the woman an entrancing smile.

'Can't you guess?'

'No.'

'Yes, you can. He came back to *you*. He always will. You know that.'

The landlady looked directly at her. 'You're… different, aren't you?'

'Why do you say that?'

'I thought you were… at first, I mean…'

'A tart?'

The woman blushed. 'No.'

'I don't mind,' said Deirdre. 'It's what I do. I help people, if I can. However I can.'

Deirdre had thought that she would fall asleep very quickly. She was physically very tired from riding the Vincent and had had quite a lot to eat – and drink – in the bar that evening. But she had forgotten that travellers sleep lightly and that they dream vividly. This day had been so different from the norm. The recent norm, at least. It was not just the hurt she had suffered at the hands of her unwanted visitors, nor that her mind was busy absorbing the sensations of the day just past – the rush of air over her leathers, the deep throb of the engine, the swish of rubber on tarmac. It was change. Overdue change. And something else as well, which she identified some time around dawn as the light grew behind thin curtains. It was uncertainty. Essential uncertainty.

'Deirdre, old girl,' she said to herself. 'You've been getting into a rut. You need to take a step into the unknown for once.' And the dreams agreed with her.

It was twelve o'clock the following day, and the weather had changed. Deirdre had ridden for three hours down slow, twisting country roads and had finally reached the very end of the mainland. Through the raindrops that dashed themselves against her visor she could see nothing but more water; the grey Atlantic, stretched out before her all the way to America. 'Oh, well,' she said to herself, 'we won't get anywhere just standing here. Come on, let's get on with it!' She twisted the throttle grip over as far as it would go. The engine roared and earth spattered behind her rear wheel. The Black Lightning was doing over ninety miles per hour when it cleared the cliff-top. It hit the surface of the sea like a stone and was instantly swallowed up by the water, before returning to the surface, sleek and chine-hulled.

It left a wake a hundred yards long.

* * *

There was this boy; firm-muscled, lithe and beautiful. Deirdre sat under a white parasol on the harbour side of the café, sipped at her weak Campari and orange, and watched him.

He was working on the deck of a sardine-boat, hosing down the scuppers, pulling on ropes and coiling them up, stopping from time to time to take a drag on a cigarette. 'Tut-tut,' said Deirdre to herself and took another sip of her long cool drink. She might have to do something about his smoking, if she decided to take him under her wing. She returned to her examination of the boy. He was stripped to the waist, wearing a pair of cut-down jeans and dirty sneakers. Whenever he took a break from his work he stopped and turned himself towards the sun. It glinted on his skin.

His skin... Deirdre felt the blood begin to rush with increased energy through her body as she gazed at his fabulous skin. It was a rich brown, polished perfectly smooth with glossy highlights of perspiration on shoulders and back. She thought she could smell him from where she sat, although in this busy, noisy port where the lambent afternoon air was already richly scented with fish, drains and diesel smoke, that must have been impossible. All the same, she could already taste his sweat on her tongue and feel, if only in her imagination, the touch of his skin against hers and the pressure of his fingertips on her body.

He was whistling a tune she had heard booming up to her hotel bedroom from the club in the basement. Everyone was playing it this year. Its simple refrain was quite inescapable. As she watched the boy move and turn, as she began to feel his jet-black hair bunching up between her fingers, as he pressed himself against her, as she began to respond to his rhythm with an urgent beat of her own... She opened her eyes.

He was looking directly at her. He knew he had her. He could take her whenever he wanted, for she was already his. Presently he would skip across the row of boats, come up to the café table and ask her to go with him. There would be a place he knew... But why wait? She got up and walked over to him. 'Hi,' she said, smiling.

'Pah! American!' He spat his cigarette-end into the harbour and turned away contemptuously. She was easy meat – too easy for him.

Too vanilla-white. There was nothing she could offer him, Deirdre reflected and, anyway, she had been concentrating too hard on her own needs and neglecting his. That was not what the witches did. Her Eileen-mother would not approve of her lusting after a carefree, attractive boy who doubtless had plenty of notches carved on his bedpost already. There would be others who needed her more.

Deirdre finished her coffee and returned to her hotel room. It took no more than five minutes to pack her things and only another five to check out. Her boat waited by the harbour wall. She threw her bag into the cockpit and jumped in after it. The engines fired up at the first press of the starter. Deirdre cast off fore and aft and steered the black-hulled cruiser through the harbour and out onto the open sea, where she gunned the throttle hard.

There was this girl, lost and pale, huddled over a screen in a library cubicle. If she wasn't reading Baudelaire or Rimbaud, Deirdre thought, she should have been. But no.

Deirdre had never bothered much with the Internet, although the study at home contained an up-to-date computer which she used to fill in her tax returns. It was not that she was a Luddite, more that the Web offered her nothing she wanted. The Light Programme and the Home Service, Tit-Bits and the Manchester Guardian gave her all the news she could possibly require. The twins Ashley and Mitchell had a big plasma screen in their room, but she only watched it with them, never by herself. If she needed information there was a perfectly good public library in Camberley and if she wanted to talk to someone she would go round and see them or – and this happened remarkably often – they would come round and see her.

But she knew about the Internet all the same. Many of her visitors would sit with her in the kitchen and ask if they could check their email, or they'd take out their iPhones or their BlackBerrys and scan them for new messages. Deirdre observed that they consulted their gadgets almost subconsciously, as if making sure they were still connected with the electronic world had become as necessary as breathing.

'I'm terribly sorry,' she would say, 'but the signal's absolutely dreadful around here. We must be in a dip, you know? But look, it'll wait, won't it?'

Her visitor would look forlorn and Deirdre would have to find something to distract him. It was nearly always a man, she'd noticed. Some of them became quite twitchy – they were the ones who needed her help the most. But this was not a man, it was a girl and she was not looking at Google or Amazon or Facebook or Twitter but something much darker. Not porn; Deidre was often visited by users of pornography. They were usually men too. But it was clear from a short glance that she needed help.

But how? Deidre's home was thousands of miles from this East Coast university town, so it wasn't very likely that this girl – darkly pretty, wearing a long-sleeved white blouse over a blue mid-length skirt – would pop in and see her any time soon. And Deirdre did not know if there were any of her sisters living nearby. The witches had been terribly persecuted here in the past; hunted down, branded, flogged and burned. The memory of their torments lived on, scorched into the fabric of the land. The witches forgave – that was their nature – but they found it hard to forget Salem.

Deirdre watched the girl. It was not part of the witches' credo to offer help directly. The needy ones had to find their way to them as a rule although, like most rules, this one was open to negotiation.

There was this man – late forties, grizzled hair, Stetson hat – sitting by himself in a Midwest diner marooned in a sea of cornfields and missile silos. She should have known better, but Deidre could see his unhappiness and loss the moment she walked into the brightly-lit room, so she took a seat in the booth next to his. It had been a long day's drive; she needed a break and somebody to talk to.

'Coffee, please,' she said to the waitress.

'Pastry with that, miss? We have great Danish, pancakes also.'

They would be mass-produced, stodgy and bland, made in a factory back East and shipped in frozen. But anything would do.

'Pancakes would be lovely,' Deirdre said. She was wearing blue jeans, a denim jacket and a John Deere baseball cap over her long dark hair. Her truck was parked outside.

'Maple syrup, strawberry sauce, raspberry sauce, chocolate sauce, pecans, hazelnuts...?'

'Maple syrup, please.'

'Thank you, miss. Coming right up.'

'You have a ladies' room?'

'Left of the counter and through to the back, miss.' Deirdre found the restroom and made a few necessary changes to her appearance.

He was still there when she returned. His eyes followed her as she took her seat at the table where her coffee and pancakes were waiting. Soon, as Deirdre had planned, they were talking. They left the diner together.

'That your truck?'

'Sure is.' What was it about men and motor vehicles, anyway?

'It's a '54 F-100, right?'

'55 actually. Belonged to my grandpappy. I had it restored. You want a look?'

'Sure.'

It was, as Deirdre had said, a 1955 Ford F-100 truck, with a 239 cubic inch Y-block V8 engine developing a modest 130 horsepower. The man opened and closed the doors and admired its shiny black paintwork and all-original interior.

'Like a look under the hood?' Deirdre asked.

'Sure. Say, my place isn't far from here. We could...'

'Why not? You could have a real good look...'

Deirdre wanted to help the girl if she could. But how? Would it be a good idea to meet her online and talk to her there? Or should she find her in real life? Either way would be difficult. If the girl thought Deirdre was stalking her she would reject her help instantly. Online or in real life; it would make little difference. But Deirdre had seen the marks, despite the long sleeves of the blouse the girl wore. She knew about her unhappiness.

'Do you want to have me now?' Deidre was standing at exactly the right distance from the man. He could put his hands on any part of her body with no trouble. He could, if he wanted, stand up and kiss her. 'I wish you would,' she added. 'I'm getting awful wet – I've not had a real man for ages.' Deirdre turned and slowly, button by button, undid her checked shirt and dropped it on the floor of the barn. She was wearing a black, lace-trimmed bra underneath. The man breathed in audibly. He was interested, then.

Deirdre wished she had chosen to wear a skirt rather than jeans. She was sure the man would have enjoyed slipping his hand inside a gingham skirt, belled out with frothy layers of petticoats, and discovering smooth, soft thighs and a warm sex within. Instead, she took his left hand and placed it on her denim-clad leg. She reached behind her back and unclipped the bra, lowering her arms so that it slipped from her shoulders and released her breasts from their confinement. They were larger than she usually wore them and their nipples were tall and erect. The man took in another deep breath.

'What would you like to do with me?' Deirdre said. 'I'll do anything you like. Just a minute.' She kicked off her boots, undid the belt of her jeans and wriggled out of them. 'There. That's better.' She put his hand against her panties so he could feel how damp she'd made them. 'Why don't you pull them off me?'

All this time, while Deirdre performed her striptease, the man sat silent and motionless on a hay bale, his face expressionless. The only clue to his arousal was his shallow, rapid breathing. Deirdre knelt down in front of him, allowing her breasts to brush against his face while she undid the zipper of his trousers and carefully drew out his member. She leaned forward and took it into her mouth, rolling her tongue around it, sucking it and letting her teeth nip it. The man panted and gasped. He grabbed her hair and pulled her head over his crotch, forcing his sex deep into the back of her mouth.

He came almost immediately. It was as Deirdre had guessed in the diner – he had not been with a woman for a very long time. That pent-up hunger she thought she had seen in him had been real. He was just like so many of the sad, abandoned men she had received in her house.

'There,' she said, lifting her head and swallowing. 'That's better, isn't it? Now, why don't you take those unnecessary clothes off? And why don't you show this girl what you can really do? Take your time, hey?' Deidre pulled her panties down and tossed them on top of the rest of her things. She knelt down in front of the man once more and removed his shirt with a few deft movements. She dug her nails into his back. He flinched and put his hands to either side to steady himself. His member was becoming stiff once more, so she straddled him where he sat, impaling herself on him.

'Mmm. That feels nice.' She put her hands on his shoulders, lifted herself slightly and let go suddenly, so that he penetrated her more deeply.

'Ahhh...'

Deirdre returned to the library often. She made a point of being in the vicinity when the girl spoke, so that she learned her name, which was

Ella, and where she lived, which was in an all-girl dorm on the east side of the campus. But it was hard to discover more. She didn't know how to reach her. And although she said hello and goodbye when they passed, Deirdre never saw Ella eat. And she never saw when she cut herself.

She began to lose weight.

The man stood up suddenly, pushing Deirdre away. She rose to her feet. Was she doing something wrong? The answer was not long in coming. 'Down,' he said, pointing to the earth floor of the barn. Deirdre took two steps back. Which way did he want her? Taking a wild guess, she got on her hands and knees and lifted her rear, presenting her sex to him.

'Hell, no! What do you think I am; an animal? Do it like a Christian, for God's sake!'

Deirdre turned over onto her back and opened her legs wide. The man tore off his pants and threw himself onto her, forcing himself deep inside and pushing hard. Ah... So he liked to be on top. Right.

It was Deirdre's duty to take care of her visitors, to maximise their enjoyment. So, while letting the man think that it was he who was in control, she subtly manipulated him, gasping and crying when he seemed to be becoming less firm, and slackening off when he started to approach his climax. She had skills and muscle control that most mortals had never heard of. The ground was hard and scratched her back, but she could deal with that quickly and easily enough.

Eventually, with him thrusting above her and she bucking beneath him, he reached the point of *little-death*, as the witches called it among themselves. She cried out to make it appear that her orgasm had coincided with his. Except, of course, that she had no orgasm.

Good, she thought. *That was well done.* True, the man was still a widower and his children still lived with his sister Jean in another state. But she had brought something to him, had she not, even though it was fleeting. She was sure he would not forget their encounter in a hurry. And... there must be some of her sisters living nearby, even in such a God-fearing part of the country as this. When she got home she would do a little research.

A week passed, and then ten days. Deirdre and Ella discovered they took some of the same classes and covered many of the same assignments. Deirdre confessed that she was having difficulty with her essays, and Ella volunteered to help her. And Deirdre always made sure that there was never any doubt which was the prettier girl, although it went against her instincts. She enjoyed being beautiful.

But, even with all the hanging out together that they did, she could get no closer to Ella. And despite her best endeavours, Deirdre still attracted attention where Ella did not. At parties, in the cafeteria (where Ella chose little and ate less) despite being pretty Ella's plain friend, it was Deirdre who had to shake off the boys at the end of the evening or when it was time to return to classes. And when Ella went back to the dorm or the library and hung out on the pro-ana and pro-suicide forums and found people in chat rooms whose feelings meshed with her own, Deirdre could only stand by and watch. She did not dare press the girl or ask questions that could not be answered for fear of tipping her over the edge.

All the same, they had this conversation one day while taking a coffee break between lectures:

'You know what a con this all is.' Ella, waving a hand at the cafeteria counter.

'What do you mean?'

'All this food, all this *stuff*.'

'It's just food.'

'It's not. Oh, it is, but it's more than that. It's a trick.'

Deirdre took a sip of coffee. 'Go on, tell me.'

Ella leaned forward. 'Go back in time. Two hundred years or so. What did people eat?'

Deidre knew the answer to this question from direct experience. 'Whatever they could.'

'That's right. No refrigerators. No bulk transport. No out-of-season food. No raspberries in December.'

Deirdre nodded.

'And we evolved to deal with it. When there was plenty to eat we ate it, before it could go rotten. We stored what we could for the winter. It was a survival thing. When winter came, we were fat. Come spring we were thin. But now...'

'Yes?'

'Now there are no seasons. You can get anything you want, any time. But our bodies, our hindbrains, they don't know that. They say eat now, while you can. Eat as much as you can stuff down yourself.

Supersize it. And those bastards know it, don't they? They sell us cheap fatty processed trash that blocks us up and kills us and they know all the artificial flavours to add and all the sales tricks to use to keep us coming back for more.'

'But you don't have to eat it...'

'No! You don't! We know that! But look... it's operating below the conscious level. And it's all a lot of us can afford.'

'That's true.' Deirdre had been shocked to see so many poor and malnourished people in such a rich country.

'And they don't want the people to know how much they're being taken in.'

'It's a conspiracy, you mean.' Deirdre smiled.

Ella's eyes flared. 'Don't fuck with me. It's not funny. This isn't Mulder and Scully. This isn't Fox News. This is big business destroying people's lives for profit. This is real.'

'Have you had enough of screwing me yet, you bitch? You whore?'

The man stood above her, pulling his pants back on.

'Sorry?' *Oh no.*

'You heard me.'

'Don't you like me?' Deirdre put a little-girl note in her voice.

'I like you fine, harlot. Now get the hell off my property.'

'I thought we could go inside. I'll fix you something to eat. I'm a real good cook.' Deirdre got to her feet.

The man came up to her. His face was red with anger. 'I wouldn't allow you anywhere near my house. That's for decent folk. Not for whores like you. Now – get out! Before I set my dog on you!'

Deirdre picked up her things. 'You'll let me get dressed?'

'You can do what the hell you like. I don't care.' The man turned his back on her and stamped out of the barn. Deirdre left not long afterwards.

They found Ella in the Connecticut River two day later. The marks were fresh on her body, but she had a history and no third party was suspected, not even her new friend.

I couldn't let anyone see me – I'm so fat, it said in her last status update. *Look – I'm absolutely bulging!*

But oh! Why hadn't she stayed and fought?

Deirdre wore a red bracelet in Ella's memory and continued on her westward journey. The road was long and hard and strewn with broken lives.

* * *

Deirdre parked the Clarity next to a row of Winnebagos at the Marin County end of the bridge. It was a popular viewing point. She got out of the car, walked up to the fence and looked out across the bay. There it all was – the island of Alcatraz, the Coit Tower, the Transamerica Pyramid and, to her right, the red ochre piers of the Golden Gate. The City, they called it – as if it were the only city in the world – and today it was fog-free.

She had reached the West. Not the extreme West – that would mean a journey north through Oregon, Washington, Canada and Alaska to the Bering Strait. But the deep-blue Pacific lay just on the other side of the bridge just as only a few weeks ago – or however long it had been – the Atlantic Ocean had waited for her at Land's End.

A small girl came up to her. 'Hello,' she said. 'My name's Annabel. What's yours?'

'That's such a pretty name. I'm Deirdre. Pleased to meet you. Isn't it a lovely view?'

The girl started to reply, but her mother called out from the driver's seat of her van, 'Belle! Come here! Don't bother the lady.'

'It's no bother,' Deirdre began, but Annabel had gone. Oh well. Time to move on.

Deirdre drew out onto Highway One. The northern coast road turned off to the left after a mile and she was tempted to take it. But no... She took the first exit to the right and followed it. She was going back east.

The boy was standing next to the city limits sign, wearing cowboy boots over Wranglers and a Jack Daniels tee under a vintage flying jacket. He raised his thumb as Deirdre passed and, wanting company after a lonely night spent in a Motel Six, she pulled over. Perhaps this boy would help her with what she needed to do.

You don't run, you don't ride. That's the rule. The boy jogged up to her, hitched his holdall to the bike's cissy bar, and swung his right leg over the pillion seat. There was a spare helmet hanging off the pannier rail. He unclipped it, pulled it over his springy bush of ginger hair and fastened the chinstrap. He was nineteen or twenty years old with freckles and a scruffy beard. His eyes were hidden behind a pair of Aviators.

'Handle's behind you,' said Deirdre. 'Hang on.' She twisted the throttle and the Indian grabbed tarmac and pointed itself down an infinitely straight, undulating desert blacktop.

Deirdre drove at a steady fifty-five. The big four didn't appreciate being revved. 'Where're you headed?' she called over her shoulder.

'East,' the boy replied.

'OK.' They rode east, past telegraph poles and gas stations, across a wide landscape of stumpy mesas, yellow grass, billboards and scattered settlements. The boy sat back and enjoyed the ride. He kept his hands to himself.

That night, after two hundred miles of blue highways, they stopped in a small wooden town and ate in a family restaurant – steakburger, Coke, fries, apple pie with ice cream, coffee – at a red Formica table under glaring tube lights.

'Do you have money for a hotel?' the boy asked. This came not long after, 'You're English, right? I'd know that accent anywhere. I love Monty Python, don't you?' Deirdre smiled and nodded.

'Yes, I can afford a room. Can you?'

'No, but that's OK. I'll find somewhere.'

Is he angling for a bed? 'You're sure? I'll lend you fifty if you want'

'I'm sure. I don't need the money. I'll be OK. See you tomorrow?'

'I'm leaving at eight.'

'I'll be there.'

And he was, leaning against the Speed Twin with a sideways smile on his face. The bike had decided to be a Triumph today, it seemed. It must have decided to reflect the boy's anglophilia. 'If we're travelling again today I guess it's time we swapped names. I'm Charles Foster.' He held out his hand.

'Deirdre.' They shook and for the first time she noticed the smell of him – dry and dusty, sweet and corrupt, redolent of sage-brush and roadkill. There were, she noticed, bird-feathers stuck to his jacket and traces of blood on his stubbly beard.

'Had breakfast?' she asked.

'Yes, thanks.'

Deirdre kicked the Twin into life and they followed the telegraph lines eastwards. The road stretched on, never-ending. And as they rode, and Deirdre settled into the automatic routine of throttle-brake-clutch-shift she had time to think. And time to see signs and read what they said. And time to *realise*. And to make a decision.

They lay side by side on top of a mesa, unspeaking, surrounded by ultramarine sky, under a brilliant sun that scorched the rock but did them no harm. Time passed – quick-slow-quick – and sun gave way to stars and blue to black.

'Coyote?' said Deirdre at last.

'Ah, so you know me.'

'Yes, of course I do. How could you imagine I would not?'

The god turned onto his side and smiled. 'How indeed? I'm Mister Notorious, no? But go on; what did you want to ask me?'

'I think,' and Deirdre looked directly towards the stars, 'I think I would rather like to die.'

'That is a grave request.'

'Trickster!'

'Sorry.'

'No, you're not.'

'And if I were, how could you tell?' Coyote waved his left hand and they were both naked under the heavens. 'Like this?' He smiled.

And it was all for her.

'You think I'm going to change my mind just because you're a great fuck?'

'Don't be coarse, dear. Instead… follow me.' Coyote was uncovered except for a loincloth. Deirdre wore white cotton overalls.

They had left the Speed Twin at the foot of the mesa, but it was not there when they climbed back down. Instead... Deirdre gasped. She had rarely seen an object so full of purpose.

'This is the trainer version. Dual cockpits. You're in front. Jump in.'

The Blackbird stank of JP-7 fuel. It was leaking visibly onto the desert floor. 'Don't worry,' said Coyote. 'It's by design. By the time we reach Mach 3 air friction will have closed up the joints.'

They took off on a wave of rolling thunder. Somewhere around the fifty-mile line that separates air from space the plane became an Ares-1 second stage, lit its J-2X engine and accelerated further. And as they entered orbit it transformed itself into a General Products #3 hull, with external antigravity thrusters and a warp driver embedded in the floor.

'Black is so last year, don't you think?' said Coyote. The hull was as transparent as optical glass.

'Have you brought me here so we can do it in zero-g?' asked Deirdre. The idea tickled her.

'It's overrated,' said Coyote. 'Nothing to push against. All thrash and no thrust. But, if you're curious...?'

'Presently,' she said.

'You said you wanted to die.'

'Yes.'

'Why? For the novelty of it?'

'Don't be facetious. Look – how old are you?'

'As old as...' Coyote pointed downwards. The nacreous Earth rotated below them.

'Billions of years.'

'Yes.'

'And how old do you think I am?'

'Not a year over ninety-nine, and looking good!'

Something splintered inside Deirdre and she back-slapped Coyote hard across the side of the face. His head jerked to the left and his right foot swung up, driven by instinct. Its claws missed ripping a huge gash in her side by a mere quarter of an inch.

'Don't try that again! I'll kill you next time. Or is that what you want?'

'Then take me seriously, damn you!'

'I take nothing seriously.'

'Then why are you here?'

'To offer help.'

'Then help me!'

'By killing you?'

'Yes.'

'You didn't want to be killed just now. You dodged me very neatly.'

'I am too old. I want to die, not live maimed.'

'But you can heal yourself. You did so before, when the demons and the witch-hunters came. It is an uncomfortable thing, this power we have.' Coyote's form flickered before Deirdre's eyes. 'It doesn't always work for us, does it?'

'A demon or human can only hurt me. They cannot kill me. A god can. Will you give me a swift, clean death?'

'I would need a very good reason. For a start, can't you kill yourself?'

'No.'

'Have you tried?'

'Yes. I was willing myself to die the day I met you.'

'But it didn't work. Can you guess why not?'

'Because it's not allowed, I suppose. It's so unfair! That girl in Amherst… Ella. She was able to end herself.'

'It that why you want to die? Because you failed to save her? Because, you know, we fail all the time. You, me, all of us. Even the demons. They failed with you, didn't they? They could not make you one of them.'

'I want to end the pain.'

'Look down there.' The ship was passing over Europe. On one side, sunlight, on the other, darkness, dotted with sodium and mercury. It was *l'heure bleue* in Paris, *zwielicht* in Berlin. 'Look at all those people, in all those cities. And all of them failing. Every day, in thousands of ways, great and small. A misstep here, a false word there. A momentary slip, and the consequences may be terrible. Everywhere you look, people are wounded; they're damaged, hurt and unfulfilled. There's pain – they all suffer pain, every one of them, even when there's no need for it. They are mortal. That is what it means to be mortal – to feel pain. We who are old, but immortal, should not forget that.'

'Of course I don't forget it! What do you think I spend all my time doing? You've no idea, have you? They have needs that I have to try to meet as best I can. I have the power to help their pain – I've got to use it. You have the power to do nothing at all, except mess things up.'

'Because I'm Coyote. Of course, that's what I'm for. But look, Deirdre, you're talking about power.'

'I mentioned it. Don't say you've actually been listening to me.'

'I have. But look; what *is* power?'

'I don't know. Why are you asking me?'

'Because I want to hear what you think. We're both pretty powerful, wouldn't you say?'

'You are. That's probably because you're a god.'

'And you're a witch. God, witch, witch, god – there's not much difference when you think about it. Hey – come here. Come on.' Deirdre floated free of the spacecraft's floor and drifted weightless into Coyote's arms.

'That's better.' They hung in mid-air, entangled. 'Now – are all mortal prayers answered? Reasonable ones, I mean.'

'No.'

'Why not? Why do we gods – who have infinite power – allow mortals to suffer? Is it because we're such mean bastards?'

'You certainly are.'

'If you say so. But let's put it another way. What happens when a mortal acquires power? Don't bother – I'll tell you – he uses it. However appalling the consequences may be, however much he fears them, in the end he uses it. Give him a gun, a knife or a bomb – he'll use it to kill someone. Give him economic power – he'll use it to starve someone. They can't help it. It's just the way they are, poor dears. Not to say they don't occasionally use it to do good, of course.

'And that's why they can't understand why we don't spend all our time fixing their problems. We have the power – why don't we use it? They would. But we know that the true essence of power lies in *not* using it.'

'What a philosopher you are, Coyote.' Deidre remembered the demons, perhaps for the last time. She could have sent them back to the Pit with the merest flick of an eyelash, but…

'So I am. Now if you'll just put your hands down here and here… and pull… Right! Hold on! I told you zero-g was tricky stuff!'

There was a lengthy hiatus in their conversation, while perspiration formed a small cloud around them. Then:

'You see? Novel, yes, but ultimately satisfying? I'm not convinced.'

'You're too modest.'

'It's not often I'm told that. But after all, I am the Charlatan God.' His skull-necklace rattled as he spoke. 'Now then; you were talking about pain, I about power. I am Coyote – I cannot feel pain. I can only see it. I understand it, but it does not reach my heart. That…' and he looked directly into Deirdre's eyes, 'is your job. But you should only take it so far.'

'Are you telling me what to do?'

'I'm reminding you of something. It's time you behaved more like a god and less like a mortal. Look, we've got a starship here. Why don't we spin up the warp engine and take a holiday somewhere more interesting?'

'Like where?'

'I don't know. How about Glory, or Terminus, or the Kefahuchi

Tract?'

'Would it make any difference if we did? Wherever you go, there you are, you know.'

'Platitudes from you, Deirdre? I would've thought you'd have more originality than that. You ought to be ashamed of yourself.'

'I'm not. And you know I'm right. Don't you?'

Coyote sighed. 'OK. Whatever. You win. Shall we go home then?'

'That's a much better idea. And... you *are* a great fuck!'

'I know.'

Deirdre bustled by the Aga while Coyote sat at the kitchen table and tried to talk to Ashley and Mitchell, who were drinking Baileys and blackcurrant and reading webcomics on their Vaios. They had chosen to be fifteen years old today. It was funny, Deirdre thought, how the Internet always seemed to work perfectly for them when it was so unreliable for her visitors. Coyote was dressed in a suit from Top Man, with a white shirt and a blue tie, and his hair was short and gelled back. It made him look like a junior estate agent.

Deirdre gave him a cup of tea.

'Do you really want to settle here?' she asked, pulling back a Windsor chair and sitting next to him.

'Yes, why not? It'll do me good to become a bit more serious for a while. And it'll do you no harm to cut loose and have some fun. Real sod-the-consequences fun. Express your power.'

'I don't know if you'll run the place properly. I can't trust you.'

'Of course you can't trust me. That's the beauty of it.'

'I'd better leave you my phone number. Me, I don't think you'll make it past two weeks. When did you last go shopping? Or pay your Council Tax or your gas bill? Or catch a bus? Are you going to be male or female? You must be the least adult immortal I've ever met!'

'And you're the most grown-up. Now bog off and leave me to it. This pair will soon let me know if I'm getting it wrong. And you...'

'Yes?'

'Let go! Screw your way around the world. Join the circus and learn to juggle. Trip elder statesmen as they get out of planes. Plant bugs in the code, and gremlins in the operators. Live wild in the woods and shit on the tourists as they walk under the trees. Untwist their DNA when they're not looking. Play neu-guitar in a hash-soviet band. Fuck a professor or two. Design a new mathematics. Do nude yoga on TV.

Become a porn star or join a girl group – it makes little difference. Go seetee. Have great sex wherever you go. Help people out if you think they deserve it, or even if you don't. Be Coyote-girl, or Coyote-boy if you prefer. Be a legend. Be free.

'And when you're ready, come home. We'll be waiting for you.'

'I still don't trust you.'

'Then you must become untrustworthy yourself. Now, vamoose! There's a world of Twelfth Nights and Winter Carnivals and Fat Tuesdays and Days of the Dead out there and they'll fall flat without a really great party organiser behind them. What? You didn't think you were going to have nothing to do?'

Deirdre smiled lop-sidedly. 'No, I suppose not. Goodbye, children.' A silent pause. 'I said, goodbye.'

The twins put down their glasses and looked up reluctantly from their screens. Ashley belched loudly. 'Goodbye, Mummy.'

'Be good for Uncle Coyote.'

'We won't.' They poured themselves another shot each and returned to their comics.

Deirdre shut the front door behind her and walked down the garden path. She stopped at the gate and turned for a last look at the house. There it stood, set back from the main road, stone-solid and secure but blurred and insubstantial too; ready for her homecoming and yet indifferent to it. Behind her the traffic crawled up and down the London Road in a hushed, foggy haze. A deep breath; and the desert perfume of herbs and carrion washed through her. She clicked the fingers of her right hand twice.

She felt a curious lightness beneath her feet.

MEN AND GODS

THE YOUNG OLD YOUNG WOMAN
AND HER DEATH

The Young-Old-Young Woman and her Death

THERE WAS ONCE A BOY WHO, BECAUSE HE WAS THE SEVENTH SON OF a seventh son, had no family inheritance to look forward to. In its place he possessed a gift, both wonderful and terrible, for he was a prophet.

It was said that his prophecies were so uncannily accurate that, rather than have him be proved wrong, the Multiverse would change its shape to match his predictions. Now, there came a day in this boy's nineteenth year when a woman, who was both young and old, dark-haired and grey, smooth-skinned and wrinkled with age, came to him where he sat in the shade of the courtyard of his father's house, and put to him a question. That question was, 'When shall I die?'

The boy had heard this question many times in his life, young though he was, and he always gave it the same answer: 'Madam,' he said. 'You will die when you find your Death, and he finds you.'

'Then I shall never die, for I have locked my Death away in a dark place far below the surface of the Urth. He will not be able to find me, and so I shall live forever and not die.'

'Does your Death have hands?'

'Yes, he does.'

'Then he will be able to scratch his way through the rock and gravel and soil and grass until he reaches the surface, and then he will be able to find you.'

'He will not, for I have buried him many thousands of leagues from here, in a grotto underneath the sea-bed.'

'Does your Death have feet?'

'Yes, he does.'

'Then he will be able to kick his way up though the sea-water until he reaches the surface, as the divers do who compete in the Great Thracian Games, and then he will be able to find you.'

'But still I shall not die.'

'Why so?'

'Because, before I buried my Death in a cavern deep below the bed of the Peaceable Ocean, I blinded him with a bar of red-hot bronze. He will not be able to see me, and he will not be able to find me, and so I shall live forever and not die.'

'Did you remember to seal up his nostrils?'

'Yes, I did. I also blocked his ears with spermaceti wax. He will not be able to see, hear or smell me, and so he will not be able to find me, and so I shall live forever and not die.'

The boy sat and considered the young-old-young woman for a minute or two. Then, 'Wait here,' he said and stood up and walked over to the door of his father's house. The woman heard a terrific crashing and banging from inside the house, and the sound of store-cupboard doors opening and closing. Eventually the prophet emerged, covered with dust and carrying a hessian sack over his shoulder. 'I have brought you the things you need,' he said.

'But I did not ask you to bring me anything. I do not want you to bring me anything. I do not need anything.'

'Nevertheless, I have brought you the things you need. Behold!' And the boy emptied the sack onto the ground in front of the young-old-young woman with a loud metallic rattle.

She stared in astonishment. 'What are these things?' Scattered across the flagstones of the courtyard were a pair of antique iron-shod leather sandals, a spade of tempered steel and some aeronaut's goggles.

'They are what you need. You have buried your Death a very long way off, so you will need these hard-wearing shoes to carry you there. He lies many fathoms below the waves, so you will need these goggles to help you navigate your way through the water. And you have buried him deep under the sea-bed, so you will need this spade to dig your way down to his grave so that you may find him. For, my lady,' and the boy fixed the young-old-young woman with his emerald-facetted gaze, 'most assuredly the time will come when the thing which you desire most above all things will be to find and embrace your Death, for he was made for you and you were made for him. When that time comes, I should not wish to come between you, nor be the cause of any undue delay in your union. Now go! And take that stuff with you. It is blocking the path.'

The young-old-young woman replaced the sandals and the spade and the goggles in the sack, and threw it over her shoulder, and went out of the courtyard and into the street, to her home and her husband and her children. She put the things that the prophet had given her on display in her house, and when anybody asked her why she had done so, she replied, 'As a reminder.'

And it was said in the later days that she was a woman who knew how to die well, and that she had made a good death for herself.

THE MAN AND HIS GODS

The Man and his Gods

THERE ONCE LIVED IN THIS TOWN – OR IT MAY HAVE BEEN THE CITY OF Orm, which lies not sixty furlongs from here as the eagle flies – a man whom many counted the most fortunate of his generation, for he was beloved of the most beautiful woman in all the world. Of her it was said – and said truly – that she was so lovely that whenever she went forth from her house, even though it were at the brightest time of the day when the regal Phoebus Apollo surveys the kingdoms of Urth from his flying chariot of beaten copper, the moon and stars would foregather and walk beside her, that they might share in the golden scattering of life-essence which glittered in her train.

It might be supposed that this man was not only very fortunate but also supremely happy; but the more astute among you will have come to realise that lasting happiness is a rare gift – not rarer than beauty, perhaps, but of a different kind. And so it was that this man was indeed, despite his great good fortune, not content.

As is the way with men who carry a burden of unhappiness, he looked around for a means of lessening its weight. 'See if you can find someone to share it with you,' said the man's anima. This advice seemed wise to the man, so he went out into the streets, squares and taverns of the town and showed his burden to the people he met there, and asked them if they would carry it for him or, if not, take a portion of the load upon themselves, so that his share would be correspondingly reduced.

You, my wise reader, will not be surprised to learn that the man was disappointed in his search for help. 'You fool,' said one whom he approached and, 'I should have such a problem,' said another and, 'Stop bothering my customers,' said the owner of the Boar's Head Inn.

So the man returned home no less heavy of heart, but certainly lighter in the purse. 'If I can get no help from Men, then I shall have to send my problem up the line,' said the man to his anima, and she agreed with him.

In one corner of the man's house there stood, as I have no doubt there stands in the house of even the most unwise reader, an altar to the small god in whose care he lay. The man made the customary sacrifice of perfumed woods and dried juniper berries on the zinc plate within the shrine and waited for his god to manifest himself; which he did with no little delay, being somewhat busy with other matters.

'Hello,' said the small god. 'How may I help you?'

'I have a grievous burden to carry and I desire your advice as to how I may reduce the pain that it is causing me to suffer,' said the man, bowing deeply to the small god's manifestation.

'What is your burden, Man?' said the god.

'It is Fear,' said the man.

'Ah yes,' said the god, allowing his manifestation to settle down in the shrine and get comfortable. 'What do you fear? Tell me, and I may be able to help you face it and overcome it. Did you, for example, have a bad experience in your childhood?'

'No,' said the man. 'My childhood was very happy.'

'Nobody abused you?'

'To my certain knowledge, no.'

'Ah,' said the god, slightly disappointed. 'Perhaps you had better express your fear in your own words. Reveal your inner child to me, and let us deal with it together.'

The man had no intention of letting the god deal with his inner child, so he gathered his thoughts together and spoke:

'You know that I am beloved of -----,' he named his lady friend, 'and that she is surpassingly beautiful.'

'Her?' said the god. 'You lucky -----!' He named a denizen of the Other Place. 'That's your worry? I should have such a problem!' He thought. 'Let's see... Is she, perhaps, easily roused to anger?'

'No, she is very sweet-natured.'

'Does she, perhaps, neglect matters of personal hygiene?'

'No, the perfume of her skin is more seductive than the blooms of Elysium and her breath is sweeter than all the comfits of Araby.'

'Hmm. Perhaps, then, she is dull of wit and tedious in company.'

'No, she sparkles in conversation. She can contrive to make the most foolish man believe himself to be wise.'

'So she is not cruel or heartless?'

'No, she is kindness itself.'

The small god considered the matter. 'In what way then, Man, is she a burden to you? You tell me that she is kind, witty, and altogether delightful to know. How good is she in bed?'

'You mind your own business,' said the man.

'I'm sorry. Did I touch on a sore point?' said the god, quite unabashed.

'Never mind,' said the man. 'The thing is...'

'Yes?' The small god's manifestation rested his hands in his lap.

'I am but one man among many. I am not rich, nor am I particularly good-looking or intelligent. My fear is that my beloved will find another man who does not share my deficiencies and that she will abandon me for him. If that were to happen I do not believe that I could go on living.'

'I see, said the god, crossing his manifestation's legs. 'What do you want me to do about this? You know that I am not permitted by the laws of Olympus to make you more personable in any way.'

'I know that,' said the man.

The god thought briefly. 'I know! I will send a plague of cysts to your lady-friend. She will become altogether loathsome in the sight of men. No other man will want her and you will be able to keep her for yourself.'

'No!' said the man. 'Do not do that to her. She does not deserve it.'

'Very well,' said the god. I think I shall have to send your problem up the line. Would you hold for a minute? Your call is important to us.'

The small god's manifestation flickered and disappeared. The man waited, and presently the senior god on duty that day, who happened to be the sun-god Phoebus Apollo, appeared before him. The god's manifestation was as terrible to behold as if the mighty star Arcturus had landed upon the surface of the Urth. His face glowed from within with incandescent light and his hair streamed and crackled about his head like the tail of a fiery comet.

'Eh-up, lad! What ails thee?' said Phoebus Apollo. The man explained his problem to the sun-god who thought for a moment with his chin resting in the palm of his white-hot hand.

'I've got it!' he said, leaping to his feet in scintillating glory. 'Look into my eyes, lad. I will take away thy sight and thou shalt forget thy lady's beauty, and the cause of thy grief shall be taken from thee.'

'No!' cried the man. 'I would not wish to be made blind to the wonders of Urth and Sky. That is a terrible idea!'

'Oh,' said Phoebus Apollo, quite crestfallen. 'I see that I shall have to send thy problem up the line. Half a mo.' And he left in an effervescence of flame.

The man marvelled at the splendour of the sun-god's manifestation and departure. 'Who could possibly be more transcendental than he?' he thought. He did not have to wait long to find out. With footsteps heavier than the Pillars of Hercules and more relentless than Fate itself, came the Father of the Gods, great Saturn himself. When he spoke, it was as if the weight of all the spheres of heaven had descended upon the man, and he felt that he was being crushed into the soil of the Urth.

'What is all this fuss about?' the god said, and his voice boomed and rolled about the land of Jaed, in which stood the city of Orm, where the man lived. The man shook, and his bowels were loosened; but he was a man yet and he told the god of his fear.

'You call it Fear,' pronounced the god, 'but I have another name for it. It is called Jealousy, and it is a small, mean and nasty thing. Let me tell you what will come of it.'

'Are you an oracle, then?' asked the man who, up to this point, had not considered making a pilgrimage to Delphi to seek a solution to his quandary.

'Enough already!' thundered the god, 'I am Saturn, who was once known as Chronos. I am Time, and I see everything that has happened, everything that does happen and everything that will happen, for to me all times are one. I tell you, Man, that if you cannot look upon your lady with the same love and trust with which she regards you, then you will lose her. For in all the comings and goings between men and women there is nothing more important than Trust. Without Trust, love and beauty are nothing and fade and die too soon, as do all things that are washed away from the shores of Time if they are not well-founded on the rock of the Urth below.

'Now stop bothering me with little matters. I have to count all the atoms in all the grains of sand of all the beaches of all the worlds of all the stars in all the galaxies in all the universes of the Cosmos, and that is quite enough to be getting on with.'

Saturn departed, and lightness returned to the Urth. 'That told us,' said the man to the small god, who had re-manifested himself.

'He's a… difficult person to deal with,' said the small god to the man.

Phoebus Apollo returned in a blaze of radiance. 'Father hasn't got much time for his children,' he said to them both. 'Let me tell you, it's quite a worry. In fact, it's eating us up…'

The wise reader will appreciate his concern.

A God called Neville

THERE WAS ONCE A DISCONTENTED GOD. THE WISE READER WILL ASK why the god was discontented or, more probably, how he was discontented, or possibly how discontented he was. Those of you who are very wise – or who have read the kind of book which affords the reader a semblance of wisdom – will smile and ask if the god was suffering from "divine discontent". Be that as it may, the god was not happy.

This god – his true name was not to be spoken by those who were merely human – had been suffering from a form of spiritual malaise for quite a long time. The concept of Time, rather like the idea of Name, can be a slippery matter when it comes to the consideration of the lives of the gods. As, indeed, is the association of Life – with its inevitable linkage with Death – with the occupation of god. As a rule, the gods have no regard for Death – it is something that only happens to other people.

In fact, any discussion of the affairs of the gods quickly comes to resemble the navigation of a dense jungle or a minefield. The slightest deviation from the path of true religious orthodoxy when speaking to – or of – the gods may lead to an unexpected and potentially fatal explosion of divine wrath; or the imposition of a judicial sentence of eternal confusion and repeated retracing of the same fruitless track in the Forest of Theomancy. You never know who may be listening.

Therefore, in order to relieve the reader – however advanced he may be in the acquisition of wisdom – of the discomfort from which he may suffer when considering the comings and goings of the gods, we will say here and now that this god's name was Neville and that he had been feeling mildly, but increasingly, hacked off for the past six months or so.

To answer the wise reader's second question; Neville was suffering from a stress-related disorder. His life (for so he has permitted me to describe it, as if it were a linear, Point-A-to-Point-B, birth-to-death sort of thing) was lacking in zip, zest and pizzazz. Partly this was because he was but a junior god. There is a hierarchy in the Celestial City, just as there is on Earth. This should be clear even to the most unwise reader. Do not our human, mortal institutions derive their structure and meaning from the divine order which they reflect; as a sheet of hammered bronze presents a dulled, dimmed and distorted image of even the most beautiful of women? Truly is it said, "On Earth, as it is in Heaven."

Neville's position in the theocratic hierarchy was a lowly one. Not for him the Great Council of the Most High, where cosmic matters are weighed in judgement and the future courses of the creations which comprise the Multiverse are determined. Nor was his a managerial position; charged with executing the Will of the Council and with all the resources – both material and metaphysical – of the Kingdom of Heaven at his command.

No – Neville was an Agent. He lived in one of the many accommodation blocks which ring the Outer Walls of the Celestial City; in a tenth-floor inside apartment with two small rooms – a sitting-room and a bedroom. There was no need for a kitchen in his flat, for Ambrosia – the sustenance of the gods – was regularly delivered by an angel pushing an insulated handcart. Nor was there any requirement for a bathroom as the gods do not get dirty and Ambrosia is a zero-residue food. It was said by some that many of the middle-ranking gods equipped their residences with kitchens and bathrooms so that they could keep the "common touch" or, to put it another way, increase their understanding of the human condition. Others said that they clearly did not have enough to do with their time. Whatever that may mean.

The divan in Neville's bedroom was cloud-soft and covered with silken sheets, but this story does not go there. His sitting-room was furnished with an Eames chair complete with footstool, a nice teak coffee table, a small library of crime fiction and a large plasma screen on which he could view, among other riches, perfect restorations of the VistaVision films of Alfred Hitchcock and the best of the MGM colour musicals. Neville's favourites were *Rear Window* and *On the Town*. He was a New York City boy at heart.

There is perhaps one other thing I should mention, and that was that – like many of the gods – Neville enjoyed the company of animals. He did not keep pets, for hutches, cages and kennels are anathema in Heaven. But his window was always open, and next to it stood a perch on a stand and if a passing siskin, robin, starling or dove happened to pass by and alight on it he would welcome the creature and, if it was willing, engage it in conversation.

Some Earthly theologians like to insist that if – as they claim – animals have no souls, they can have no immortal part to occupy the Holy City and its environs and are therefore not to be found there. This is patent nonsense. Even if it were true that:

> The jocund cow
> Does not reflect on the why or how

it would nevertheless be grossly unfair on the denizens of the Blessed Place if they were to be forced to spend all the days of Eternity without the companionship of the creatures they had loved in their mortal lives or to be forbidden from talking to them. The skies of Heaven were full of wings, and animals great and small – the lion as well as the lamb – ran and grazed in its parks and wild places.

To the unwise reader who dares to ask whether Neville had a girlfriend and if she ever stayed the night in his apartment I would suggest – while standing at a safe distance for fear of thunderbolts – that the gods are not carnal; which is not the same as saying that they are not interested in carnality. And that is all I am going to say on the matter.

Now; to return to Neville's unhappiness. His humble position as a foot-soldier in the Legion of the Blessed was not the direct source of his dissatisfaction, for he was not an ambitious god. He did not aspire to the Council of the Wise. He knew his limitations and was content to work within them. But indirectly, it was. Let us see how that came to be.

Neville's day began – as they all began – with a sweet chime from a set of porcelain bells hanging from the wall by his bedside. He arose refreshed from his bed of finest cumulo-cirrus – doing his best not to disturb the nymph who still slumbered there – dressed himself in glowing raiment from the armoire, drank a quick grail-goblet of

Ambrosia and left the apartment; pausing only to leave a goodbye kiss on the forehead of his latest conquest. At the very moment he reached the tenth-floor lobby the elevator's doors opened for him and he was whisked to the ground floor in an instant, just in time to catch the tram which stopped outside the front door of his block. The streetcar carried him quickly and comfortably from the outskirts of Olympus, along the expansive boulevards which, lined with bookshops, pleasure gardens and cafés, are among the principle tourist attractions of the Holy Metropolis, to the employees' entrance of the Ministry of Mortality. Along the way he caught up with the latest news and chatted to his fellow passengers.

The streetcar pulled up and Neville stepped down from it and entered the Ministry by the wide rotating doors which led from the street into the central atrium. From there he strolled across a wide marble concourse to one of the crystal elevators which serviced the building and let it carry him to his floor. It was but a short walk to his desk, which was positioned at the end of the twenty-third row of the forty-second rank of the thirty-seventh tier. Neville had earned his privileged position at the end of the row in recognition of a particularly difficult, but ultimately successful, Intercession he had accomplished a month or two previously. The other junior gods were still coming up to him by the Ambrosia cooler and saying, 'I expect you'll be leaving us soon, Neville. Going Upstairs, I shouldn't wonder.' Whenever this happened Neville smiled and nodded before returning to his desk.

A large light-up board was suspended from the ceiling at one end of the office. At the time Neville signed in that day it read:

1,426,789,125 CALLS WAITING
AVERAGE RESPONSE TIME 37 SECONDS

It was a quiet morning.

Neville's desk was made of the finest figured walnut. It was fitted with a video screen, a headset and a numerical display with two buttons mounted on the top, labelled NEXT and REFER. Some kind acolyte had placed a vase of white lilies from the Elysian Fields next to the screen. Neville put it carefully on the floor next to the pedestal, for fear of accidents. He donned his headset and turned the screen on. According to the numerical display there were twenty-six calls waiting for him. He drew a deep breath and pressed the button which was marked NEXT. The screen lit up, showing the face of a middle-aged woman in a green toga. She looked worried. So did most of Neville's callers.

'Speak, my daughter, for your prayer is heard,' said Neville into the headset's microphone.

The woman, who had been casting fragranced dust onto the family altar, bowed her head. 'Oh god of our household, grant that my baking may go well today, for Livia Fortesque, the Senator's wife, is coming to tea and she will sneer at me if my Victoria sponge is not well risen.'

This was a nice easy start to the day. 'My daughter, your prayer is answered. Do not open the oven door until the time is ready, not even for the tiniest little peek, and verily your cake will be a masterpiece of the baker's art.' He pressed NEXT. The woman disappeared and a schoolboy's face appeared on the screen.

'Speak, my son, for your prayer is heard,' said Neville.

'Please sir, I've not done my homework, sir, and it's due in this morning.'

'Who is your teacher, my son?' said Neville.

'Sir, it's Mister Hardwicke, sir. He'll thrash me, sir.'

So he would. Mister Hardwicke was also on Neville's register and the god knew of his harshness. Neville's finger hovered over the REFER button. There was a possible conflict of interest here. But no. Household gods were expected to deal with as many of humanity's problems as they could by themselves and not send them up the line to their superiors unless it was strictly necessary.

'My son, your prayer is answered. Do as much of your work as you can on the way to school. Sit neither at the front nor the back of the class. Do not call attention to yourself and it is possible that Mister Hardwicke will not ask you for your homework.'

Neville pressed NEXT. According to the display there were now forty-two human souls requiring his attention. It looked as if was going to be a busy day after all.

All that morning Neville listened to the prayers of his supplicants. There were children with lost cats. There was an account executive worried about meeting his monthly sales target. There was a widow who, two years after her husband's death, still laid his place at table every morning. There was a child whose parents' marriage was breaking up and who thought it was all his fault. A mother in an

African village who needed to find the strength to make the ten-mile return journey to the nearest clean well. Another whose son and daughter were dying of AIDS. A faithless couple in a motel bedroom. A man lying on a Bristol pavement, clutching at his stuttering heart. A nursing sister drawing the curtains around a cancer ward bed. A priest who was losing his faith. A tired housewife with her head inside the oven door. A boy whose uncle was visiting that afternoon, and who dreaded what he would be asked to do for him. A workless man, riding his bicycle through the streets of a deserted mining village. A baby – her prayers vague and unformed but shot through with pain – lying in a freezing doorway, abandoned.

There were billions of human souls on Earth. There were many hundreds of thousands of household gods in the Ministry of Mortality busily engaged in answering their prayers. A continual torrent of worry and fear flowed from Earth to Heaven and a corresponding stream of reassurance, and the occasional Intercession, travelled in the opposite direction. For a junior god like Neville it was the whole scale of the operation that was the most appalling thing – the overwhelming tide of suffering that swept his way, the pitiful banks of consolation he piled up against it. It all seemed so pointless, so inadequate; and so did he. It hadn't always been like this. He could still remember, somewhere in the backwash of Time, when he had first come to the Ministry. Then every day had been new and challenging and every mortal's problem an opportunity for redemption. In those days it had seemed to him that he was making a real difference to the well-being of Humanity. He had felt that he was, in his own small way, helping to steer the souls in his care along the sure and certain path to Heaven.

But now... There was nothing special about this day. It could have been any routine day in Eternity. Neville pressed the NEXT button and a red-faced man appeared on the screen.

'Speak, my son, for your prayer is heard,' said Neville.

'That bastard, he's just cut me up. Fix him!' said the red-faced man.

'I'm sorry,' said Neville, 'but I don't know what you mean.'

'I mean,' said the red-faced man, speaking very slowly and one-word-at-a-time as if to an imbecile, 'that a fool in a Ford Capri has just cut into the lane in front of me. I want you to sort out the presumptuous idiot.'

'Has he harmed you?'

'No, of course he hasn't harmed me. But I had to jam on my brakes.

There could have been an accident. Now damn well sort him!'

'How would you like me to sort him?'

'Oh, kill him or something. You're a god, aren't you?'

'But if I kill him now his car will stop or veer into the path of the traffic coming towards you. Either you will have your journey interrupted or some innocent person will be hurt.'

'Kill his wife then. Or his kids. I don't care. Just make the creep suffer.'

'I am very sorry, but I can't do that. It's not in our joint service level agreement. You have to be a head of state or a Mafia don before you can have someone killed for you.'

'All right, bloody Holy Joe,' said the red-faced man. 'I suppose you think you're so effing moral. You bleeding heart liberals get right up my nose. Forget it – I'll deal with him myself.' And the screen went blank.

Neville sat back in his chair. He sighed and ran his hands through his hair. The digits on the display counted up; 51, 52, 53, 54 souls urgently needing his help. He shook his head mournfully, got up and walked slowly to the end of the office (whose walls were covered with perfect copies of the greatest masterpieces of human art) and stood by the window. The Glory of the Highest shone out from the Holy Citadel beyond, illuminating the streets and squares of Olympus with a living amber radiance. Such delight up here in Heaven. Such ugliness down below on Earth. The utmost beauty was here for him to enjoy, each and every day. It was his, forever. He felt a little sick.

The god Neville could stand it no longer. He opened the window and leapt into the golden air beyond. The ground rushed up towards him, bearing oblivion in its arms.

The reader may ask how this could possibly be; that a god would try to kill himself. That is a good question and one which Neville had not considered before he jumped from the ten thousand, six hundred and fifty-fifth floor of the Ministry of Mortality. Nor had he thought about what might come next, which is odd for someone who had positive proof of the existence of the afterlife.

It seemed to Neville that the discontent that had been festering within him was like a boil; nasty, unsightly, uncomfortable, but nothing to be worried about. The red-faced man's obscene demand was no more than the squeeze which had burst it. But if that was all it was, why did Neville not go and have a quiet word with his supervisor or take a couple of days' compassionate leave? It was this; that he knew that when he eventually returned to his desk it would be the same thing all over again – the flood-tide of human woe overwhelming the pathetic ramparts of belief – and that sooner or later he would crack again, and that all this would go on forever.

For what is Forever but another word for Despair?

Neville had not fallen more than half-way to the ground when the duty angel who had been patrolling the skies above shot past him in a power dive, opened his wings with a *swoosh* and a *crack*, and caught his plummeting body in their snow-white embrace. The angel spun in the air, wrapped his arms around Neville and carried him back up towards the tower-tops of downtown Olympus. The god gasped in shock. It looked as if his life was not going to end today after all. He felt breathless and not a little dizzy. It was too soon for him to feel relieved at his escape from destruction.

At first Neville thought that the angel would take him back to the window he had jumped from; then he thought he was being taken to the Divisional Manager's office for a good talking to. But the angel continued to climb, beating his wings against the supportive æther. Higher and higher they went, and as they ascended they changed direction so that they were flying away from the Ministry of Mortality and towards the Citadel itself. What could be going on? Was his offence so serious that it could not be dealt with by his immediate superior; an experienced sea-goddess with an excellent track record in the field of personnel management? Surely he was not being sent right to the Top?

The angel's wings dipped and rose in a steady rhythm. The fortifications of the Holiest Place came ever closer, bulking up in Neville's sight, and then slipping beneath him as he passed over their walls. He caught a quick glimpse of the battlements of Heaven, with their rows of spearmen, archers and grenadiers, and then they were descending again. They touched lightly on the ground and the angel released Neville. He looked around. They were standing in a high-windowed courtyard of polychrome granite. 'Over there,' the angel said, pointing to a gothic archway to the left. 'Go though.'

'Thank you,' said Neville, but the angel had gone and was already no more than a spark of living fire in the cerulean arch of the sky above. He shrugged. Angels were flighty creatures, weren't they?

Although he had all Eternity at his disposal, Neville realised that the Person he had been brought to see might not be very pleased to be kept waiting, so he walked quickly across the courtyard and under the archway. A long passage stretched ahead of him into the distance. There were oaken doors set into the walls at regular intervals. Was he meant to pass through one of them? If not, where should he go? He hesitated.

'Go all the way to the end,' cooed a soft voice at his right shoulder. Neville turned his head sharply and nearly dislodged the creature which had settled there. It was a dove – perhaps one of those which Neville had welcomed to his apartment.

'I'm sorry,' he said. 'I didn't know you were there. I wasn't trying to push you off. All the way? It looks like miles.' That was true. The corridor blurred into the distance. 'It's going to take a long time.'

'You had better start now, then,' said the dove.

Neville squared his shoulders and began to walk. The dove's presence was reassuring, for if she had not been there he would have felt very alone and – despite his godhood – very afraid.

'Am I in a great deal of trouble?' he asked the dove after a few minutes.

'That is not for me to say,' she replied.

'Why are you here? Are you my guide?'

'Yes, I am.'

'I am glad you are here to guide me, even though the corridor is so straight that I hardly need to be shown the way. Tell me, please...'

'Yes?' said the dove.

'I am a little lonesome, here in the Fortress of the Most High. I feel very small and not a little frightened. Will you stay with me when I meet whomsoever I have come here to meet? Will you speak for me? Will you be my friend?'

'Yes,' said the dove. 'That is why I am here.'

They walked together, and the dove rested the side of her head against Neville's cheek and opened her left wing and wrapped it around his shoulders. And so he was comforted.

They walked together down the corridor and came at last to a great gate, made of lapis lazuli and bound with gold and silver. An iron knocker hung down from it, crafted in the form of a unicorn's head. Neville took hold of the unicorn's horn, lifted it on its hinges and let it fall again. The gate boomed and shook with the impact and the sound reverberated up and down the passageway. Neville and the dove stood and waited for a response. Nothing happened for a very long time.

Then a small door which had been let into the great gate, but was so cunningly made that its seams were quite invisible, opened and a finger beckoned Neville and the dove to come in; which they did, ducking their heads slightly. They emerged on the other side. A void opened up before them – a void so vast that it was both unseeable and unknowable, so black that it was only after his eyes had adjusted to the darkness that Neville saw that it was sprinkled with planets, stars, nebulae and galaxies. He turned. The little door swung to and closed behind him. Neville gulped. Was this the Other Place? Had he been condemned to Hell for his crime? Was that not the fate of human suicides – would it not be his fate also?

'Courage,' said the dove, and kissed him gently on the cheek. Neville raised his hand and let it rest upon her velvet-soft head.

'Come along now,' said a voice. It belonged to the person who had opened the door. He reached into his pocket and pulled out an electric torch, which he clicked on. 'Hmm, now, where is it?' he said, directing the torch's beam around the ebony dome of the chamber. 'Aha!' he said. 'Here it is!' And he took a bronze key from a clip on his belt and inserted it into the image of a glorious violet-ringed planet. A door opened in space.

Neville and the dove followed the gatekeeper through the door and into a small office. It had faded green walls and was furnished with a desk, three dirty grey metal filing cabinets, a flip-chart with an electronic wiring diagram drawn on it in red marker, a white telephone, a somewhat elderly computer and two plastic chairs. The doorkeeper invited the god to take a seat. Neville sat down and the dove left his shoulder and perched on the desk next to him.

'Thank you,' said Neville to the gatekeeper. 'Will someone be along to see me shortly?' But he had gone.

Neville looked around the office. It was a scruffy room, well-used and much in need of redecoration. He took some solace from that. Clearly he was not here to meet someone of any great importance. Whoever used this office could not be a very senior person and would surely not have the authority to hand down a severe punishment to him. But then he remembered that the most dreadful torments in the worlds of men were often inflicted by the most junior officials. It had not been Adolf Hitler who had operated the gas-ovens of Belsen, but the privates and corporals of the Waffen SS. The tortures of the Spanish Inquisition had not been administered by the cardinals of the Roman Catholic Church, but by working priests in their service. Perhaps the poor condition of the room reflected his own lowly status, and not that of his judges. This shabby place was probably quite good enough for him.

Neville picked up the telephone's handset and put it to his ear. There was no dialling tone. not even after he rattled the cradle rest. He replaced the receiver. Would it be worth trying to log on to the computer? No, probably not.

'Dove?' he said. 'Is this it? Is this my punishment?' A terrible thought had struck Neville. Perhaps he was being punished already. He would have to stay in this office forever, kept waiting for all Eternity. But no, that could not be it...

'No,' said the dove. 'Not while I am here.'

'Not while you are here to be my friend. And to look after me. To love me... Oh, wait a minute. Yes, I see...' Why had he not realised before?

'You know it now, then,' said the winged being whose name was Love.

At last he did. He knelt and did obeisance to the Dove and begged forgiveness of Her. His tears fell freely upon the scratched and marked linoleum which covered the office floor.

'That was a terrible thing you did,' said the Dove presently. 'To throw away the gift I gave you.'

'My life, you mean. Yes, it was an awful thing to do. I am truly sorry. You know that.'

'Yes. I have always known it, but you had to say it yourself.'

'It was my heart that told me. It knew the truth before I did.'

'That is often the way.'

'What shall I do now?' A cup of tea had appeared on the desk and Neville, feeling more composed now, took a sip. It was made from the finest high-altitude Darjeeling and was utterly refreshing. 'I don't think I could go back to the Ministry. Not yet, anyway. Do I presume too much, Ma'am?' He looked anxiously at the Dove.

'No, Neville. You should not go back. You see, I think that your talents were possibly not being used to their full advantage there.'

'Perhaps, Most High, I could take a less demanding job? There must be any number of administrative tasks that need doing. Building maintenance? Gardening, maybe?'

'Due humility is one thing, my son. Dodging your responsibilities is quite another. Is that not where we came in? With you trying to duck out of doing the work I gave you?'

'Yes, Ma'am. I'm sorry, Ma'am.' Neville bowed his head. The Dove continued:

'There is a bargain – a compact – between men and us. It is this – to reward prayer with reconciliation, worship with transcendence, trust with certainty. Men and gods – we need each other equally. Neither of us could exist if it were not for the other. Do you see?'

'Yes, Most High, I do.'

'Now; this bargain is sealed with Duty. When Time began, men and gods took a Duty upon themselves, to serve each other in the best way they could. It is in this that you erred, Neville. You failed in your Duty to the souls in your care. You left them with no access to us, alone in their world. That is a grievous sin for a god to commit.

'But I forgive it, as I forgive all sins, because I know why it was that you failed. It lay in this, my son, that you felt the sorrows of men so deeply, and took them so much to heart that you could see no end to them. Is that not right?'

'Yes, Ma'am.' The Dove was very beautiful. Neville could hardly bear to look at Her, but neither could he take his eyes off Her.

'You feel in a *special* way, Neville and in a way that's not so very unlike the way I do. You understand belief, not as an intellectual does, but in your heart. You know of its weakness, and in that understanding lies your strength.

'Neville, I have a job for you. A very special job. You know that there are many worlds in the Multiverse. Some of them are fine places in which to live, many are only tolerably good. Some are poor, and a few are very bad indeed. They resemble the Other Place. They are abominable worlds, my son. They are all the worse because they have been made abominable by the very people that they were given to. I did not want these worlds to turn out the way they did, but there it is.

'But that is not the worst thing about these worlds. The people who live in them suffer, true, but so do people in many of the worlds of the Multiverse, even those we call blessed. No, the worst thing is that they are alone. They can no longer speak to us, nor we to them. The link between men and gods has been broken. We can no longer reach them or help them, and they have lost touch with us and turned against themselves. They are sealed in. Their world has closed in on them and become their prison.'

The god shuddered at the Dove's words. He could picture such a world all too easily. How dreadful it would be to find himself in such an awful place... He felt even more the magnitude of his offence. He too had left his people alone.

'There's a particular world out there – a world of terrible suffering and desolation. It is a world that has lost its way. They need someone to help them, Neville, the souls who live in that world. Someone to Save them. Could that be you? Would you do this thing for Me? Will you be these people's Saviour?'

'Most High, do you mean...?'

'Yes. If you can find it within yourself, I want you to let go of your godhood for a while and enter this world. I want you to become one of its people. I want you to try to restore the relationship between the men of that world and us.'

'But...'

'It is very likely that they will not want to listen to you. They will probably hurt you. They may even try to murder you. But Neville, there is no other of My children that I would rather send in your place. No one whose heart does not feel the pain of mortality more keenly. None that I love more. Will you go and live with the men of this world and be one of them for a short span of Time? Will you let them torture and kill you, for My sake? Will you suffer and die for them?'

Neville managed a lop-sided smile. 'Is that all You want of me?'

'There will be no end to what I want of you, and that is something of which you should be very glad. But it is all I want from you for now. Will you do it for Me? Please?'

Work continued as ever in the Ministry of Mortality, following its endless daily pattern. Every morning the household gods on the day shift arrived by car, tram, bicycle or on foot, sat down at their desks and took their calls, and handed over to the evening shift when their day's labours were done. At the end of the office the Calls Waiting board counted its digits up and counted them down again as the tide of the sorrows of men ebbed and flowed in its eternal rhythm. The toil of the Ministry's staff was constant and unremitting.

Busy, busy, busy... The desks were all busy, except for one. One special desk – positioned at the end of the twenty-third row of the forty-second rank of the thirty-seventh tier – remained empty and unused, fenced off by a rope of soft, braided silk. It was a kind of shrine.

For the gods had found that they missed Neville much more than they had thought they would, so they kept his desk free against his return and whenever they passed it they stopped and bowed their heads and were quiet for a moment. Neville's headset lay unworn on the desk's walnut top and his screen was dark and cold. Next to it someone had placed a small wooden cross, and twined about that cross there grew a single red rose.

234

ANOTHER PLACE

Another Place

BY THE TIME MELANIE ROBERTS CHECKED IN TO THE NORTH Midlands Airport DriveInn it was a quarter to ten in the evening. She was exhausted, so it was more of a relief than a disappointment to find that her arrival was registered by a computer rather than a human being. It made no real difference – either would have followed the same robotic script – but she could work out her frustration on a machine in ways that would be socially unacceptable if directed at a person. She was in a foul temper after a bad planning meeting and the stop-start journey from the office to the hotel had not improved her mood.

'Thank you, bellend,' she said to the machine's display as it returned her credit card and disgorged a magnetic key to Room 406. 'And if you've put me next to the lift shaft, I'll be back, I promise.' She stuffed the key and the credit card into her purse, picked up her overnight bag and crossed the purple-carpeted lobby floor to the elevators. Unseen and unheard, the check-in system wished her a good tonight and a great tomorrow.

Despite her irritation, Melanie had taken a certain pride in managing her interaction with the register quickly and efficiently. There had been no queue of weary hotel guests building up behind her, no impatient muttering at her time-wasting female ineptitude. Get it done, get it right, don't mess about. That was the way she went about her business.

The key carried the slogan *Sweet Dreams, Miles of Smiles*™ embossed on the back in corporate script. It slipped easily into the door lock, a LED glowed green and the latch clicked. Melanie pushed the door open and lugged her bag after herself into Room 406. The light turned on automatically, revealing a standard-grade room decorated in the same mauve-and-green colour scheme as downstairs. Someone had once told her that the reason chain hotels were so garishly tasteless was to prevent the guests from being tempted to make off with the contents of the bedrooms. Those that weren't screwed down, at any rate.

Melanie dropped her bag on the bed and considered her options. Should she take a shower, go to bed, and let the TV lull her to sleep, or just leave her stuff and go down to the bar? She was feeling so tired and a nightcap might help relieve the accumulated stresses of the day. A double cognac would be just the thing and she could probably slip it through her expenses without anyone noticing, not even that suspicious cow Harriet Smyth in Accounts. On the other hand, she needed to check through her PowerPoint for tomorrow's Amsterdam meeting and you met some pretty obnoxious characters in late-night hotel bars. That decided her. She had had quite enough bad experiences with off-the-leash middle-aged sales managers.

The shower was hot and sufficiently forceful to sluice away the grime of the day. Melanie dried herself off with the room's sole bath-towel (Only one towel? In a double room? That would be going on the feedback form), pulled on cotton pyjamas, got into bed and fired up her laptop. Just one last run through her presentation and a final check on the next quarter's forecast. Oh, and set the alarm on her phone. That was her checklist before turning in. Fail to prepare, prepare to fail. Get it done, get it right, don't mess about.

Sleep came easily. Tomorrow would be a busy day, but Melanie thrived on busy days, and she no longer allowed the prospect of hard work and tough negotiations to disturb her rest. She had done her preparation, she was ready, she knew what she was doing.

Melanie woke in broad daylight and immediately realised that something had gone badly wrong. It should still be dark. She should have been up hours ago. She checked her watch. Nine-thirty. Her flight was due to leave at half-past ten. How could she have forgotten to set her alarm? Oh shit, shit, shit!

She had one hour to make her flight. It was barely, just barely, possible. She had once caught a plane within fifteen minutes of reaching the airport. Her boarding card was ready-printed in her bag. If there was no security alert, if the airport wasn't clogged with clueless holidaymakers and their screaming brats, if the departure gate wasn't somewhere out in the boondocks, she could still do it. Melanie threw on last night's clothes, grabbed her bag and crashed out of the door. No time to wait for the lift – she flung herself down the stairs and into the lobby. Fifty minutes left. Still possible, but probably not if she had to find somewhere to park at the airport. She'd have to take a cab. There was a phone in the lobby. She lifted the receiver and tried to dial the taxi firm whose number was prominently displayed above it. No answer. She rattled the phone. No dial tone.

'Fuck!' Melanie dropped the receiver on the floor. She'd have to chance the airport car park after all. It could still be done. The taxi would probably have been late arriving anyway. No good calling them on her mobile. She ran out of the door and hared across the car park to her car. Knowing her luck today she'd have dropped her keys somewhere or left the lights on. A flat battery would really sink her. But no, the doors unlocked and the lights flashed and the engine started. At last something was working right.

Forty-five minutes to go. Melanie smoked the tyres out of her parking space, narrowly missing a Mondeo on one side and a Vectra on the other. She floored it down the narrow road to the exit. There was a barrier. 'Open!' she shouted. She wound down her window and pressed the button under the speaker grille. 'Could you open the barrier please?'

No answer. Melanie thumped the grille. Still nothing. Then she saw it. There was a notice: INSERT TOKEN TO EXIT, and beneath it: TOKENS AVAILABLE AT RECEPTION.

Damn. That had probably finished her. Forty-two minutes to departure. But the plane might be late leaving. They might hold it for her. She couldn't quit now. Melanie backed up to the hotel entrance and dashed into the lobby. Just like last night there were no staff on reception. Would there be a supply of tokens, on a plate, perhaps, or in a jar? No. Nothing.

At this point Melanie came close to giving up. But… there was a bell push on the desk, so she leaned on it. And waited. And leaned on it again. And felt the panic that had been surging through her begin to subside as her hopes of catching her plane receded and she started to think about alternatives. She needed a Plan B. Should she give up, return to the office and phone into the meeting? Or do it from the hotel, so nobody back at base would know how badly she'd fouled up? Or take a later flight and try to reschedule the rest of the day? After all, most of the real work on these foreign jaunts was done in the bar afterwards. The rest was mere box-ticking. But boxes were still important, and they still needed to be ticked.

Thirty-seven minutes left, and at last someone answered the bell. A man wearing a DriveInn uniform appeared through a door behind the desk. 'Good morning,' he said. 'How may I help you today?'

'Car park token,' Melanie said. 'I need a token. Could you give me a token please?'

'Token, token,' said the man. 'Oh, yes. Just a moment. They're round the back. With you in a minute.' He disappeared through the door.

Five minutes later, at thirty-two minutes to take-off, he returned. 'Sorry to keep you,' he said. 'I thought we'd run out, but I've had a bit of luck and found you one in the back of a drawer. Here.' He held out an aluminium disc. Melanie took it.

'Thank you,' she called over her shoulder.

Her car had been blocked in by a wheelie bin, but after some frantic manoeuvring she extricated herself and drove back to the barrier. She inserted the token and the machine swallowed it with a solid clunk. The barrier rose. At last; now if the traffic wasn't too bad… Melanie let out the clutch and pressed her foot on the gas.

The car stalled. It did that sometimes. No panic. Just depress the clutch and turn the key. The starter motor spun, but the engine didn't fire. Try again. Whirr-whirr-whirr. Again. Whirr-whirr-whirr. And at last the motor caught. Melanie revved it hard to stop it stalling again.

And the barrier lowered. It had timed out to prevent tailgaters slipping out behind bona-fide guests and stealing free parking from the hotel.

The man was still behind the desk when Melanie returned. 'I'm sorry,' she said, not feeling at all apologetic, 'but I need another token. The barrier lowered before I could get out.'

'That's odd. People don't usually have problems with the barrier.'

'I stalled it, OK?'

'I see. Just a minute, I'll try to find another one for you.' He disappeared again.

Another five minutes later, with twenty-five minutes left until departure time, he came back with a shake of his head. 'Sorry,' he said, 'but we're all out of tokens. Tell you what, though, I've got a code that'll open the barrier for you. I can't give it to you, but if you take me out there I'll sort it.'

'Oh, thank you,' said Melanie. Could this state of affairs get any more humiliating if it tried? She must look ridiculous – face flustered, hair everywhere, rumpled clothes, no make-up – to this little DriveInn employee in his green and purple uniform, his white shirt and his chrome tie pin. They went out to her car.

'Lexus, isn't it? My brother's got one of these,' said the man. 'Diesel. Very economical to run. Goes well, too.'

When they reached the barrier, the man got out and tapped a long list of numbers into a keypad. The barrier rose. 'There you go then.' He gave her the thumbs-up. 'Have a great today!'

The car lurched forward and stalled. The barrier fell and landed on the bonnet with a metallic thump.

'Never mind,' said the man. 'I expect it'll polish out.' He leaned in at the driver's side window. 'There's your problem,' he said, pointing to the dials. 'You're out of petrol. See?'

Yes, she was out of petrol.

'Do you have any petrol I could buy?'

'Sorry, madam. We're a hotel, not a garage.'

Back in the hotel, Melanie hauled her bag into the coffee shop and ordered a late breakfast. It looked as if the establishment had a staff of only one, or maybe it was run by twins, because the man who took her order looked exactly like the one on the reception desk. She glanced at his name badge. He was a Keith, apparently. Now, time to get on the phone while the Keith fussed about with juice cartons, coffee pots and toast racks. Had she thought about it, Melanie might have realised he was doing her a favour. Breakfast at places like the North Midlands Airport DriveInn was usually a self-service affair.

Ten-thirty passed and her plane left on schedule. Melanie took out her phone. There were some awkward calls for her to make. Her idea, she realised, of phoning Amsterdam directly was out of the window. She'd only show herself up in front of the customer, and that'd be goodbye to the performance-related pay rise she'd been hoping for. Actually, after this fiasco she'd be lucky if the firm let her operate the photocopier. But the best thing now was to phone home and get them to send a deputy or postpone the meeting. They could say she'd been taken ill. She keyed in the office number. Best get it over with. But there was no reply, and when she looked at her phone there were no bars. The battery was OK – at least she hadn't forgotten to charge it – but there was no signal. What? No signal in the vicinity of an airport? In a transit hotel? Just a minute... She'd heard stories about hotels jamming mobile frequencies to force guests to use their overpriced room phones.

'Keith!' The little man came running up. 'I can't get a signal. You wouldn't know anything about that, would you?'

'No. I'm sorry, madam. Our guests don't usually have any problems. Are you sure your phone is all right? Topped up and all?'

'Yes, of course I'm sure.' But all the same, perhaps she could ask to borrow someone else's phone. She looked around. The coffee shop was empty, except for Keith and herself. In fact she hadn't seen another living soul all morning. Or last night, for all that.

'Keith? You don't mind if I call you Keith?'

'Not at all, madam.'

'There's something funny about this place.'

'I sometimes think that too, madam.'

'I know I had half a tankful in the car when I got here last night. Are you sure there aren't petrol thieves in your car park?'

'Can't really be sure of anything, madam.'

'And my phone doesn't work. The phone in the lobby doesn't work either. Does your phone work?'

'Last time I tried, it did.'

'May I borrow it?'

'It's against the rules. But… all right. Bring your cup into the office.'

Melanie picked up her coffee and followed Keith into a small room, fitted out with wood-effect furniture and crammed with piles of emergency sewing kits, hair shampoo, toilet tissue and towels. Oh yes, she was going to complain about the towels. Not now, though, because there was a phone which buzzed expectantly when she picked up the receiver. She dialled and, thank god, got through.

'I'll leave you to it,' Keith said. He closed the door behind him.

'Hello, this is Melanie Roberts. Can you put me through to Brian Davies?' Brian was her boss. Best to get the hardest part over first.

'I'm sorry, Mr Davies is out.'

'Julia Henry?'

'Ms Henry is out too.'

'Adrian Wordle?'

'Gone to Glasgow.'

'Jaz Saleem?'

'Not taking calls.'

Melanie was stumped. 'Is there anybody from Product Development in today?'

'I'm sorry, they're all out. Can I take a message for you?'

'No. No, don't worry about it.'

'Thank you.' The line clicked. Melanie put the phone down.

Keith's head popped around the door. 'Did you get through OK?'

'Yes. No. I'm going to... to walk to the airport. It's not far.'

'It can be dangerous, madam. The roads are busy. Better to get a bus. Every hour, on the hour. Go out of the entrance, fifty yards down to your left. You can't miss it. Oh, and that's ten pounds fifty for breakfast. Shall I charge it?'

A quarter past one and Melanie staggered back into the lobby of the DriveInn. She was shattered. Two hours of carrying a heavy bag up and down access roads that ended in dead ends, of waiting for buses that never came, of flagging taxis that didn't stop. She hadn't got within a mile of the airport. Keith rushed out from behind the reception desk. 'Ms Roberts! You're back!'

'Yes.' *Yes, I'm back.*

'Didn't you catch your bus?'

'No.' *What does it fucking look like? Would I be standing here like a drivelling idiot if I'd caught the fucking bus?*

'I'm sorry. People don't usually have any problems catching the bus.'

'Oh, shut up! Shut up with your "people don't usually have any problems" you brainless little squit!'

'I'm sorry, madam. Would you like something to drink?'

'A glass of water, please.'

'I'll bring you one in the coffee shop. Don't worry about your luggage. I'll take care of it.'

Melanie dumped her bag on the bed in Room 406. She sat down next to it and, now that she was by herself, buried her head in her hands and cried. Cried until the tears ran between her fingers and dripped onto the purple counterpane of the king-size bed.

I'm forty-eight years old. I'm a successful product development executive. I'm competent. Actually, I'm better than competent, I'm bloody good. I've fought my way up to a senior position on the basis of ability and sheer hard work. They were going to make me a VP next year. Why is all this happening to me? I shouldn't have to put up with this kind of shit any more!'

A hot bath made things better. A change of clothes made them better still. She got her laptop out of her bag, opened it and stood it on the desk next to the television. It picked up the hotel Wi-Fi straight away and she logged in to the Internet. There. She was more than half-way back to normality already. She could read her emails and, more importantly, send some. Something could still be salvaged from the wreckage of the day.

But there was something funny about the Internet. She could read her emails, but she couldn't send any. The server connection was denied. She tried her Facebook. Yes, that was OK, but she couldn't post on her wall or make any comments. Twitter seemed to be blocking her messages. LinkedIn looked like it had forgotten about her.

She picked up the room phone. 'Hello? How can I help you?' It was Keith, of course.

'The Internet's not working properly.'

'That's funny. People don't usually —'

'Have any problems accessing the Internet. I know. Tell me, Keith, can I get something to eat?'

'The coffee shop is open from six-thirty am to eleven-thirty pm daily. We have an exciting grill menu, also salads, seafood and Chicago-style pizzas. Would you like to order?'

'I'll come down.'

There being apparently no other guests in the hotel – perhaps it was still too early and the overnighters would start to turn up in another hour or two – Keith was happy to sit with Melanie while she ate a gourmet cheeseburger and side salad. He brought her a glass of sparkling water to help it go down and pointed out the wide variety of tasty relishes available on the serving counter.

'Funny about your car,' he said. 'Must be something wrong with the fuel sensor.' When Melanie returned it to the car park the gauge had shown half-full, just as she'd expected. Her attempt at calling someone out to look at it had been just as unsuccessful as all her other attempts at connecting with the world beyond the hotel. Nobody could come for at least two days. There'd been a bad crash on the M42 last night and there were still hundreds of wrecked cars with children and old people in them who needed rescuing. She seemed to be stuck for the moment.

Soon they'll be wondering where I am. I won't have turned up in Amsterdam, but the office will know I tried to get in touch. Wait – no they won't. I didn't say who I was when I called. How daft was that?

So the last anyone knew of her was when she left the office yesterday. Nobody was going to do anything serious about finding where she'd got to for at least a couple of days. Some people vanished for weeks without anybody noticing they'd gone. People who'd been murdered, or who had died alone. Messages would be piling up in her voicemail, but that wouldn't help if she couldn't read them or respond to them.

Ah! She had a brainwave. She'd got herself too wrapped up in technology. Snail mail! She could write a letter, put a first-class stamp on it and post it to the office. The hotel must get post. Even if she couldn't find a letterbox, she could ask Keith to give it to the postman. She mentioned it to him.

He shook his head. 'Sorry, madam, but all our post is internal. It comes from the depot in Chesterfield, on the supply lorry. We're not allowed to send private post through the company system. It's against policy.'

Policy! It's against policy! Don't talk to me about policy, you funny little Keith with your funny little balding head and the hairs poking out of your funny little nose. I write my company's policies! I know all about them.

'Would you like me to bring you another towel?' said Keith.

Melanie was sitting in her room watching the television when there was a knock at the door. 'Only me,' said Keith. He was standing in the corridor holding a stack of white towels in his outstretched arms.

'Thank you. Do come in.'

Keith entered the room and put the towels down next to the complimentary teas, coffees and shortbread biscuits.

'Thanks. I only wanted one, but thanks.'

'Glad to help. Is there anything else I can get you?'

'I'll be needing something to eat later.'

'The coffee shop's open until eleven-thirty pm and we have a distinctive range of beers, wines, cocktails and soft drinks in the bar.'

'I'll be down in a while.'

'OK.' Keith pointed to the television. 'We have a channel showing movie classics and all the latest releases, and there is adult entertainment available after ten o'clock tonight, for a small supplementary charge.'

'Thank you.'

It was after he'd gone that Melanie remembered that she'd only intended to complain about the towels once she'd left the hotel.

Later she went down to the restaurant and chose a chicken Caesar salad and a bottle of Cabernet Sauvignon. Keith brought the food over to her solitary corner table. He declined her offer of a glass of wine.

'Not when I'm on duty, madam, thanks all the same.'

He also refused to call her Melanie, again citing company policy.

She had been too frazzled to notice it earlier, but the food was remarkably good – much better than you might expect to find in an identikit hotel where the menus were created in a centralised kitchen and subject to strict portion and cost control. She wondered who had cooked it.

The restaurant and bar were deserted. No guests had arrived while she'd been upstairs in Room 406, or if they had they were keeping strictly to themselves, and while the car park was full of vehicles of all kinds there were no sounds of televisions playing, baths running, people speaking or toilets flushing. Nobody banged their luggage against the fire doors, no lifts rose and fell. There was nothing but the gentle hum of the air-conditioning and the clatter of a loose extractor fan in the bathroom. Perhaps everybody who'd been staying at the hotel had gone off on the same charter flight and all the usual staff – chambermaids, housekeeper, maintenance man, receptionists, night porter – had been laid off until their guests returned from Lanzerote, Minorca or Sharm el-Sheikh.

'Keith!'

The man came over to her table. 'Yes, Ms Roberts?'

'I'm curious. How did you know my name? That first time?'

'You registered under it, madam.'

'But I could have been someone else.'

'But you weren't, madam.'

'Do sit down.'

'Thank you.'

'Are you the only staff here at the moment?'

'Yes, madam.'

'So you're the manager.'

'Duty manager, madam.'

'But you're in charge.'

'Yes, madam.'

'Well, could you please pass my compliments to the chef? This is very good.' Melanie realised how silly this sounded as soon as she said it. Keith didn't seem to notice.

'Thank you, madam. I will, madam. Would you like to see the dessert menu? The tarte tatin is popular or we have low-calorie chocolate ice-cream if you prefer.'

'Tarte tatin, please.'

'Coming right up, madam. Coffee to follow?'

'Yes please.'

That night, the calm which had settled over Melanie during the evening began to crack and fray. The veneer of normality flaked away and in the close-curtained darkness of Room 406 her situation's underlying oddity became ever more apparent, and then threatening. After a sleepless three hours she turned on the light, got out of bed and watched television. When that bored her, she tried to read a book on her laptop. Between paragraphs she thought about what she should do tomorrow. For she had to do something. To do nothing was not in her nature. She hadn't got where she was by doing nothing.

Melanie woke in broad daylight. Her watch said it was half-past ten. She was in bed, which surprised her, because she was sure she'd fallen asleep in her chair, although she had no idea of when that had been. No matter, although she expected she'd pay for it later in aching joints. Sleepless nights led to confused days, she'd found, and bad decisions. She had made enough bad decisions yesterday. Today she would have to get everything right. So; slow and steady. Don't rush. Rushing was for yesterday morning, when she was still trying to get to her meeting. Today, she could take her time. All she had to do was have a shower, eat breakfast and drive slowly and carefully home. There she could relax and start to plan her recovery from this ghastly shambles.

Keith greeted her in the coffee shop. 'Good afternoon, Ms Roberts!' he said. 'Fancy a spot of late lunch?'

Late lunch? Breakfast, more like. Melanie checked the time. Half-past two. What? She looked up. The wall clock agreed with her watch.

'I could run you up a toasted sandwich,' said Keith. 'Ham and cheese? Minute steak and onions? Half of lager with it?'

'Thank you,' said Melanie and sat down. 'Steak sounds good.'

The sandwich was savoury and delicious, the lager was cold and refreshing, and when Melanie returned to her room at half-past seven she was ready for a little snooze. She lay on top of the duvet and dozed off. At ten o'clock she stirred herself, brushed her teeth and got into bed where she slept but fitfully.

Melanie woke in broad daylight. She took a shower, got dressed and went downstairs. Keith was waiting by the lift. 'Good morning, Ms Roberts. Breakfast? We've got some beautiful haddock in today. Arbroath Smokies, they are, direct from Scotland. I could poach a pair for you, or you could eat them cold. Yes? You'd like some? Wholemeal toast and coffee? Fruit juice? I could squeeze a fresh mango for you.'

'Yes, thank you. That sounds very nice.'

After breakfast, Melanie took the lift to the first floor. Starting at Room 102 she knocked at every door in turn and waited for an answer. She even knocked on the service hatches and cupboards. Then she walked up a floor and did the same. Room 201 to 256. No answer.

No answer. Seems to be the story of my life.

She repeated the process on the third floor, with the same results.

Finally she tried every door on the fourth floor. And at last she got a reply. 'Come in!'

The door opened and she walked in.

Oh.

It was *her* room – Room 406 – and it was Keith who had let her in. He was holding a duster in his right hand and there was a mound of sheets and pillowcases heaped up in the far corner, next to the window. 'Hello Ms Roberts. I'm just making up your room. I hope you don't mind.'

'No, I don't mind.'

'If you'd like to wait downstairs? There's coffee in the machine. Help yourself – I won't tell anyone if you don't.'

'All right.' Melanie turned and walked downstairs.

Damn him! Damn him to hell! Damn all insignificant little Keiths! Useless jobsworths, the lot of them. She'd get out of this, whatever it took. She'd do it with, or more likely without, the help of this time-serving drone. She'd work it out herself, the way she always had. Plan A, Plan B or Plan Z, it made little difference. And that night she thought of something.

* * *

Melanie woke early. It was still dark. Good! Now the scheme she'd thought up at a wakeful three o'clock that morning had a chance of working. She dressed herself quickly, picked up her bag and tiptoed out of the room, being careful not to let the door bang. To take the lift was out of the question, so she crept down the stairs and, reaching the door at the bottom, opened it gradually and peered into the lobby. There were probably CCTV cameras and infrared sensors hidden there, but she would have to take that chance. If she moved very slowly she might not trigger them.

Melanie knew the barrier would block her car, and there was no way she was going to try walking to the airport again. However, there was another possibility. Keeping her face to the wall, she shuffled crabwise around the lobby until she reached the main doors. Would they be locked? If so, she would have to find another way out of the hotel – through the kitchen, maybe, or perhaps there would be a window in Keith's office. But no – the door opened when she pushed against it. Surely an alarm would go off now? Apart from anything else, the management would want to know when people entered and left the hotel although, it struck Melanie, with every room being paid for in advance they had no need to worry about moonlight flits. She imagined a bell sounding in the office or in Keith's bedroom, wherever that might be. Assuming, that was, that he slept at all.

OK, she was outside now. Where should she wait? There must be a goods inwards entrance or a loading bay. Somewhere she would find the lorry that delivered supplies and internal post from the depot in Chesterfield.

It was cold and still dark. Melanie let the backwash from the sodium lights that illuminated the facade of the hotel guide her round the ground floor. She didn't want to risk straying into the car park, where there would definitely be security cameras, so she kept close to the building. The ground next to it was planted with the same kind of spiny bushes that protected the boundaries of motorway service stations. They tore at her tights and snagged on her skirt, pulling threads. At least she'd had the sense to drive in flatties. She was wearing them now; her heels were safely stowed in her bag.

Round she edged, and at last she found a wide stretch of tarmac with a concrete platform next to it. A pair of metal doors stood above the platform with a hasp and a large padlock linking them. This must be the right place. All she had to do now was wait and try to keep awake. She should hide somewhere – yes, there was a clump of bushes next to the perimeter fence. The driver wouldn't see her if she kept her face out of sight and she'd be able to slip into the back of the lorry while he unloaded it. She wouldn't try begging a ride in the cab. Too risky – the driver might turn her in – and apart from anything else she'd read stories in the newspapers about what happened to unaccompanied women in lorries. She crossed the tarmac and concealed herself. She checked her watch. Seven twenty-eight. OK, she might only have to wait a few minutes, or it might be several hours. The sooner the better, though. Keith would miss her when she didn't come down to breakfast and he might come looking for her. He'd probably check the CCTV tapes. She just had to hold on patiently and hope for the best…

Shit! She'd fallen asleep, and now she was colder than ever and had a bad cramp in her side. But – thank heaven – there was the truck that had woken her. It had backed up to the loading platform and its rear doors were open. Right. This was her chance. Where was the driver? She had to know where he was. Ah. A uniformed man emerged from the inside of the hotel with a hand trolley. He pushed it onto the truck's tailgate and disappeared inside, reappearing a minute later with a pallet loaded up with cornflakes and toilet rolls. Melanie gave him fifteen seconds, then sprinted across the loading bay, hauled herself up onto the platform and threw herself into the back of the truck. There must be somewhere to hide… yes! There, in a corner by a stack of milk cartons. She crouched behind them and ducked her head. She stopped breathing.

Ten minutes later, they were on the road. At last! Just hold on and wait until the truck's next stop. She'd be out of the back of it before the driver knew what was happening. She'd dial 999 and if the driver made a fuss she'd threaten to tell the police he'd been harassing her. How long would that be? Chesterfield was in Derbyshire; that couldn't be more than thirty minutes away. Forty minutes at the most. That was good, because she hadn't appreciated that the lorry would be refrigerated. She was already feeling colder than ever.

It was more like an hour and a half, as it turned out. The nerve-fraying whine of the truck's gears came to a halt, the boom of its exhaust ceased, it stopped its sick-making swaying from side to side. OK. This was it. Melanie pulled herself upright, praying that her legs hadn't seized up with the cold. The lock rattled and the doors opened with a clang. She got ready to run and jump.

But it was no use. No use at all. A complete waste of time and effort. For there was a concerned-looking Keith, holding out his hand to support her.

'Oh, Ms Roberts, you poor thing! You look frozen half to death. Come in and have a warm. I'll light a fire in the bar. You could do with a hot toddy. Your clothes are in a bit of a state, if you don't mind my saying so. If you let me have them later I'll see what I can do about tidying them up. Do a bit of darning, run an iron over them. I'll give you a spare duvet to wrap yourself in.'

There was Melanie, and there was Keith. Little Keith, with his comb-over and his piggy eyes and his nasal Brummie drone, and his badly-fitting uniform and, most infuriating of all, his endless kindness and consideration. One more than usually exasperating day she tried calling him Fuckwit. Continually, all day – hello Fuckwit, goodbye Fuckwit, bring me a glass of iced tea, Fuckwit. He smiled and called her Ms Roberts, and was as helpful and attentive as ever. And it wasn't he who pointed out the notice behind the reception desk that reminded guests that verbal or physical abuse of the employees of DriveInn plc was subject to a zero-tolerance policy and could lead to a denial of accommodation and possible prosecution.

One day she had a flash of genius. There was an inch of lipstick left in her handbag. She stood on a chair and wrote on the window:

But, and it was inevitable, she supposed, Keith wiped it off with a damp cloth. It would attract the birds, he said, and they would leave white streaks all over the outside wall. The glass was smeary for the next day or two.

She undid the top buttons of her blouse one evening and let her skirt ride up when she sat down. Keith paid no attention to her dishabille, but merely offered her a rare malt whisky on the house. She trashed her room, but all that happened was that she had to spend the night in Room 404 instead. (It was the mirror image of Room 406; a symmetry she found strangely unsettling.) She tripped herself and woke at the foot of the staircase, to find Keith fussing about with a sling and a bottle of soluble aspirin. One particularly bad day she took off all her clothes and ran up and down the corridors, shrieking at the top of her voice and banging on the doors. Another day she squatted on the reception desk and fouled it with her excrement. But however badly she behaved, it made no difference to Keith. He quietly tidied up the messes she made and asked if there was anything she needed or if there was anything he could do for her. She had long conversations with him but she never discovered a thing about Keith's background, or his family, or his upbringing, or even his employment history with DriveInn plc.

If she'd had Internet – real working two-way Internet – Melanie would have started a blog. As it was she could only write down her experiences at the North Midlands Airport DriveInn in a Word file on her laptop. Perhaps she would publish it some day, the way that call-girl had. As it was she tried to keep a diary, but after the first week of her stay she realised that every day was so like every other day that any potential reader would lose interest after the first few pages. So she soon gave it up and all that was recorded in it, apart from a detailed account of those first two or three days when things still seemed to be happening in order and with some sense of sequence and progression, was a list of the films she had watched and, for a while, what she had had to eat:

The Third Man (Where is he, anyway?)
Sole Véronique
Fantasia (Trippy!)
2001(Trippier!)
Mystic Pizza
Beef Wellington (Fab!)
Groundhog Day (Ho-ho, very funny!)
Flash Gordon (Saviour of the Universe!)
Chicken Tikka Masala
Ding-Dong (That's what they call adult entertainment around here?)
Prawn Cocktail

The Bride of Frankenstein (I know how she feels)
Beef Chow Mein (Yum!)
Aguirre, Wrath of God (What the hell was that all about?)
The Magic Roundabout
Fried Green Tomatoes at the Whistle Stop Café
The Matrix (Is that what's actually going on here?)
I Know Where I'm Going (If only!)
Fish fingers, beans and chips
The Prisoner

'Keith,' Melanie said one day. 'Have you heard of something called the Stockholm Syndrome?'

'I'm not sure I have, madam.' Keith was stuffing brochures into the tourist attractions rack. 'What's it about? Not something nasty, I hope, like a disease.'

'No, not really. No, it's what sometimes happens when someone is kidnapped. You'd think if someone took you hostage you'd hate your captors, especially if they did awful things to you, like locking you away in a dark room or starving you.'

'Hate... that's a strange thing, Ms Roberts. I'm not sure I understand hate.'

'But you'd not be very fond of them, would you, even if they treated you decently. And suppose they were on the other side – in a war or something?'

'I'm not sure I understand war, either.'

'Oh Keith! What are you like! Look, what I'm trying to say is that there's this thing called the Stockholm Syndrome where people in a hostage scenario start to take on the mindset of their warders. Join their side, identify with them. It's rather unexpected, don't you think?'

'There are many things we don't expect, madam. There, that's finished!' Keith stood back and admired his work. 'Would you like a cup of tea? I'm just about to put the kettle on.'

Whether it was due to her previous failures, or because she had somehow lost interest, Melanie made no further attempts to escape. Of course, escape might not have been the right word. She knew that nobody would stop her walking out of the door, but that there was probably no point in doing so. She knew it was no good trying to phone or send letters and when she asked Keith to call her a cab he told her it was more than his job was worth to do so, in case the taxi driver turned out to be a criminal. 'Security, madam,' he said with a smile. 'Gets in the way, it does. That, and health'n'safety. Bane of my life, Ms Roberts, bane of my life.'

She spent a lot of time, insofar as time had any meaning in this place, lying on her bed and trying to remember her old life outside the North Midlands Airport DriveInn. She'd had a job and a nice flat with a riverside location. Friends – yes, she'd had friends and the occasional lover and they had come to stay with her and she'd shown them around and cooked bœuf bourguignon for them and she'd gone to visit them in turn. She'd enjoyed going to the cinema and reading nineteenth-century novels. She had tried to write a novel once, but it had failed to gel.

Every few weeks she'd gone to see her mother in the family home in Ipswich. She had always enjoyed being next to the sea, and her mother and she still liked to go down to the waterfront and look at the boats. Her father had said he'd buy a boat when he retired, but a coronary had claimed him before he could collect his pension.

Work had always been busy. Melanie had worked hard all her life and got results. It would have been easy for her to have stayed in her office and sent a wingman to the Amsterdam meeting, but she was too hands-on for that. She wondered how Product Development was getting on without her. There was – there had been – a launch in Birmingham, set for the week after next. Who was handling it? She should call. But she'd tried calling and that hadn't worked. She was never able to get through to the right people.

She would get out of all this somehow. She'd work out a way to get her life back. Why had she become so passive, anyway? Was this all there was left for her? Was this it forever? Of course not – everything had to come to an end sooner or later – but it looked as if that end were still a long way off. Unless, and she'd considered the possibility quite early on, she'd died and gone to Hell. That made some kind of sense, but there were one or two objections. First, there was Keith. He made an unlikely demon, didn't he? The last thing she'd heard, demons spit-roasted you over slow fires or whipped you with scorpions or buried you in ice, and they mocked you while they tortured you. Keith didn't mock or torture her, unless you counted his constant presence as mockery and his tireless attention to her needs as torture. The other thing that was missing from the Hell theory was despair. She knew that the damned realised their torments were eternal and that with eternity came the loss of hope and the onset of despair. She didn't feel either hope or despair, only a dull blankness interspersed with outbreaks of randomly directed rage. Some days she was so angry she found it impossible to speak and she communicated her wants to Keith in a series of grunts and pointings of the fingers. On others she was possessed by a calm resignation, quite Zen in its acceptance of her predicament. And always there was Keith; kind, willing, helpful Keith, ready at a moment's notice with a cup of tea and a sandwich. He was, she supposed, her jailer. She should have hated him, but that good old Stockholm Syndrome got in the way. Sometimes, just sometimes, she caught him looking at her with she could only describe as pity.

An indefinite amount of time passed. It could have been months, it could have been years. Melanie had no idea. But however long it was, that period naturally split itself into discrete days and those days passed, quickly or slowly as they chose, with no shape or form beyond that laid down by the simple order of repeated events that comprised each one and no sense that anything was leading anywhere. It was not until the night she asked a particular question that Melanie realised how much of a rut she had let herself fall into. When the breakthrough came it was all but invisible, and only Keith knew exactly when it happened.

'Keith,' Melanie said, one evening, over sweet sherry in the bar and *Crossroads* on the television. 'What am I doing here?'

'There's a question, Ms Roberts!'

'Do you know the answer?'

'The question really is, do you?'

'Don't try to change the subject! Don't you think I don't know all about diverting one question by asking another? I'm a businesswoman '

'So you are, Ms Roberts.' Keith picked up a glass and began to polish it.

'So, what am I doing here?'

'You mean, why are you here?'

'Yes, of course that's what I mean!'

'I'm not sure I can answer that.'

'But you're the manager!'

'Duty manager, madam.'

'You have a boss, don't you? A supervisor?'

'Yes, madam. That'd be the regional manager.'

'Could he answer my question?'

'She's a woman, madam. No, I'm afraid she couldn't.'

'So who could?'

Keith put the glass down slowly and carefully. His hand shook slightly. He took in a deep breath and held it. 'Hmm. That'd be someone from HQ.'

'Could you call him or her?'

'I could.' The television picture froze and the sound stopped. There were no sounds to be heard anywhere. Nothing moved.

'Would you? Would you help me? Please, Keith, please, won't you help me?'

'I'd be happy to.' Keith gave Melanie a broad, angelic smile and let his breath out with an audible whoosh. 'Very happy. Ms Roberts, you've no idea how happy that would make me.'

'I'd be so grateful.'

'I'll put in a request first thing tomorrow. It's getting a bit late now.'

Melanie woke in broad daylight. She got out of bed and crossed to the window and drew back the curtains. And it was different. Melanie recognised the difference instantly – it was something in the refraction of the air – and she showered and dressed and took the lift to the ground floor of the DriveInn with no thoughts of meetings or phones or airports or cars or motorway service stations or anything other than toast and coffee and poached eggs and walking out of the front door and, especially, saying goodbye and thank you to Keith.

'Goodbye, Ms Roberts,' he said, and held out his right hand. Melanie took it and considered giving him a hug, but thought better of it. She didn't want to embarrass him.

'Goodbye, Keith,' she said. 'Thank you for everything.'

'It's been a pleasure, madam.' Melanie rather doubted that, but she gave Keith a smile, set her shoulders and turned and walked through the hotel's entrance, across the car park, past the barrier and into the lively thoroughfare that lay beyond. The roadway was busy with buses, trams, cabriolets and bicycles, and the pavements were bordered by gaily-canopied shops and cafés, art-deco theatres, open gardens and playgrounds, fountains, and groves of cypress trees. Tall buildings were set well back on either side, made of glass and white marble and topped with winged figures glinting golden in the sunlight. Melanie turned to look behind her, but the North Midlands DriveInn had disappeared. That was a shame. She had thought to wave back to Keith. Unexpected, too, as despite the traffic the air was alpine-pure and so clear she could see everything, however near or far, in the most exact detail. After the narrow beige corridors and cramped artificial lighting of the DriveInn these wide-open spaces and broad blue skies came as a marvellous liberation of the spirit.

What should I do? she asked herself. How to use this new freedom?

The answer was obvious. *Explore. Have a look around. Work out what's going on.*

Melanie walked a few hundred yards, and, suddenly not sure if she was going the right way, found a bench which encircled the trunk of an elm tree, sat down, and watched the people come and go. Several of them noticed her watching them, and she dropped her eyes, not wanting to offend anyone or cause trouble, but all she got were smiles and the occasional raised hat. It seemed nobody minded her looking at them.

She rested quietly and let the physical sensations of this place – the brilliance of the light, the warmth of the air, the gentle chatter of the leaves moving in the trees – permeate her soul. She believed she knew where she was, but she had expected something rather more mystical and less matter-of-fact than this city, which to her eyes resembled Paris on a bright day in early summer. Paris, yes, but without the incessant blaring of car horns and the Parisian attitude, which she always interpreted as disdain, and the terrible rushing about. She couldn't help noticing that everybody, whether walking quickly or slowly, seemed to be moving at exactly the speed they wanted, not one that had been imposed on them by clocks, timetables and appointments. Perhaps, then, somebody would be able to spare her a moment. Let's see... Melanie stood up and stopped a middle-aged woman whose outfit of long green skirt, white silk blouse, elegant court shoes and purple cloak made her own grey business suit feel horribly dull and drab. The woman smiled. 'Hello, dear,' she said.

'Excuse me,' Melanie said, 'Have you got a minute? I'm new here. I wonder if you could help me.'

'New, eh?' said the woman. 'That's nice.' She held out her hand. 'Welcome to the City. Now, what can I do for you?'

'I'm not sure. I think there's someone I need to see. I've got some questions I ought to ask.'

'Yes, that's very likely. Most new people are absolutely chock-a-block with questions. I expect you're finding things a little strange.'

'I am – that is, I mean it's rather different... but strange? No, not really. But please, could you direct me to someone who could help me?'

'Of course. I know the very person. Look, here's a tram that's going the right way. Let's hop on board. I'll make sure you get off at the right stop.' The woman raised her left hand and the tram halted next to them.

'I'm afraid I don't have any money for the fare.'

'That doesn't matter.'

'Really? Are you sure? Well, all right, I'll pay you back as soon as I can. But – don't you have something else you need to be doing?' Melanie blushed. 'Sorry, that came out all wrong. I didn't mean to be rude. It's very kind of you to offer to help me.'

'Not at all. Would you like me to show you the sights as we go along?'

'I'd love that. If it's not too much trouble, that is.'

'Oh, nothing's ever too much trouble, dear. Not for me. Now – come on! Mustn't keep everybody waiting!'

They linked arms and boarded the tram.

PAN
AND
THE
RIVER

Pan and the River

I T'S NO GOOD LOOKING FOR THE GREAT GOD PAN IN THE CELESTIAL CITY of Olympus because he moved out several years ago. His house was shuttered, the furniture was covered with dust sheets, and the carpets were rolled up pile side in while the water, gas and electricity supplies were disconnected and their direct debit accounts discontinued. Outside the elegant front door, with its Doric columns and broken pediment (for the god had never forgotten his Hellenic roots) a sign, engraved in an angular script, informed prospective callers that all enquiries should be directed to a certain Post Office Box. Despite this clear and unambiguous notice an ever-increasing pile of catalogues, telephone directories, special offers and television licence reminders built up on the tiled floor behind the letterbox and every few months (as the gods count time) someone came with a master key, forced the door open against a heap of junk mail and disposed of it.

The cultural life of the City was somewhat diminished by Pan's departure. He had been a significant patron of the arts and had actively encouraged the creation of new work, heading many committees and sitting on the boards of the City's major orchestras and opera companies while, on the quiet, making sure that those of the younger gods who were more interested in guitars, drums, decks and loopers got an opportunity to express themselves in their own ways. This was an extremely worthwhile thing to do. The gods were kept very busy looking after the affairs of mortals and often lacked the time or the inclination to do much more than flop out when they got home. True, the boulevards and alleyways of the City were full of cafés and bars and there was singing and dancing in them; but they were more often than not mortal songs and human dances.

The gods sometimes asked if good art could only spring out of suffering. Was the creative impulse inevitably dulled by happiness and contentment? Was eternal bliss the reason so few of the gods, living as they did in the light-drenched streets and towers of Olympus, made so little significant work of their own? Maybe – but consider that every day they answered the calls and prayers of the multitudes of the many worlds, and experienced, if only by proxy, the tribulations of mortal life with all its frustrations and failures. Humans spoke of compassion fatigue, but that was a human failing. The gods truly felt the agonies of their supplicants and they could not have become gods had they not done so.

Perhaps it came down to a matter of taste. It was considered rather bad form for a god to bring his work home, so to speak, or try to profit by it. The taint of exploitation could quickly come to haunt the immortal who sang of human fears, who painted images of human misery or whose dance steps spoke too eloquently of love unrequited or love lost forever. It was strange, was it not, that life in the City of the Most High should so resemble, in its mores and customs, that of the worlds and that a god should experience social discomfitures that were readily understood by any enlightened person, however mortal.

As for Pan; his opulent town house had become a prison to him. He was a senior god and therefore not responsible for the day to day well-being of a panel of humanity, unlike the desk staff who sat by the phones and screens of the Ministry of Mortality. Not for him the daily commute, the fixed spell of duty and the weary return, on foot or by bus, bicycle or tramcar to apartment, hotel, club or restaurant. His time (whatever that may mean to a god) was his own to dispose of as he wished, and apart from regular attendances at the Council of the Wise and an occasional but rare audience with the Most High in the Citadel, there were no demands made upon him.

He would not have said that he was bored, but merely that town life did not suit him. The parks, squares and gardens of the City were passing beautiful, but they were fixed in size and their borders were strictly circumscribed by streets, houses and apartment blocks which, regular and formal as they were, contained within themselves the spirit of orderliness – that spirit which was so foreign to his nature. From time to time he would call up his old friend Bacchus and they would go out on the razzle and roister up and down the streets and crossways of Olympus; but it was never enough, however wildly exuberant their rampages and however much work they made for the City's road sweepers, rubbish collectors and purveyors of headache cures. (Headaches in Heaven? But of course! The remedy is a mixture of tomato juice, Angostura bitters, Worcestershire sauce and Ambrosia.)

The Most High – whose name, essence and chiefest joy are Love – understood the roots of his discontent as She understands the hearts of all, mortal and immortal alike, and when Pan came to Her, shamefaced after a notably spectacular (not to say orgiastic) binge, She suggested that what he needed was a change of scene.

'Have you heard of a place called Glyndebourne?' She asked 'It exists in many of the worlds of men.'

'I think so,' said Pan, fiddling nervously with his beard. 'It's an opera house, isn't it?'

'That's right. It's in the countryside. People – wealthy people, or people who have saved up for a special treat – go there and listen to opera in a purpose-built auditorium. In the interval they eat a picnic on the lawn.'

'That sounds very nice,' said Pan.

'It is. They're particularly good at Mozart. I wonder if you might not like to set up such an establishment yourself. I can think of some splendid locations not too far out of the City. It would be a new venture for you. Something fresh.'

'That's marvellous, Most High, but I must say it sounds terribly refined and civilised and I fear it might not be altogether my kind of thing. Begging your pardon, of course.'

'Hmmm,' said the Most High. 'I see what you mean. Tell you what—'

'Yes?' (Giant stars orbited the chamber where they spoke. Bright flowers bloomed, grass swayed in a gentle breeze. The zephyrs sang of motion and delight.)

'Even if you don't want to set up an out-of-town opera house and arts centre I still think you should move away, if only for a while. There have been a number of complaints and it's hard, as I am sure you will appreciate, for the junior gods to stand up to you when you're in one of your moods. You can be rather overbearing, you know.'

Pan bowed. His tail lay flat on the greensward between his hooves

'So we're agreed. I've got just the place for you. It's nothing like as plush as your present accommodations and I'm afraid you'll have to leave your retinue behind. They've had enough, to be frank, and it'll do you good to fend for yourself for a change. I think you'll like it.'

'But... my orchestras! My theatre companies! My superstar DJs!'

'Will learn to do without you. They need a break.'

Pan considered the Most High's offer. Perhaps he had rather been pushing the limits of acceptable behaviour. And maybe, just maybe, a change of scene might be just the thing he needed. Nobody had said anything, but he had the feeling he'd been repeating himself lately. He nodded.

'And You need a break too. All right. Do as Thou willst.' Pan knelt and kissed the Most High's hand.

And She was gone.

Pan's new home was, as he had been warned, rather less than grand. It was so much less than grand that the first time he passed it he missed it altogether. It was only when he saw a letterbox inscribed *Pan* standing next to an oak tree and looked up to see a wooden platform surrounding its trunk that he realised exactly what he had let himself in for.

'Bloomin' 'eck,' he muttered; and if the kookaburras in the branches overhead seemed to be laughing at him, that was surely in the nature of their song and nothing to do with the Most High's notoriously dry sense of humour. He shrugged, hoisted himself up onto the platform, and looked around.

The first thing he noticed was that there was a spiral staircase on the other side of the tree-trunk which led down to ground level and up to a further platform above his head. He felt foolish for not having spotted it before. Looking further, he found a door in the trunk which opened into a larder and utility room, and on going upstairs he found a compact bedroom, sheltered from the elements by willow screens and a reed thatch. A convenient and deceptively spacious en-suite shower room occupied the hollow in the trunk above the downstairs larder. Its shelves were stocked with his favourite shower gel and shampoo. (Jojoba and aloe vera, if you must know.)

Pan returned to the first platform and sat back in the orange La-Z-Boy recliner which took up much of its floor space. His manifestation was not a small one and he was relieved to find that the chair appeared to have been custom-made to fit him, despite its second-hand appearance. In fact, all the tree-house's furnishings had acquired quite a bit of wear and tear before being handed down to him. The sideboard was covered in a faded teak veneer and the table lamp which stood on top of it had a dented and discoloured shade. An old rag rug covered the floor and the coffee table rocked on unsteady feet.

'Dulce Domum,' said Pan, and laughed. Home, sweet home. Now, what was there to eat?

There was no sign of an Ambrosia dispenser anywhere, but the fridge in the larder was stocked with milk, butter, ham and cheese and the cupboard next to it yielded several bottles of Old Burton and a crusty cottage loaf. These were just fine as far as Pan was concerned. He made himself a couple of doorstep sandwiches and took the top off a bottle with his teeth. Ignoring the foolish staircase he leapt down from the platform, taking care not to drop the beer, and set out to find somewhere to sit and enjoy his lunch. His tree – for he already thought of it as being his personal property – stood at the southern edge of a sizeable wood of mixed conifers, oak and beech, while before him, and sloping away from him, was a scrubland of yellow flowering gorse which quickly led down to green fields and meadows. This was no part of Olympus or its environs that he recognised. The trees were different and so was the colour of the sky. It looked as if the Most High had sent him somewhere a very long way from home. And yet it was oddly familiar too, as if remembered from a dream.

Pan was in no hurry to map out his new neighbourhood, so he let the ground carry him down through grassland and hedgerows while taking alternate swigs from the bottle in his right hand and bites from the sandwich in his left. An even-tempered air ruffled the hairs of his legs and chest and his hooves lifted a little dust from the pathway to which the gravity of the hillside had guided him.

The path widened as he sauntered downhill. It never quite became a road, but it would have made a fine bridleway, if he had had a horse to ride down it. It sank into the land, so that the hedges to either side, which had until then reached only to shoulder height, soon became impossible for him to see over. So much the better, Pan thought. At least he was in no danger of losing his way home.

The bridleway passed through a band of trees; then suddenly stopped and broadened out into a T shape. It had reached an obstacle

The River.

Naturally there was a river in Olympus. No human or godly settlement is complete without a watercourse of some kind, and the river (which had no name, but was fed by the Styx, the Acheron, the

Cocytus, the Phlegethon, the Lethe, the Ganges and the Jordan) was a broad and stately stream which rivalled the Rhine, the Mississippi and the mighty Amazon. It was crossed by twenty-five superbly engineered bridges, three chain-ferries and numerous tunnels. It was remarkable, it was magnificent, it was the scene of some of the greatest public celebrations in Heaven, but it was not especially lively.

This river was *made* of life. It sizzled with it – it ran with a sinuous athleticism that said Look! Look at me! See how beautiful I am! It had whirlpools and sandbanks and reverse currents and sinkholes and it knew it was dangerous. Danger was its forte – it gloried in it. It would pull you in and drown you without a second thought, and mourn your death for ever after. It would not be contained – it treated its banks as useful markers but not inflexible barriers; and if it wished to jump over those barriers it would, and damn the consequences. It was faithless; a vandal, a hooligan, a strumpet and a rake and Pan lost his heart to it immediately. He would have thrown himself into it directly and ravished it, but he had not yet finished his lunch. He would sit down first and eat, and think about how he could seduce this wild creature and make it his own. He looked around for a place to sit that would not mess up his pelt or squash his tail. Ah yes! There was a wooden landing stage and tied up to it a small white rowing-boat nudged back and forth against the current. That would do. Softly, softly. He would try the gentle approach first.

Pan sat on the edge of the landing stage and let his hooves dangle flirtatiously in the water. Its coolness was a relief after the hot dust of the path, and the way it flowed around his legs was an agreeable novelty. It felt like skilful hands massaging him. Pan leaned against one of the mooring posts and relaxed. He finished off the sandwich, broke wind tempestuously and took one last draught of Old Burton. Unthinking, he hefted the bottle in his right hand and tossed it into the river. It made a considerable splash, bobbed up and down a couple of times and slowly sank into the stream, vanishing from sight. Silence fell – a country silence, made of water and shadows and leaves and air.

In the opposite bank something moved. A dark circular hole that the god had not seen before suddenly became visible, because a light – two lights, quite close to each other – appeared within it and defined it. The lights grew and between them there was a deeper, but smaller, darkness. More motion, and there was a face, with a whiskered nose and a narrow mouth surrounded by brown-grey fur. The mouth opened, and a small but determined voice spoke. It sounded cross.

'Hey, you! What the bloody hell do you think you're doing?' said the Water Rat.

'Eh?' said Pan. 'You talkin' to me?'

'Stay where you are. I'll come across and fetch you.'

It was a simple matter of good manners, the Water Rat explained, pouring the tea and indicating the biscuit barrel with his left paw. It just wasn't done to throw glass willy-nilly into the river. Somebody could get hurt, and empty bottles littered the riverbed and disturbed the sticklebacks who lived there. Chucking stuff around like that was the kind of thing steam-launches did; and they were unutterably vulgar and nothing better was to be expected of them.

'You're lucky the moorhens haven't got wind of this,' he said. 'It'd be all up and down the river by now and your name would be mud from Pangbourne to Mapledurham. You'd never live it down. Oh, by the way, I don't think we've been properly introduced. I'm the Water Rat, but you can call me Ratty.' He held out his right paw.

'Honoured, I'm sure,' said Pan. 'I am Faunus, son of Dionysus, although that is but one of my names and the tales of my conception, birth, death and rebirth are as many as the stars in the sky. I am potent and mighty and altogether to be feared.'

'Impressive,' said the Water Rat.

'But you can call me Pan,' said the god.

'Pleased to meet you, Pan.' They shook.

'Before I forget, are you all right for digs?' asked the Water Rat. 'I've got a chum stopping with me already, but I'm sure we can squeeze in one more.'

'Yes, thanks. The Most High gave me a tree-house up the path that way.' Pan jerked his thumb over his shoulder. 'Across the river and up the hill.'

'Next to the Wild Wood?'

'Is that what they call it?'

'Yes.'

'It seems pretty tame, if you don't mind my saying so.' Pan smiled. 'Compared with me, anyway.'

'I see.' The Water Rat was silent for a moment. Animal-etiquette forbade the discussion of possible future trouble.

'Don't worry! I'll be fine. Now, what about that river-trip you

267

promised me?'

Pan settled in pretty well over the next few weeks. The Most High (or someone in Her service) had arranged to keep the tree-house's fridge and cellar well stocked, so Pan never had to go shopping (which he detested.) The water supply was reliable and pre-softened; a luxury in the valley of the Isis, which collects lime as it passes through the Chiltern Hills. The jojoba and aloe vera shampoo foamed deliciously in his beard and helped keep his horns free of unsightly scale build-up.

On his first night there had been a certain commotion among the denizens of the Wild Wood – eldritch screeches, sinister rustlings, beady eyes peering out from behind trees and bushes, that kind of thing. It was presumably intended to frighten him off, but of course it had no effect whatsoever. Pan had only to climb out of bed, walk a few yards into the wood and bellow the chorus of a hunting song from the Late Pliocene Era to shut the racket up.

His nights were peaceful thereafter. His days were spent in rambling around the lanes, ditches, fields and hedgerows of the Riverbank, discovering the lie of the land and meeting its inhabitants. They were an hospitable crowd and Pan enjoyed visiting them in their homes, nests and burrows. In the evenings he took up residence in the lounge bar of the Grateful Leaf in Goring and stood everybody drinks. In this way he gathered a wide circle of friends – or, more accurately, kind-of friends. The thing he soon began to notice was that, despite his splendid manifestation and charmingly robust manner, people and animals he had seen only a day or two earlier would greet him as a new acquaintance and only slowly remember that only the other day they had been vigorously discussing the best kind of fly with which to catch brown trout. Pan was rather disappointed by this. He had always thought he was a memorable sort of chap.

It was only to be expected that the Riverbankers would want to do more than just drink and talk with Pan. For example, after his weekly choir practice with the young field-mice, their mothers would hang around the tree-house, giggling and wearing their best hats and shawls. It was clear what they wanted from him, and it was hard for him to turn them down. Only the presence of the children prevented a simple chat from turning into an all-out orgy. Sometimes there were no children present and Pan, his urges matching those of his disciples, would join with them in bedroom, kitchen, haystack or meadow and show them why he was known as the god of sexuality as well as music. Human or animal, male or female, it made no odds to him.

It had always been thus. There would have been no virgins left in Heaven if the Council of the Wise, guided by the wishes of the Most High, had not given sanctuary to those who did not wish to couple with Pan and arranged for the restoration of those who had coupled with him and rather wished they hadn't. They were known as dorisdays, for reasons that were only understood by those gods who had dealings with one particular world of creation. Sex was in his nature and that was all there was to be said about it.

You might have thought those busy days of music (he had founded a light orchestra in Henley and established a techno club in Caversham, a swing band in Basildon Park and a women's barbershop octet in Wallingford) and copulation (which took place, as has been intimated, just about everywhere) would have been enough for Pan. He regularly popped across the river to see his friends, and sat patiently listening to the lyric poetry the Water Rat had recently started to write. He agreed with Ratty's companion, the Mole, that the poetry was mostly pretty bloody awful, but he was kind enough not to say so, instead applauding his host's piquant phrasing, acute sense of rhythm and vivid imagery. These quiet times were refreshment for his hectic spirit and had one of his roistering comrades from Olympus (Silenus, for example) met him in his friends' home he would hardly have known him, so grown-up did his behaviour appear to be. He would have been deceived. Pan's blood was seething and bubbling with a desire that could not be assuaged by a thousand waiting mouths and trembling thighs. Every night he lay sleepless in his bed on the top floor of the tree house, masturbating extravagantly and thinking only of his one true love:

The River.

Pan adopted the little white rowing-boat that was tied up to the landing stage opposite the Water Rat's house. He used it to visit Mole and Ratty, but he also valued it for the closeness it gave him to the water. Ratty gave him rowing lessons, but Pan scarcely needed to be told to dip the oars gently into the stream and pull slow and strong. He could be the most thoughtful suitor in the world when he chose. When he was not out on the water, he would take the pipes he had made from the cut and bound stems of bulrushes and improvise love songs and lullabies on them. These songs were among the most beautiful he had ever made and if Orpheus, who was still too stricken by the loss of his Eurydice to play the lyre, had heard them he might have discovered a fresh muse of his own. The Most High (who sees and hears all that men and gods do) became aware of Pan's new inspiration and sat by him, concealed in a ray of sunlight, and listened, marvelling that Her creation could have given birth to so gracious an offspring. The River, that coy lady, heard him too but she neither repulsed nor encouraged his advances. She may have spoken to Pan, but if she did it was in a voice that was as yet too soft for him to hear.

Weeks and months passed happily, but there came a time when the peaceful life of the Riverbank became disturbed. It was nothing to do with the fear of what the ferrets, weasels and stoats of the Wild Wood might be plotting. Pan had sorted them out, no question. Nor was it the reckless escapades of the local Bulleys, as the young aristocracy with too much money, too much free time and too little sense were known. No, it was something much worse, something to freeze the heart. A young otter had gone missing somewhere along the river.

Let it not be forgotten that the river was perilous. There were locks, there were weirs, there were cross-currents, there were whirlpools, there were a million and one dangers waiting to crush and drown a young and inexperienced creature. Otters were the most naturally gifted of water-mammals, but little Portly was less than a year old and had never been out of his father's sight before. Otter tried to pretend that nothing was wrong and that his son had just popped up-river for a sleep-over at a friend's house, but nobody believed him for a moment. The other animals organised search-parties, while Otter took to standing watch day and night at the place where he had first taught Portly to swim.

Pan learned of the pup's disappearance one afternoon at Ratty's. Both the Water Rat and the Mole seemed unusually subdued and it didn't take long before one of them blurted out their worries.

'It's a beastly thing,' said the Mole. 'Otter's such a nice chap – a bit abrupt sometimes, but aren't we all – and it's breaking his heart. He'd only just begun letting Portly go out by himself, you know. He must be feeling just awful about it.'

'We must do something,' said the Water Rat.

'Yes, we must. I say we get out our waterproofs and search up and down the Riverbank tonight. All the way through from midnight to dawn.'

'Don't tell Otter. He'll think we're interfering.'

'No, of course not. And don't you, neither.' He glared at Pan.

'No, Moley,' said the god.

It was twelve o'clock, midnight, and the last of the bells of St Andrew's church had faded into silence. Pan hid in the bushes and watched while the Mole and the Water Rat, warmly muffled, set out along the towpath. A waxing moon threw the darkest of shadows onto the water.

The two animals spoke only to guide one another. Pan followed on muffled hooves, unheard behind the ever-present sounds of the river. This was the quietest time – birds warmed their eggs, mice hid in their holes, safe from swooping owls and patrolling cats, insects ceased their chitter and rattle. Pan sensed his friends' tension – it showed in the way they placed their feet, their whispered conversation and the set of their shoulders. Their fear – fear of what they might find – crossed over to him; even he, immortal Pan.

Soon they heard the bustle of a weir and saw, against the limb of the setting moon, Otter's silhouette. He was standing at the water's edge, his head moving from side to side, searching, searching. 'Poor chap,' Pan heard the Rat say, and felt the animal's sorrow as his own. He responded with silent anger. This should not be! This must not be! This small life, so precious, so full of hope for the future, should not be ended so soon. But what could he do? He watched as the Water Rat and the Mole sat and waited and scanned the surface of the water for any sign – a ripple, a wave, a glimpse of a whiskered snout or fur-tufted ear – of the pup. Pan had never felt so helpless.

Hours passed. The moon set and darkness fell, broken only by a few stars and the nightlights shining in the windows of moored narrow-boats and pleasure-craft. Nobody moved. Pan dozed off and woke, furious with himself for breaking his watch. Downstream the edge of the sky was shaded into grey. Dawn was coming and the birds were waking and beginning their early song. Their song... And suddenly Pan knew what he had to do. It was the only thing he could do. He stood, stretched, took out his pipes and began to play.

He turned to the River and sang to her of his sorrows and his fears. He played a song of longing, of yearning, of love mislaid and never to be found again. The song dipped in and out of a minor key, resonant with the colours of desolation. He sang of sadness and death and waste and unfulfilled promise, and the willows turned their branches aside and wept to hear him. He sang of a cold northern sky streaked with blood and a woman weeping by a poisoned well, of the dark patch on the x-ray and the shaking of the doctor's head, of the blighted life and the long falling away of the spirit. All these terrible things he evoked in his song and between its verses he cried, *do not allow this terrible thing to come to pass.* At last, exhausted and soul-stained, he stopped to rest. He listened. Had his song been heard? Had the river heard him? Had he touched her? Would she reply to him? Would she share his anguish and help him to end it? But no. There was nothing. Nothing but the muted chirrups of the unheeding morning birds.

It was no good. His musical talent, which he had thought was the greatest gift he possessed and which was the envy of the gods of Olympus, was worthless if it could not save the least creature on Earth, a mere otter-pup, from being drowned in a weir. He threw the pipes down in disgust and stood with his hands by his side, feeling utterly wretched. Along the towpath, the Mole and the Water Rat were stirring. They too had failed and would soon have to go home to an empty house and a cold fireplace. Tomorrow night they would try again, and the night after, and the night after that, but sooner or later they would have to give up. Portly would be lost and his life ended before it had truly begun. His father's life would be tainted with regret for ever after. Pan could not bear that. He scrabbled around by his hooves and found the fallen pipes. He lifted them to his lips. He had to try again. He had to play a different song. Only a new song could defeat the intolerable pain and despair he and his friends were suffering.

Pan took a deep breath, set his sorrow and fear aside and played a song of joy. He put everything he had ever known of happiness, of light, of friendship and good company into its melody. He sang of the open road, of radiant noontide, of lanes and pathways, and destinations no more precious than the journey but always waiting at twilight's coming. He sang of the mystic depths of the quiet hours, when love is the essence, when there are no secrets, when oneness is all. He sang of the rising sun, while the sky grew pink in the east, and he sang of life; life eternal, life irrepressible, life that illuminated the universe, life that would not and could not be cast down, blotted out or pushed aside. The morning stars heard him and joined in with the chorus.

'River, River,' he sang, 'hear me. Believe me. Come with me. Live with me and be my love. We will do marvels together. And please, please, please, return this lost one to his father. If not for my sake, do it for the sake of the Most High, in whom there is no shadow of fear and for whom all things are possible.'

Pan stopped playing and listened. He played a few more phrases. Still nothing. That was it, then. His last appeal had come to nothing. It had been rejected or, worse, ignored. He turned away, not sure where he should go now. Back to his tree-house? Or the City? Silence fell. He could no longer hear his own breathing. Perhaps it had stopped. Silence... but yet? Somewhere below the threshold of hearing, hidden in the gaps between the atoms, breathed across the strings of the tiniest particles of creation...

'Look down, Pan. Look down.'

Pan looked, and between his hooves he saw a small form, curled up tightly and fast asleep. He rested a hand on its fur and felt warmth and a light, quick pulse. The creature lifted its head to him and blinked.

'Go, little one,' he whispered, scarcely able to speak, 'Daddy's waiting for you. Look! Just over there. Do you see? There he is. Run along now.'

Portly got to his feet and scampered across the grass to where Otter was standing. Pan heard a joyous bark and saw Otter take his son into his paws and hug him closely to his chest. 'Look!' said the Water Rat to the Mole. 'Look!' They turned away quickly and left the pair to their blissful, private reunion.

'Pan,' said the River. 'Hear me.'

'I hear you,' said Pan.

'You have won me. I will give myself to you. I will be your love. But first, there is something you must do. Do you know what it is?'

'Yes,' said Pan, 'I think I do. My song... it was too strong for these small mortals. It will destroy them. It will burn them up.'

'Then play to them now. Play them one last song.'

And Pan played his song. It sang of calm, of readiness for bed, and soft sheets and coverlets, of pyjamas and warm milky drinks, of a good book and sleep. Dreamless sleep, sleep floated on the waters of Lethe. Sleep of oblivion. His friends would never remember – or if they did, only as the ghost of a dream – the songs they had heard on the banks of the river Isis at the gates of dawn.

'Forget,' he sang. 'Be at peace, and forget. Go home and know only that the child is safe and well and that your vigil helped restore him to his family. Be happy, be safe, be content.

'And forget.'

Pan is different now and his misadventures no longer feature in the gossip columns of the Henley Standard and the Bisham Times. You might say he was a reformed character and someone who would be welcomed back without question into the cultural life of the Celestial City of Olympus. This is true, but it only takes the matter so far. The whole story is that Pan had always been a rustic god and had never truly fitted in with City ways. He was born to live on open hillsides, among trees, fields and hedges, and to take his rest in woods and copses. He knows this, because every year he makes positively his last farewell tour of the concert halls, clubs and discos of the City and, as you might expect, he goes down a storm and is fêted in cocktail lounges, pubs and salons from the cosy suburbs of Elysium to the highest towers of Anova. But he never turns up for the last, or even the next-to-last gig of the tour. The promoter bangs in vain on the starred door of his dressing room and pushes it open to find nothing but an empty chair and an untouched dish of oysters. There's no point in sending out a search party or making frantic phone calls, for Pan is offski, sitting in a corner of the guard's van of the last train to Oxford, stopping at Twyford, Reading, Goring, Pangbourne, Wallingford and Abingdon, playing blue notes on his pipes. And nor is it any good leaving him messages via a certain Post Office Box or ambushing him at Oxford station and waving a contract under his nose. He's long gone, walking the moonlit lanes back to his house next to the Wild Wood and stopping only to embrace his undine mistress before heading up the wooden hill to Bedfordshire.

The Most High keeps in touch, naturally. She has no favourites and every creature in all the manifold realities of the Multiverse is of equal importance to Her but, just the same, even the Supreme Being needs a holiday every now and then. At these times, when the to-and-fro of the worlds is running smoothly, She leaves the Citadel and travels to the Riverbank, where She may often be seen, cast in the reflection of a kingfisher's wing, listening to Pan play songs of sweet desire to his Lady Isis or waiting patiently nearby while they make slow, ecstatic love beneath the willow trees.

Godhead and Goodness

WHILE EDITING THE PRESENT EDITION OF *THE BOY* (AND WRITING the two new stories which, together with the new cover and illustrations, distinguish it from its electronic predecessor) I've been struck by how many of the people in it are good. Not good-but-with-a-dark-past or good-but-conflicted or even bad-but-with-some-goodness-in-them-somewhere-and-needing-redemption-in-act-three but just plain good. Given that I inhabit the same messed-up world as everyone else on the planet this seems extraordinary. I must be some kind of cockeyed optimist.

The other thing is the odd way religion keeps turning up.

Me, I'm not religious. If asked, I'll say that religion is the kind of thing that entities like us construct as a form of consolation against the sure and certain knowledge of our own mortality. I don't believe in God. So why write about Him (or Her)? And what's with the capital letters? Surely a good secularist – even a Church of England secularist such as myself – should eschew these genuflections towards a being whose very existence he denies. And yet, belief in a Higher Power is endemic amongst humanity. We seem to need there to be a God.

Voltaire famously said, "Si Dieu n'existait pas, il faudrait l'inventer". So, passing over the aphorism's assumption that God does in fact exist, which necessity is the mother of His (or Her) invention?

I think it comes down to stories. We are story-telling beings. Every time we see something happen, we build a narrative around it. We need characters, causation and outcomes. What just happened? Who did it happen to? Why did it happen? What may happen as a result? We make narratives out of random events as readily as we do from streams of genuinely linked circumstances, simply because that's what we do. It's the way we work. Oh, and because it allows us to do something that, while it is by no means unique to humans, is something we've become very good at – to project ourselves into the future. It happens all the time. It's a survival thing. For example, consider Ugg the caveman. He's out hunting bison one day when he looks up. Ah – that rock just rolled against that bigger rock which is now falling. I'm not in danger at this very moment, but if I don't skip two feet to the left – *pronto* – future-Ugg will get a nasty bump on the head. Move! And he moves, and the rock falls harmlessly at his feet and there is a good outcome. An unhappy story, in which Ugg is killed by a falling boulder, is replaced by a cheerful one in which Ugg goes home to his cave and tells his family and friends all about his lucky escape. And if he bigs up the tale a little as he tells it; well, why not?

And so, by virtue of millions of years of experience and remembering we have become a time-dwelling species, whose lives are stories which, as we are taught in school, have a beginning, a middle and an end, a plot and a purpose.

It's hard to conceive of a story – a purposeful story, at any rate – that has no author, and so behold! here is God, just as Voltaire said, with Her pen poised and ready to write our personal narratives for us – with their title pages and chapters, plot developments and final paragraphs – and maybe, just maybe, give them a part in some greater, more epic, story. It's been fun to reverse that process, as the ancients did, and have a go at telling a little of God's story instead.

Debrief

THAT WAS WELL DONE,' SAID THE MOST HIGH.

'Thank you, Ma'am,' said the minor god sometimes known as Keith.

'No, really, I mean it. They can be the hardest ones to save, the ones who think they've made it all by themselves, through their own merit. The ones who can't envisage ever asking for help – who see it as a sign of weakness.'

'Yes, Ma'am.'

'I'm sure you wouldn't make that kind of mistake.'

'No, Ma'am.' Keith sat up straight.

'Oh, do relax! You're not here for a telling-off!'

'No, Ma'am. Thank you, Ma'am.'

'Anyway, what did you think of her? Melanie Roberts?'

'Annoying, Ma'am. Angry and annoying. Annoying as all He—'

'Quite.'

'But sad, too. I felt so sorry for her. She was so cut off, so isolated. She had built such a high wall around herself. She wasn't sick, was she?'

'No, I'd have taken that into account. Just cut off, as you put it. But it all turned out all right in the end, didn't it?

'Now, is there anything else you'd like to ask me about?'

'Er, yes, oddly enough. That night she tried to seduce me. Should I have let her?'

'It wouldn't have done any harm, as it happens. Perhaps you should have given me a quick call.'

Keith blushed. 'Sorry, Ma'am.'

'Don't apologise! As I said, you did a good job. In the meantime, I've got a little proposition for you.'

'Oh yes?' Keith braced himself. The Most High's little propositions were well known throughout the Celestial City of Olympus.

'Young Melanie. She's got a good head on her shoulders and once she's rid herself of that foolish attitude of hers I reckon she'll make quite a reasonable household god.'

'Most High?'

'But she'll need a mentor.'

'A mentor? Oh... I see.'

'It'll be good for both of you. I can probably arrange you a promotion on the basis of the extra responsibility you'll be taking on and she'll get a useful outlet for her abilities, once she's been through Training. Don't worry! I'll make sure you don't have to give up your field work.'

Were it not for the fact that it was impossible for anyone to feel fear while in the presence of the Supreme Being, Keith might have shuddered at the mention of Training.

'Is that all right with you, Keith?'

'Yes of course, Most High. As Thou willst, Most High.'

'Then we're done. Again, thank you. Oh, and just one last thing while I think of it...'

'Yes, Ma'am?'

'Next time she tries to get you into bed...'

'Yes, Ma'am?'

'Don't hold back, old fellow. This *is* Heaven, you know. We're all entitled to our fair share of bliss.'

'Yes, Most High. Thank you, Most High.' Keith bowed his head and put his hands together in the ancient Hindu gesture of *namaste*.

And She was gone.